FINAL TRANSACTION

A NOVEL BY

DIANE DICKINSON

Black Rose Writing | Texas

ISBN: 978-1-68513-351-1
Library of Congress Control Number: 2023942568
PUBLISHED BY BLACK ROSE WRITING
www.blackrosewriting.com

Printed in the United States of America
Suggested Retail Price (SRP) $21.95

Final Transaction is printed in Adobe Caslon Pro

*As a planet-friendly publisher, Black Rose Writing does its best to eliminate unnecessary waste to reduce paper usage and energy costs, while never compromising the reading experience. As a result, the final word count vs. page count may not meet common expectations.

This book is dedicated to my children,

Christine Bowen, and Regan Dickinson.

FINAL TRANSACTION

CHAPTER 1

"Dammit! I've been suckered again." Lara muttered as she hammered a Drake Properties *Open House* sign into the unrelenting ground.

Another Sunday working my ass off!

She knew ahead of time that this two-million-dollar home would attract a crowd. Mostly women. Today was their chance to meet the handsome hunk of a realtor, Todd Drake, co-owner and broker of Drake Properties. The icing on the cake.

Normally Lara didn't mind assisting other agents with open houses. Today was not normal. Today she wasn't assisting, she was doing it all. Todd had asked her to help him far enough in advance for her to say no, and she almost had. But then he had dangled the juicy possibility of working with a high-end buyer. As Todd had put it, "No realtor in her right mind would pass up this chance."

Even though Lara knew from past experiences that most people at an open house were just curious, looking for design ideas, or the real downer, already working with an agent, she said yes. Once again, she succumbed to Todd's charm, agreeing to work on her rare Sunday off.

"When will I learn to say no?" she mumbled as she straightened the sign, pointing the arrow toward Crestline Drive where the open house would take place.

After slogging through Houston's oppressively hot, swampy summer air, driving signs into the ground, and tying those damn balloons to each sign, she made a mad dash through the grand two-story home to turn on all the lights. Grabbing the slick brochures and the sign-in sheet, she stacked them neatly on the kitchen's granite countertop next to the floral arrangement of roses, foxglove, and poppies. Many home-owners baked cookies before an open house to evoke a warm, homey feeling. This owner placed fragrant fresh flowers in strategic places throughout the house.

Nice touch.

She paused at the entry, took a deep breath, then fanned her face with a brochure while inspecting the house one last time for any im-perfections. She found none. The highly polished hickory staircase opened up into the wide, welcoming foyer. She walked into the spa-cious great room with streak-free floor-to-ceiling windows looking out on the infinity pool, and lushly landscaped back yard. She wondered if the maid got hazardous duty pay for cleaning those windows.

Shaking her head, she turned toward the kitchen when an unex-pected chill made her shudder. The hair on the back of her neck lifted. Her head snapped around toward the French doors.

Someone's in the house.

Lara walked quickly to the doors. She reached out and turned the handle. Locked! Perhaps she had imagined it.

To be certain it wasn't her imagination, she removed her shoes, and silently walked through the entire first floor. Her heart raced as she opened closets, and peered around corners. Every small sound brought her to a halt. No one.

Stop freaking out.

She breathed deeply, gave a short laugh at her empty house jitters, then rushed back to the kitchen where she placed a stack of her business cards on the counter. After stowing her purse in a cabinet, she felt her scalp begin to tingle.

"Crap!" she said, her voice echoing through the empty room. The familiar first sign of sweat. A bad omen. This was the beginning of a fashion breakdown.

In no time at all the moisture on her scalp gathered. Large drops of perspiration ran down her forehead, and into her eyes destroying her meticulously applied makeup. Her arms began to sweat under the tailored blue striped suit she always chose for such a high-end open house. She retrieved her purse, and grabbed a compact mirror.

The image she saw was not the face of a cool, competent, hot-shot realtor. Her shoulder length red hair had frizzed. The black mascara she applied to highlight her green eyes ran down her cheeks, leaving dark smudges under her eyes.

Shit! I look like Orphan Annie with a hangover!

She threw the compact back into the purse, tore several paper towels from a roll on the counter, and began patting at her blackened eyes. Taking another deep breath, she glanced at the wall clock. In ten minutes, everyone would arrive.

Where the hell is Todd?

It was then she heard a loud thud above her head on the second floor. Her heart raced as she walked toward the stairway. She looked out the side window, and saw Todd's car pull into the drive. There wasn't time to go back upstairs.

I'll check it out later.

Todd burst through the door, then called out in his buoyant voice, "Hi Lara!"

Lara's back stiffened.

The star has arrived.

She turned and stormed into the kitchen, while Todd sauntered behind her, totally oblivious to his sodden, pissed agent.

"Wow, everything looks perfect. Good job!" he beamed, raising his right open hand toward her.

Lara moved to avoid the ex-football player's huge high-five. His six-foot-four frame dominated the room. Everything about Todd was large. His body, personality, and energy overpowered the average mortal.

He dressed impeccably always keeping in mind how dark gray suits, and pastel shirts set off his hazel eyes, and long black eyelashes. Many women would kill for those eyelashes. He wore only tailored suits from Nordstrom's in the Galleria, a prestigious area frequented by oil men, professional athletes, old money, new money, and fashionable women.

"I'm glad you finally made it, Todd."

"Oh yeah, the traffic was horrible," he said distractedly.

Typical Houston excuse.

She watched Todd stroll around the kitchen checking to make sure everything was in place for the afternoon's rush. Glancing over at Lara, he gave her his sexy, crooked smile showing off flawless white teeth. His hair was tousled, giving an air of whimsy to his appearance without detracting from the fact that he was so well put together.

In the recent past his smile alone made Lara's heart skip several beats. That was then. This is now. Today it was simply irritating.

"Looks perfect, Lara."

"I could have used your help, especially with those signs," she said through clenched teeth.

Todd smiled, and put his arm on her shoulder. "Aw, come on, Lara. Lighten up. This is going to be a great open house."

Before she could reply, the doorbell rang. Todd dropped his arm, and clapped his hands.

"Show time! Let's sell this house."

Lara instinctively put on her I'm-so-happy-to-see-you realtor smile. What a pair they made. Cool, dry Todd standing next to clammy Lara, who was discreetly patting her face with a limp paper towel, while silently praying she could keep the sweat from dripping off her chin.

"Come on in folks. Out of the heat, and into cool luxury," Todd crooned, capturing everyone's attention with his welcoming smile, and charm.

Lara stood back secretly admiring his easy way with people, the way he made them feel at home, as if he was shootin' the breeze at his favorite sports bar. She listened as he warmed to his audience. His I's became ahs, as he slipped into the vernacular of East Texas. "Ah think y'all will lahk this big kitchen, dontcha think?"

For two long hours Lara smiled, answered questions, and played second banana to Todd's starring role. She also corralled unruly children, and a couple's scraggly puppy.

Who in the hell brings an animal to an open house?

Rather than have the dog run loose, Lara smilingly offered to hold the puppy while its owners took a leisurely stroll through the house. When they returned, the puppy was so excited he hadn't been abandoned that he peed on the side of Lara's blouse. Fuming internally, she pulled her jacket across the stain, and continued her job as the charming, chatty realtor, capable of handling any situation.

A few people took her business card, but none seemed interested in her, or in buying the house.

The open house went into overtime. Finally, everyone left. Lara closed the front door, kicking her shoes off before limping toward the kitchen where Todd was going over the sign-in sheet.

"My feet are killing me," she said. "It's time to close up and go home."

"Here's to another great open house, Lara. I couldn't have done it without you. I'll go upstairs, and shut everything off if you'll get the signs," Todd said, waving his hand in dismissal. "Be sure to come back before you leave. See you in a few!"

"Hey, wait a minute…" Lara stammered, but Todd was already taking the stairs two at a time.

Here I am again, sweating like a pig, and picking up these damn signs.

The last sign stood on a stretch of flat, hot, dry road, and was a bitch to pull out of the ground. Lara gave one last full force tug, and the spindly wire legs popped out of the ground. She threw the sign with the deflated balloons still attached into the trunk of her Infiniti, then sank into the driver's seat trying to cool off.

Son-of-a-bitch it's hot! Will this day ever end?

Lara dreaded returning to the house. She knew she would have to endure the inevitable dissertation by Todd on how great he did, and how Lara could have done better. She had always believed that Todd's know-how along with broker, and co-owner Megan James' cool and aloof perfectionism, helped the agents at Drake Properties become productive, aggressive real estate pros admired by their peers. A good thing. The overarching need to produce or get out of the business turned some agents into neurotic money-grubbers. Not a good thing.

Fear of failure. The great motivator.

Lara pulled into the driveway behind Todd's sleek, red Lexus.

What if I just pulled that Open House sign out of the front yard, and left? No! Be strong!

Lara got out of her car, adjusted her limp skirt, pulled her shoulders back, and walked into the house.

"Hey Todd!" she called.

The only sound she heard was the air conditioner cycling on. She felt the rush of cool air as she walked through the kitchen toward the front staircase.

"Todd, let's wrap this up," she yelled.

She heard the A/C hum, and detected a strangely sweet, smoky, metallic odor as she rounded the corner to the prime bedroom suite. When she entered the room, she saw what appeared to be a coat on the floor. She bent over, and immediately recoiled. It was Todd sprawled out face down on the oriental carpet.

"Todd!" she screamed as she dropped beside him. "What the fuck!"

Blood spilled out on the rug as she pushed him over. His eyes stared blankly.

"Oh God, help me," she shrieked, then pressed her ear on his bloody chest. *Nothing.* She pressed her fingers on his wrist. *Nothing.*

She yanked her cell phone from its holder, and pushed 911.

"Nine-one-one. What is your emergency?"

"Todd's hurt. I can't find a pulse. 8413 Crestline. Doors open. Hurry! Please!"

After being assured help was on the way, she turned her attention to Todd. She looked at all the blood soaking his beautiful suit, inhaled the sweet, heavy tang in the air, and wept uncontrollably. Blood was everywhere around her, the carpet, her legs, and Todd's body. She glanced at his blood-soaked chest, then to his head. Clumps of gray scattered around a huge bloody mass at the side of his head.

The front door burst open.

"Medics!" a male voice yelled.

"Over here, in the bedroom!"

Two paramedics rushed into the room, and unceremoniously pulled her up off the floor, ordering her to leave. Lara bolted out the front door, and onto the impeccably mowed lawn.

"Shit, shit, shit," she yelled, feeling a sharp pain in her stomach. She wrapped her bloodstained arms around her waist, and threw up all over the red and gold balloons waving festively atop the *Open House* sign.

CHAPTER 2

The heat, nausea, and smell combined into one blood-red haze as Lara collapsed on the lawn. She heard sirens in the distance as she briefly drifted off to a better world. It was then she felt strong hands grab her under her arms, and knees. She sensed a forward motion, and then a sudden rush of cool air. Two paramedics unceremoniously laid her limp body on a long sofa. Opening her eyes, she tried to focus on the fuzzy image of a man who passed a small piece of brown paper under her nose. A strong odor of ammonia jolted her out of the fog, and back into the real world. The medics strategically placed cold compresses on her wrists, ankles and forehead, then left without a word.

"Unbelievable," she moaned closing her eyes praying this nightmare would go away.

"Ms. Maxwell? Lara, are you awake?" asked a silvery, cool female voice.

Lara slowly turned her head. Sitting beside her was a small dark-haired woman in a tan pant suit. She scanned the room, and saw tall white oak bookshelves. She realized she was in the library, her favorite room in the house. The chocolate brown walls, the vermilion-colored sofa cluttered with pillows gave Lara a feeling of peace. Without warning, the detective's voice interrupted her reverie.

"I'm Houston Homicide Detective Edie Ross. I would like to ask you a few questions."

"Homicide? Oh God, it's true, isn't it? What kind of hell is this?"

Edie glanced at the dried blood on Lara's hair, hands and arms. She got up from the couch to speak to the policeman who was standing in the doorway.

"I need the medical examiner in here with a residue kit," she said.

A woman, who appeared to be in her early fifties wearing a lab coat over a lavender skirt, entered the room. She nodded at Edie, then turned to Lara.

"Hello I'm Dr. Mary Craddock from the medical examiner's office. I'll need to scrape some blood from your skin, and swab your hands. Have you washed your hands in the last four hours?"

"Uh, no, I don't think I have." Lara said.

"Good. I'll run a swab test now."

"Why are you concerned about my hands?" Lara asked.

"It's just standard procedure to make sure there's no gunshot residue."

"What? I didn't shoot a gun. I've never shot a gun!" Lara exclaimed. *What type of person do they think I am?*

"Please be cooperative," said Edie. "This won't take long."

Craddock quickly swabbed both Lara's hands and scraped a sample of blood from her palm before depositing the sample in a plastic bag.

"Okay Lara, let's get you to a sink where you can wash," Edie said as she helped Lara stand. She smiled at Lara, dimples creasing her tanned cheeks.

"I can walk by myself, thank you," Lara snapped. She wobbled ahead of Edie, past the cadre of police, and directly to the kitchen.

Lara closed her eyes and splashed cold water on her face, arms, and legs before taking a dish towel to dry. She looked down at the sink. Blood mixed with water streamed down the drain. Feeling light-headed, she gripped the counter for support. She looked around in time to catch sight of Edie heading for the bedroom. With nobody in the room to stop her, Lara quietly followed the detective. She tiptoed up to the slightly ajar door, leaned in as close as she could, and listened.

"How many shots were fired, Doc?" Edie said.

"Looks like two, one in the head, and one in the chest. Either shot would have been fatal," Craddock replied. "We're still looking for bullet fragments and shell casings."

"Do you have a positive ID on the victim?"

"I found his wallet in his jacket pocket. It's Todd Drake, age 36, broker and owner of Drake Properties. Apparently, the fainter is one of his agents, Lara Maxwell," said Craddock. "I found her cards on the hallway table, and the photo on the card matches what she looks like all dressed up and clean. She's a real looker with that beautiful red hair."

"Yeah, I got one of her cards, and I noticed several of the male officers put one in their pocket."

Craddock laughed. "They love thin and young."

Lara inwardly winced at the sexist banter aimed at her by, of all things, two women.

Maybe they've been working with men too long.

"Any sign of a weapon?" asked Edie.

"No. We found nothing except the victim on somebody's very expensive Oriental rug. The officers found his cell phone, and they'll take it to forensics. I'll be here for a while longer, and if I find something else, I'll let you know," Craddock said.

Lara saw the door move outward. Not wanting to be caught eavesdropping she quickly turned to leave, and ran smack into a uniform.

"Miss," the policeman said. "You need to stay out of the crime scene area."

Feeling trapped, and flustered, Lara tried to get around the policeman. Before she could escape, she felt Edie's hand on her elbow propelling her toward the kitchen. Edie's purposeful stride, and take-no-prisoners attitude commanded respect as the small cadre of police parted, allowing her to pass. Her hazel eyes, appearing darker under thick lashes, flashed with irritation. Her full mouth narrowed as she guided Lara to a stool at the kitchen counter.

"You need to stay put," Edie said. Her soft southern drawl turned into a gruff bark.

Lara sat down rigid, and ashen-faced. "I guess I just let my curiosity get the best of me."

"You need to stop being curious, and do as I say. This is a murder scene. There's evidence everywhere, and you can't be traipsing around possibly contaminating it."

Lara fought back tears of anger and humiliation.

"Now that we have that settled, I'd like to ask you some questions," Edie said. "Where were you when Mr. Drake was shot?"

Lara shuddered, and began relating the details of her nightmare day.

"There are no signs of a break-in. Were all the doors unlocked when you left?" Edie asked.

"I, I'm not sure. I locked all the back doors on my way out. Last time I saw Todd he was going upstairs to turn off lights. I'm not sure he locked the front door."

Lara thought back to when the paramedics came into the house. "Todd didn't lock the front door because the paramedics entered the house without a problem. I can tell you there were no cars in front of the house when I left."

"Do you have any idea who would want to murder him?" Edie asked.

"Who wouldn't?" Lara blurted out.

"He wasn't well liked?"

Lara took a deep breath, trying to clear her head.

What a loaded question. How does one explain all the conflicting emotions associated with Todd? Now is the time to be clear thinking, unemotional, and for God's sake, mature.

"Todd's an enigma," Lara said. "He has many friends, and his clients adore him, but he has made enemies. Most Houston realtors respect, and probably fear him. He's a reasonable, but tough negotiator. The office staff dislikes him because he's just so damn mean to them."

"Can you think of anyone who would want to kill him?"

"I'm not sure I know someone insane, and angry enough to murder. Right now, no one comes to mind," Lara said.

"What about during the open house? Any person, or persons who acted suspiciously?"

Lara closed her eyes, and rubbed her forehead. She tried to picture the people she saw, and what they did that made them stand out.

"I can't think of anyone who acted strangely," she said.

Edie picked up the sign-in sheet she retrieved from the kitchen counter, and handed it to Lara.

"Maybe if you read these names, it will help jog your memory."

Lara smirked, and took the paper from Edie's hand. "Detective, I would lay you odds that half of these names are fictitious, and the other half were scrawled so they wouldn't be legible. People on the whole don't want to be contacted after an open house, so they lie. It's a pretty useless piece of paper, but I'll try."

Lara looked at the names trying to not only remember who went with what name, but if any acted out of the ordinary. She remembered how surprised she was that the majority were young, some with young children, looking at a house for over a million dollars. Two of the couples brought their parents with them.

"Nothing unusual comes to mind. There was one couple who brought a puppy that peed on me. I've held babies and watched children, but this was the first time I held someone's dog. You wouldn't believe the crazy-ass things people expect you to do," Lara said. "I take that back. In your line of work, you probably would."

Edie smiled. "Yes, that's true. I've been with homicide for eight years, and I've seen people do bizarre things. I also know that people who have been traumatized by murder remember more than they realize. Your recall ability will increase once you've had some rest. Here's my card. If you remember anything else that was off, or odd, call me. We'll talk in more depth in a day or two. Oh, and stay in town. Don't talk to the press, or anyone else about this investigation."

"You know, I could have easily been in this house when Todd was shot," Lara said. "In fact, there is one thing I didn't tell you that seems silly, but it was odd."

"What's that?"

Lara took a deep breath, then slowly exhaled. "When I was alone in the house, before Todd got here, I had an eerie feeling that someone was in the house. I quickly went through the house to check, and found no one."

"Did you see a car in the driveway, or close to the house? Any unlocked doors, or sign of entry?" Edie asked.

"No. That's the strange thing. I just figured it was empty house jitters. Then right before Todd arrived, I heard a thud on the floor above me. Like something fell."

Edie immediately called a uniformed policeman over. "Henry, has anyone been upstairs?"

"Yes ma'am. Officer Jackson and I went upstairs as soon as we entered the house. We found no one."

Lara shook her head. "I don't know what it was, but I've been off my game today, the worst day of my life. I'm a mess. Do you think I'm in danger?"

"Just be aware of your surroundings. If something or someone frightens you call me," said Edie.

"I will. Thank you, detective, for helping me through this nightmare."

As she was leaving Lara paused at the bedroom entrance where she saw an empty gray stretcher. Her hands trembled as she fumbled for her car keys. She looked into the bedroom again. Todd's body was still lying on the blood-soaked rug. One of the policemen who was guarding the room saw Lara. He quickly moved toward her, and without comment closed the door in her face.

Lara sighed deeply, then turned toward the front door. She heard loud, angry voices coming from somewhere outside of the house. The front door opened, and two policemen escorted a tall, red-faced man, and a shorter blonde woman into the foyer. The man's height alone was imposing without the fury, and the woman's hefty, full-figured stature completed the boisterous pair.

"This is my goddamn house," he sputtered. "I don't need the police to let me in!"

Lara's heart raced as Jack and Melanie Bard raged toward her. "Mr. Bard, Mrs. Bard," Lara said. "I'm so dreadfully sorry."

"You're one of Todd's agents, aren't you?" Jack said.

"I'm Lara Maxwell, the agent who helped Todd hold your open house."

"The police told us you left Todd alone. You're the one who found him dead," Jack said.

Lara visually slumped. "Yes, that's true."

"Jack! Can't you see how upset she is?" Melanie said. "Look at her. She has blood on her hair and clothes."

"You realize we're ruined, don't you?" Jack yelled. "How in bloody hell are we ever going to sell this house?"

Lara tightened her grip on the staircase. Out of the corner of her eye she saw Edie ease alongside the angry pair.

"I'm HPD Detective Edie Ross," she said. "This is a crime scene. We need to move to another room to talk."

As they were leaving the bedroom door opened. The once empty gray stretcher was now carrying a black body bag guided by two uniformed policemen.

Edie, Lara, and the Bards silently parted, allowing Todd's corpse to be wheeled through the front door. Melanie Bard silently wept. Lara's hand shook uncontrollably as she reached out to touch the bag. Hot tears stung her eyes as she watched the stretcher being lifted, and pushed into the back of a waiting ambulance.

Edie gently closed the front door. "Okay folks, let's all go into the living room."

Lara followed reluctantly, and took a straight-back chair across from the Bards who sat on the couch, fuming at the world. She knew the distraught couple was in for a hard time. Here they sat in a home where they had raised children, entertained friends and family. A home they'd left just hours ago, only to return to a place soiled, and destroyed by murder. Melanie's knees were shaking, and Jack slumped down, arms across his chest, eyes blazing.

At Edie's insistence, Lara went through the day's events adding at the end how sorry she was that this tragedy happened in their beautiful home.

"We love Todd," Melanie said.

Jack narrowed his eyes, then turned to look at his wife with a flicker of a glare.

Melanie glanced away, and continued. "I can't believe he's been murdered. Have you seen the news trucks outside? This is going to be all over the city in no time. It won't be long until everyone in Houston knows our home is a murder scene."

Lara stood to look out the front windows. She saw four broadcast news vans parked in front of the house, and along the street. Neighbors milled around, gathering in small groups, whispering together, and stealing glances at the house. Reporters with pads, and pens in hands talked to a few people drawn from the group, while video cameras taped other newscasters interviewing police.

"Oh great," she moaned.

Lara heard the familiar ring tone she'd set up for her newest boy-friend, David King. "Excuse me, I need to get this," she said to the room.

"David, I can't talk now," she said in a whisper. "Can you come to my place?"

"Yes, but what the hell? Are you okay? Todd's death is breaking news on all the local channels."

"I'm okay for now. It's so horrible. I'm talking to the detective, and the homeowners. I hope to leave soon."

"I'll meet you at your condo." David said before hanging up.

Gathering all the strength she had left, Lara re-entered the living room where Edie was going over the open house sign-in sheet with the Bards, who didn't recognize any names on the sheet, fictitious or real.

She took her seat, and like a good realtor smiled, and asked what she could do to help.

Jack turned to look directly at Lara and said, "Maybe now is not the time to talk about this, but we may never sell our house. We are faced with the expense of a hotel room, clean up, and last but not least, selling this house!"

Lara bit on her lower lip.

How awful this is for them. I need to be calm, and professional.

"When you are ready, we can smooth all this out. You will need to disclose a murder in the house. Patience is the key. This will blow over, and memories will fade. You will eventually sell the house."

"How long will that be?" Jack raged. "We don't have all the time in the world. I have to be in Cincinnati in a month to start my new job. If we can't sell this house, you know who we are holding responsible, don't you?"

Remain calm.

"Well, I would think the murderer is responsible for this tragedy," Lara said immediately wishing she hadn't opened her mouth.

Damn. How unprofessional.

Recovering her composure, Lara said, "Give yourself a day or two. Come to the office, and we'll talk about where to go from here."

Lara smoothed her blood-stained skirt as she stood, "I really should go now, and give you two time to be alone."

She turned to Edie, "May I leave now, detective?" Edie nodded in assent.

Lara offered her hand to Jack who reluctantly shook it. She turned to offer her hand to Melanie who suddenly got up, and grabbed Lara in a bear hug.

"Well, thank you, Melanie," Lara said shyly. "Once again, I'm deeply sorry, and grieved." She stole a glance at Jack whose look of disgust said it all.

Lara made herself walk slowly instead of sprinting to the back door where a uniformed policeman stood ready to escort her out. Once outside she thanked her escort, quickly got into her car, locked the doors, and backed out of the driveway past the media circus. As she rounded the cul-de-sac, she looked in the rearview mirror at the limp balloons drooping over the lopsided *Open House* sign.

CHAPTER 3

Lara rolled toward her incessantly beeping alarm clock. She opened one eye, and saw 6:00 in bold red numbers. Reaching over to slap the snooze button, she closed her eyes to return to sleep. Instead, images of yesterday's horror returned. A jumble of forms, and colors danced in her mind. Todd on the floor. Police in the hallway. Red and gold balloons, crimson blood, and yellow crime scene tape spun into a sickening mosaic.

Her head ached from not eating dinner last night, and drinking too much wine. Her skin itched.

"Oh, the hell with it," she fumed, crawling out of bed, and then staggering to the bathroom where she kept a bottle of aspirin. She dry swallowed two, then shed her gown. She turned on the shower, and stood under the warm water hoping to clear her muddled brain.

She normally sorted out problems, real or imaginary, while in the shower, but this morning was different. Yesterday's events were beyond imagination, and not easily sorted.

Who killed Todd? Was it someone who came to the open house? Maybe someone came in after I left. But wouldn't I have seen a car leaving?

This type of thinking could drive her mad!

What about my business? Is it murdered along with Todd?

She turned the shower off, took a towel from the rack, and began drying her hair before a mirror. She put the towel down, staring in disbelief at her likeness. Her green eyes stood out only because the whites were a blotchy red. She glanced at her stomach. She saw red welts that itched like hell.

Lara looked closer at the spots, wondering if she had stepped in a fire ant bed while she was pounding those signs in and out of the ground. No. These welts were not ant bites. Then she remembered when her childhood cat had given her a rash from his fleas. *Flea bites!* Lara's mind raced back to the open house, to the couple who had asked her to hold their dog.

That scrawny, mangy dog not only peed on me, it gave me fleas!

She flung open the medicine cabinet, and grabbed a pink bottle of calamine lotion. She found a swab of cotton in the drawer.

"Jeez, what next?" she exclaimed while lathering lotion on every flaming welt she could find.

Pulling her robe on, she stomped downstairs where her newest squeeze, David, stood pouring coffee into a cup. She stopped momentarily looking at David who was dressed in perfectly fitting khakis, a green long-sleeved shirt tucked in, and tan loafers. His sandy hair, and dimpled chin gave him a boyish look she found irresistible. They met two months ago, and soon after became a couple.

She poured herself a cup of coffee immediately inhaling the wonderful aroma.

"Your brother left a message on your land line this morning," David said.

Lara grabbed the phone, and pushed the message button. "Hi Sis! What the hell is going on in Houston? Your broker's murder is all over Austin morning news. Call me." Lara immediately pushed Randy's number, and got his voicemail.

"Hey, big brother! We're playing phone tag. I'm okay, don't worry about me. Yesterday was a day from hell," Lara said, realizing her voice was shaking. She cleared her throat, and continued. "I'm still in shock. I'm okay, and will call you later."

Lara hung up, and turned to David. "I wish Randy lived closer. I miss him."

"Well, you know I'm here for you. You don't really need big brother to protect you."

"Actually, I need Randy. He's always been there for me," Lara said, wondering if he was jealous of her brother. "Do you have a problem with that?"

"I just thought that I would be the one you turn to. Just forget it. Talk to anyone you want," David said. "How are you feeling this morning?"

Lara quickly congratulated herself for not letting David move in with her. After all, she had only known him for a little while. She'd met him at a downtown bar during Happy Hour. He was witty, regaling her with stories about his job at Shell Oil where he traveled to offshore drilling platforms. He seemed so at ease with himself. But in a short time, he was becoming needy, and possessive. David's behavior was too much to think about now. She just wanted to be alone, and go on with what would more than likely be a shitty day.

"To answer your question, I feel awful," she said calmly. "To make matters worse, that puppy I held yesterday during the open house left fleas on me. Who does that?"

"Who does what?"

"Who brings a puppy with fleas to an open house? What nerve to ask me to hold a flea-ridden dog," she said. "It just doesn't get any better than this unless I find out I'm the prime suspect in Todd's murder."

Lara walked to the couch and sat down. David sat beside her.

"Maybe you can help me decide what to do," Lara said. "I've got to get control of myself today. I have this horrible feeling that everyone in Houston knows, or will know, that I was with Todd the day he was murdered. In fact, I'll bet it's already hit the news."

"Let's see what's on the news before you go all drama on me."

What's up with him?

David turned on the TV flipping the channels stopping at the *Today Show*.

Lara muted the volume with the remote, pulled her robe tightly around her chest, and waited for the local news.

She didn't have to wait long. Todd's murder was the lead story. She turned the volume up staring in horror as Todd's face filled the screen. "Oh, poor Todd," she cried turning to David who sat motionlessly glaring at the television.

The news segment continued with video of the house on Crestline, and the body bag being loaded into an ambulance. No mention was made of Lara. The report ended with a shot of the half fallen *Open House* sign on the perfectly manicured lawn.

"Damn!" Lara said looking at David. "I feel sick. Now everyone will associate Drake Properties with murder. At least for now I'm anonymous."

David shook his head. "It won't be long before the press finds out who you are. You've worked in public relations. Should you have a statement ready?"

Lara's first job after graduating from the University of Texas was an entry-level position in public relations at Exxon. Her dream job was short-lived. After several years as assistant to the Public Relations Manager of Community Affairs she was laid off. But during her tenure she learned how to deal with the press. She remembered when bad news came down the dictate was; "Get the truth out, and get it out fast."

"It's just so unreal," she said. "I'd better write a statement before I get trapped into saying something I'll regret."

David looked at her with mild concern before glancing at his watch.

"I hate to leave," he said. "I have work piled sky high."

David reached over to kiss her. She distractedly patted his cheek. "Thanks for being here last night. You go on before the traffic gets bad. I'll be okay."

"Put some more ointment on those ugly bites," he said.

David took one more swig of coffee, grabbed his briefcase and overnight bag, and went out the door.

Well, so much for having a loving man by my side.

Lara turned the news off, and went to the kitchen to pour another cup of coffee. She wandered back to the den, and sat on the couch contemplating what to say in her press statement. She decided to make it short. Something like - I found him dead, I grieve his loss, and I don't know who did it.

The ringing cell phone jarred her back to the present. She looked at the phone, didn't recognize the caller, and ignored it.

But what if it's a client, or an agent wanting to show one of my listings? Crap!

She heard the voicemail alert tone. Her heart raced as she listened to the message.

"Ms. Maxwell, this is Stanley Cox at Channel Two News. I know this is a bad day for you, and I'm sorry for your loss. When you have time could you please call me? I would like to interview you about Todd Drake's murder."

Lara turned her phone off, jumped from the couch, rummaged through the desk drawer, found a legal pad, and began writing her statement. She was almost finished when the front door bell rang.

Now what?

She tiptoed to the door, and peeked out the side window fully expecting to see a barrage of news cameras. Clapping her hands, she flung the door open, and grabbed the stately blonde who stood before her.

"Sonya," she said. "I'm so glad you're here."

"Where else would I be, honey?" Sonya Brown said as she swept into the foyer, past the living room, and straight to the kitchen. "I hope you made a big pot of strong coffee."

Lara followed her working partner, and friend into the kitchen. Sonya was dressed to fit the somber day in a black suit, and pale green blouse that matched her eyes. She had pulled her hair up letting perfectly curled tendrils fall around her face, and the back of her neck. She looked exactly like a Houston realtor should. Beautiful, perfectly coifed, and dressed. Lara envied her style, and if truth were known, tried to emulate her.

After pouring herself a cup of coffee, Sonya turned to Lara. "Oh my God, lie down and let's put some ice on those eyes."

Lara hesitated. Sonya snapped her fingers pointing to the couch. "I'll get the ice."

Lara plopped down on the couch, and heard Sonya open the freezer door.

"There's an empty ice pack on the top shelf of the pantry," Lara said.

"Frozen peas are better. Do you have any in the freezer? Never mind I found some."

Sonya returned to the den, and gently put the package of peas wrapped inside a towel across Lara's eyes.

"You poor thing," Sonya said. "You've been through hell. Just lie back. Tell me everything. Don't leave anything out."

Lara began describing yesterday's horror story, noticing as she talked that her headache dissipated. Sonya always had a calming effect on her.

Lara and Sonya joined Drake Properties within two months of each other. Lara came first after being laid off at Exxon, and then Sonya, who had left teaching after the death of her husband. As the years passed Lara thought of Sonya as the big sister she never had.

"Sonya, what do you think this will do to Drake Properties? Megan's business partner has been murdered. Do you think she can survive this?" Lara asked.

"Oh, I imagine it'll hurt for a while. Knowing Megan, she'll come out smelling like a rose. You just watch. That woman has spunk. She's a survivor."

"You know what freaks me out the most?" Lara asked. "If I hadn't left to pull those damn signs out of the ground, I may have been shot too. That bossy detective, Edie something, said I should be careful. Do you think I'm in danger?"

"Heaven's no, who would want to murder you?" Sonya said. "I can actually think of several people who would want to murder Todd, but not you."

Sonya took a sip of coffee, and leaned into Lara's face.

"Which crazy fuck do you think killed him?"

"It's hard to finger one person when there were so many shit-bat crazies around him," Lara said. She removed the melting package of peas from her eyes, and looked over at Sonya. "Seriously, he seemed to know everyone. He also pissed off many people he came in contact with except for his clients who were crazy about him."

"If you're talking about Melanie Bard, well…"

Lara's neck stiffened. "What about Mrs. Bard? Do you know something?"

"I heard she had this thing for Todd. Silly gossip that has little merit," Sonya said dismissively. "Todd was a real charmer, wasn't he? Never in my wildest dreams did I think we'd know someone who winds up murdered. It's otherworldly."

Lara put the bag of peas back on her eyes, and sighed. "Sonya, do you remember last year when the police came to our sales meeting to talk about realtor safety? The one bit of advice I remember is, always listen to that little voice inside your head telling you something's not right."

"Yeah, I remember. Why?"

The air conditioner suddenly blew cold air through the vents directly on Lara's neck. Instinctively she lifted the robe under her ears, and shuddered.

"Something was nagging at me all day yesterday. It was an uneasy feeling. When I was alone in the house, I felt there was someone in the house with me," Lara said. "I blew it off thinking Todd's late arrival was the reason for my anxiety. The whole day seemed, uh, off kilter. Once the open house started, I got busy. That feeling went away."

"Did you see a car, or any telltale signs that someone was there?"

"No. I looked out the windows, and in the driveway. No one."

"So, how do you think it happened? Why murder Todd, and why yesterday at, of all things, a public open house?" Sonya asked.

"Maybe Todd got angry at the wrong person, and that person came to the open house. We know he has, I mean, *had,* an anger management problem that would have challenged any good therapist," Lara said. "I was in the office on Friday and heard him berating Billy Parsons for being five minutes late to show his clients a property. What a bastard!"

"I've been on the receiving end of that lunatic's anger," said Sonya. "Todd could make you feel like an utter fool. Do you think it was Billy? Do you think it was someone in our office?"

"Oh shit, I never thought of that. I suppose it could be anyone including agents, and staff." Lara's hand shook as she lifted the towel, and faced Sonya.

"How do I look?"

"Gorgeous," Sonya lied.

"Yeah, I'll bet. I'm through playing whodunit. It's time to get dressed, and ready for what will probably be, one bitch of a day," Lara said. "While I'm getting dressed will you please throw these melted peas away? Pour yourself another cup of coffee. I won't be long."

Thirty minutes later Lara appeared in her best black suit.

"I forgot to turn my cell phone on, and when I did, I had three frantic messages from Megan," Lara said. "She has arranged for, get this, a press conference at the office, and I need to be there. Will you be there? "

"Are you kidding? I wouldn't miss this for the world," Sonya said.

"As much as I dread the thought of a press briefing, Megan is making the right move," Lara said trying to remain calm. "Look how deftly she turned the spotlight on herself, and bless her little heart, took it off me. I could learn to love that woman."

CHAPTER 4

Lara slowly inched her car into the usual morning traffic jam on I-10, easing her way over to the middle lane where she sat with hundreds of her fellow Houstonians. She watched with amusement as drivers maniacally changed lanes, hoping to get a few car lengths ahead, and to their destinations faster than the person three cars behind.

After years of driving Houston's freeways, Lara was convinced that a majority of Houstonians made their way through traffic with horns honking, middle fingers waving, and mouths spewing obscenities.

Suddenly, from seemingly out of nowhere a truck cut in front of her almost clipping her right bumper. "Son of a bitch!" she yelled. "Stay in your lane!"

Breathing deeply like her yoga instructor taught her she inched along to her exit. Once off the freeway Lara sped the extra five miles to her office parking garage. Grabbing her purse, and a few client folders, she rushed into the building. As soon as she opened the door to Drake Properties, she was met by office manager, Jackie Long.

"Lara," Jackie exclaimed. "How awful this must be for you. It's unbelievable."

"I think I'm in shock just like everyone else," Lara said, noticing unusually dark circles under Jackie's eyes. She looked gaunt, and haunted.

"Jackie, are you okay?"

"No, I'm not," Jackie said. "I didn't sleep well after I heard the news. Todd. Murdered."

Lara reached out for Jackie's hand giving it a squeeze. Then she turned to enter the brightly lit work area with two neat rows of desks. Several agents were talking in hushed tones. When they saw Lara, they gathered around her.

"How are you?" Chaya Getz exclaimed. "I, I mean we are all in shock."

The others nodded in agreement. A few were openly crying. One by one they came to Lara with open arms, and heartfelt condolences.

"Lara!" Billy Parsons, Todd's assistant, called out. "Lara, sweetheart!"

Billy ran to her wrapping his arms around her neck, and wailed. "What a terrible loss. What a horrendous ordeal for you!"

"Billy," Lara gasped. "You're choking me!"

"I'm so sorry, sweetie," he said dropping his arms. "I'm so overcome with grief. I guess I don't know my own strength."

Lara rubbed her neck. How typical for Billy to be emotionally over the top.

"I understand," she said. "We're all overwrought."

Sonya emerged from her office giving Lara a small wave.

"How'd you get here before me?" Lara asked. Sonya shrugged her shoulders. Before she could reply the group silently made a path for Megan James, owner of Drake Properties, and Houston's preeminent African-American woman.

"Dear Lara, how awful yesterday must have been," Megan said. "This is such a devastating loss. I don't know how we'll get through this, but we will."

Lara stared blankly at Megan. She could count on one hand the times she had seen Megan show emotion. If truth be known Lara was intimidated by this real estate icon who ran her office with cold precision. Megan's hard-ass business acumen, and ability to cut anyone down with *the look* from those dark eyes, put fear in the hearts of all.

"Let's go into my office and talk," Megan said.

Lara followed Megan looking pleadingly over her shoulder at Sonya who grimaced, then mouthed, *good luck.*

Once inside her office, Megan closed the door, pointed at a plush leather chair for Lara, then sat behind her desk.

Lara looked at the expensively framed photos. Each one showed an exquisitely dressed, stately Megan and the mayor, Megan and the governor, Megan with a variety of city officials. Her uncluttered desk had a small-framed group photo of Megan with her agents. Everyone was smiling, looking ever so happy to be in Megan's circle. The agent photo was dwarfed by a larger framed photo of Megan and her father, a well-known local music producer.

"Losing Todd is the biggest shock of my life," Megan began. "Losing him in such a violent way has been almost impossible to bear." Her voice softened. "Not only am I grieving the loss of my business partner, but I'm also concerned about Drake Properties."

Lara looked out the large window trying to collect her thoughts.

"You'll come out on top," she said. "You always have, and you always will."

It's all about you.

Megan rose from her chair, and sat on the edge of her desk next to Lara. "We have little time to talk. The press conference is in ten minutes. I suggest you let me do most of the talking."

"That's fine with me," Lara said. "Yesterday the detective who is handling the investigation told me to keep my mouth shut. I think you need to check with the police before you say anything."

"You let me handle this," Megan said. "I'll call the detective. What's his name?"

"Her name. Edie Ross," Lara replied.

"I'll call her now."

Lara sat back in the chair, and smiled inwardly, thinking once again she had a ringside seat to Megan's stellar ability to handle any difficult person who tried to get in her way. Megan's steady, cool demeanor, intensified by *the look*, saved more contracts, and closings from going down the toilet than Lara could count. Now, once again Lara had to rely on Megan's nerves of steel to get her through a tough situation.

"Good morning, Detective Ross, this is Megan James owner and broker of Drake Properties. I just want you to know I'm giving a press conference in about ten minutes," Megan purred. "There has already been intense press coverage. I need to assure our fellow Houstonians that Drake Properties is cooperating with the police."

Megan's plastic smile suddenly disappeared, replaced by pursed lips. "But I have a statement ready. I can handle myself. But…of course, okay, yes, I will. I'll come to the station after the press conference. Goodbye."

Megan hung up, looked at Lara and shrugged. "Well apparently, I need to be careful not to say anything that will jeopardize the investigation. That rude detective basically told me to shut the fuck up. She also said when the press conference is over, I have to come to her office for an interview. Why can't they come here? I'm busy!"

Lara suppressed a laugh. Megan had met her match. Edie was one tough cop. Lara felt a strange pride in Ms. Detective Ross.

Alright, Edie! I want to be like you when I grow up.

Jackie interrupted by opening the door to say the television cameras were set up in the lobby.

"Okay, here we go," Megan said smoothing her black suit with her well-manicured hands.

Newspaper and television reporters along with several camera crews were crowded in the lobby waiting for Megan's entrance. She walked into the lobby followed by Lara, and the other agents who solemnly stood behind their broker. Megan introduced herself, looked out at the reporters making sure she had everyone's attention, and began reading her statement.

"The realtors and staff at Drake Properties are sorrowed by the untimely, and brutal death of our owner and broker, Todd Drake. As you all know one of our agents, Lara Maxwell, was hosting an open house with Todd before he was murdered. She and I have been asked by HPD detectives to not answer questions as this is an active murder investigation. All of us at Drake Properties are in shock. I ask that we be given time to grieve in private," Megan said as she paused to wipe a tear from her amber cheek. "As the co-owner of Drake Properties, I want all our clients in Houston to know despite this tragedy we will continue doing business in the professional manner to which you are accustomed. Thank you for your understanding, and compassion."

Megan gave a small smile, and regally walked out of the room.

Lara was barraged by reporters shouting questions. "Lara! Who do you think killed Todd? Lara! Do you think you're in danger too?"

Her heart beat faster as she scrambled for something to say. "I hope I'm not in danger. I trust the police will find the killer soon."

"Do you have any idea who killed Todd?" a young female reporter asked.

"I'm totally at a loss," Lara replied.

Turning abruptly, she scrambled out of the lobby straight to the bathroom at the rear of the office. Her stomach churned as she made her way to one of the stalls.

"Are you okay, Lara?"

Lara's heart skipped a beat. "Megan! Where did you come from?"

"I was already here. You were in such a hurry I guess you didn't see me."

"You gave me a start," Lara said as she went into the nearest stall.

"I came in to calm my nerves," Megan said in a trembling voice. "I hope I said the right thing out there."

"You did great, Megan," Lara said as she came out of the stall. Megan seemed uncomfortable, not at all like her hard-ass broker persona. "I was peppered with questions when you left."

"I'm sure Detective Ross will have something to say when I see her. This murder, and its aftermath scare the hell out of me."

Megan scared? How could that be? Lara had always thought of Megan as a pillar of strength. Now, to her surprise, she felt sorry for her. Wasn't it just two short weeks ago *The Houston Business Journal* crowned Drake Properties number one in sales volume among the smaller boutique firms? For several days Megan and Todd's photos were plastered over the front pages of area newspapers. Beautiful people riding high. Now that beautiful façade was tainted by blood, and murder.

"I worked so damn hard to build this business," Megan continued. "Todd worked hard. Shit, we all worked hard. Now some murderous maniac has killed Todd, and possibly destroyed me."

Lara moved closer to Megan putting her arm around her shoulder. "I know you'll survive this, Megan. All of us are behind you. We'll get through this together."

Megan stiffened, moving slightly so that Lara's arm dropped away. "I have to get ready for my appointment with Detective Ross. God forbid I should be late." She looked in the mirror, applied a soft coral lipstick to her perfectly curved mouth, and then adjusted her skirt.

"Is there still going to be a sales meeting tomorrow?" Lara asked.

"Of course," said Megan. "Jackie will send out an email to all the agents. I want y'all to get back to business as usual."

"I'm scheduled to show property this morning," Lara said. "I think these buyers are ready to write a contract."

She immediately regretted her words. Why did she feel the need to let Megan know that no matter what, even after she saw Todd in a pool of blood, she was still producing?

"Yes. Keep on making sales," Megan replied turning her back on Lara as she hurried out the door.

"I'll be damned," Lara said. Her voice echoed off the cold, tiled walls. She went over to the sink to splash a small amount of cold water around her eyes. She began thinking about how Megan's abrupt exit angered her, and made her feel like a child who is always looking for approval. She didn't need Megan's validation. She was a successful, independent businesswoman. Was it that important to her self-esteem to get warm fuzzies from Megan? Too many times she'd tried to get close to Megan only to be coldly, and yes, cruelly rejected.

Lara dried her eyes, and stood at the mirror.

Someday I'll wise up.

She stuck her chin out, looked directly in the mirror, and vowed, "I promise to never sympathize with, grovel to, or touch that woman again."

CHAPTER 5

Edie

Earlier the same morning, Edie tiptoed through her dark bedroom, and leaned over her half-awake husband. "I'm going to work now, honey."

Ted looked at his watch. "It's five-thirty, Edie. What's the rush?"

"I couldn't sleep," she whispered. "I need to clear my desk, and mind before I tackle my new case. Tell the kids I'll see them tonight."

She kissed Ted's cheek, rubbed his shoulder, and silently left the house. She needed to get to the office for some alone time; valuable time to clean off the mound of papers accumulated on her desk. She had always been a believer in the theory that a cluttered desk is the sign of a cluttered mind.

The commute to HPD headquarters was a breeze. No traffic, no stress. What a great way to start the day. She strolled into the building, greeting the few officers at the front desk before bounding up two flights of stairs, then following the caramel aroma of freshly brewed coffee. Five detectives stood around the coffee urn.

"Move aside, and hit me with caffeine," Edie said. The group stood back, and bowed in unison.

"Edie! Do you know what time it is?" asked one of the detectives. "To what do we owe the pleasure of your company?"

"Don't flatter yourselves thinking it's because I need to see your mugs," Edie laughed.

"Hey Edie," another detective called, "I see your homicide case is a major headliner. It's all over the early morning news. You'd better get this one right, kid."

Edie smiled, "You know I love high-profile cases. They make me a star."

She turned toward her office leaving behind a cacophony of good-natured groans. Edie entered her office, and emitted her own groan. "What a dump."

She mentally rolled up her sleeves, and began going through the mountain of papers on her desk, throwing some away, and pinning important sheets to the large bulletin board behind her chair. She finished in thirty minutes, then stood back admiring her work.

Order in the chaos.

"Good morning, Edie."

"Captain, you scared the shit out of me," Edie said.

"Sorry. You didn't hear me knock?"

Edie shook her head before sitting behind her desk. She really detested people sneaking up on her. An old childhood fear stoked by her brother, who found delight in sneaking up behind her, grabbing her neck, and hearing her shriek in terror.

"Knock louder next time," she said "Let's start over. Good morning."

Edie looked at Captain Mike Henry leaning against the wall smiling good naturedly, wearing a light brown suit, and blue shirt that highlighted his ebony skin, and brown eyes. She admired, and respected her captain for his intellect, and even-tempered manner.

"I'm glad you're here, Edie," Captain Henry said. "Come to my office. Yates is waiting for us. Y'all need to hear this about your new case."

So much for alone time.

Edie followed the captain to his office, and took a seat next to her partner, Ron Yates, who was slouching in his chair. He sat up straight, and gave Edie a quick nod. Ron was transferred over to homicide from vice six months ago to replace Edie's retired partner, Jake Madison. The two hit it off immediately.

"I just finished reading the medical examiner's report on Drake," Ron said. "Looks like we've got a tough one."

Edie sighed, and shrugged her shoulders. "We've been up against it before. We can handle this."

Two detectives, who Edie recognized from the Narcotics Division, knocked lightly, and entered the office.

"I think you both know detectives Steve Carter and Buzz Cline," Captain Henry began. Edie nodded at each man. Ron gave a slight wave. "They've been investigating Todd Drake."

"Our Todd Drake? The realtor who was murdered yesterday?" Edie asked.

"Yes, Edie," Steve said. "We've been watching Drake for almost a year. We were close to arresting him on drug charges. Now some asshole's gone and killed him."

"Houston's number one realtor was involved with drugs? What the hell?" Ron asked.

"It looks that way," Steve said.

"Do you think we're looking at a drug related murder?" Edie asked.

"It's quite possible," Steve said. "Here's what we know. Drake had been hosting parties for large corporation new hires in order to get business. Our informant tells us the parties involved illegal drug use. Drake apparently bought cocaine, and a mixture of party drugs from his bartender friend, Alex Ricci, and then distributed them at the parties. Do you know who Ricci is?"

Edie moved closer to the edge of her chair. "No, I don't think I've heard that name before."

"Drake met Ricci at *Ceres*, an upscale Italian restaurant in West University where he tends bar. They became friends. Our sources tell us the two of them came up with the idea to throw parties for newly hired, high salaried guys right out of college. Mostly nerdy computer geeks. You wouldn't believe the salaries those people demand." Steve let out a whistle. "Unbelievable."

"We've been watching Ricci for a long time too," Buzz said. "He's been selling drugs to some vicious clients. Drug lords, and their minions. He's lucky to still be alive and kicking."

"Odds are, Ricci won't live long enough to bounce grandchildren on his knees," Steve chuckled.

"Apparently Drake bought the drugs from Ricci. Ricci made money on drug sales, Drake on home sales." Buzz said. "We questioned Ricci on Friday. He was arrogant, and non-communicative. We still don't have enough to bring him in on charges. He's a wily asshole."

"What did Ricci have to say?" Edie asked.

Buzz shook his head before continuing. "He said Drake was his friend, and he moonlighted at the parties as the bartender. Drake was actually scheduled to come in today for questioning."

"I'll be damned," Edie said. "The bartender was Todd's friend? Apparently not only politics, but real estate makes strange bedfellows."

Ron slowly shook his head. "That's a new twist."

"Now that it's become a homicide case, we're sharing our notes with you. Anything we can do to help catch the shooter let us know," Buzz said.

Edie sat back in the chair, and sighed. After two years on this job nothing much surprised her, but this was a new one. A real estate broker involved in drugs. What next?

"Do me a favor. Keep me posted on what you learn," Buzz said while handing copies of his notes to Edie. "By the way, what's your take on this, Edie? This shit is all over the morning's newspaper. What about that agent who found his body?"

"I'm not sure about anything now," Edie said. "The agent, Lara Maxwell, is a suspect, yet my gut feeling is that she's not the murderer. She's young, smart, and observant. She doesn't quite fit the profile of a murderer. Based on her behavior at the scene I didn't see any red flags that would indicate she uses drugs. I think she was in the wrong place at the wrong time, nothing more."

"That doesn't mean she isn't in on the supply side," said Buzz. "From what I understand she's a hot-shot realtor. That shows she worked with Drake's high-end clients. Apparently, a lot of Drake's clients attended the parties. As a way of thanking Todd for a good time, they would recommend his firm to others who were looking for big, expensive homes. Hell, no wonder Drake Properties is rated number one in Houston."

"Yep, quid pro quo," Edie said, then seeing the blank looks on the detectives faces explained, "You know, you scratch my back I'll scratch yours."

"You can always make an investigation sexy, Edie," Steve said.

"I think we're done," Captain Henry said. "Let's get back to work."

"One more question for Edie, sir," Buzz said. "Since your gut feeling is Ms. Maxwell is not the perp, do you think she would be an informant? She knows everyone at Drake Properties. I would think she'd have a strong interest in helping us out with this case."

"Possibly," Edie said, thinking back to how well Lara handled herself at the murder scene. "She may just be the person we need."

"We'll talk about that later," Captain Henry said. "For now, let's continue our investigation. Maybe we can come up with a viable suspect, and won't need an informant."

"Okay, boss. Good luck you two. Let us know if we can help," Buzz said, nodding at Steve to leave.

Captain Henry rubbed his eyes, and stretched. "I'm sure I don't need to remind you both to tread carefully with such a high-profile case. I'd bet my next paycheck there are some agents at Drake Properties who know all about Todd's side business."

Edie returned to her office to read Buzz's notes, the preliminary autopsy report, and ballistic report. She was interrupted by a call from Megan James asking for advice about, of all things, holding a press conference.

What in the world was this woman doing holding a press conference?

After advising Megan to say as little as possible, Edie hung up, and continued the task she had begun earlier. She was halfway through the pile of folders when Ron burst into her office.

"You've got to see this."

Edie followed Ron into the squad room. A group of detectives were hovering around a small 1990s era television. One of them waved Edie over. As she got closer, she saw a tall, impeccably dressed black woman on the screen introducing herself as Megan James.

"Wow. She's a stunner," Edie said to the room. She watched the entire news conference, breathing a sigh of relief when Megan finished. She had done precisely what Edie had asked.

•   •   •

Two hours later a hush fell over the usually noisy squad room as Megan strolled past gawking detectives to her interview. Captain Henry hurried out of his office to escort her to where Edie was waiting.

Megan entered the drab interview room looking more stunning in person than she did on television, or in her photos. Edie introduced herself, and pulled a chair out. Megan sat, crossed her long, shapely legs, and smiled. Captain Henry knocked on the door. He entered with a cup of coffee, and handed it to Megan.

"I hope this is the way you like it, Ms. James," the captain said, smiling broadly.

Edie sat with her arms crossed taking in the scene. She waved her finger in the air to get the captain's attention,

"I'd like cream and sugar," she said.

Captain Henry gave her the get-your-own-damn-coffee look, and closed the door.

"It's good to meet you in person, Ms. James," Edie began. "Do you mind if I call you Megan?"

"Of course, you can," Megan replied. "There's no reason to be formal."

"I'm Edie Ross, the lead investigator on the Drake murder case. My partner, Ron Yates, and I will interview the agents, and staff at Drake Properties. I asked you to come in today for an interview only. Just relax, and answer my questions to the best of your knowledge."

"I am relaxed, detective," Megan said in her velvety tone. "I'm here to help in any way I can. By the way, did you see the press conference?"

"Yes, and I think you did a good job."

Megan smiled tightly.

"What were you doing yesterday between one and four in the afternoon?" Edie asked.

Megan's panther eyes narrowed. "You don't think I killed Todd, do you?"

"I need to know where anyone who was connected with Todd was at the time of the murder. It's a standard question," Edie said.

She's highly strung.

"I was at a friend's house," Megan said. "I'd rather not go into it any further."

"Megan, there are no secrets in a murder investigation," Edie said. "Where were you, and who were you with?"

Megan took a sip of coffee. "I was with Todd's father, Kevin Drake."

"You're involved with Todd's father?"

"Yes, we are privately seeing each other," Megan said. "We have not made our relationship public. Losing Todd is so painful for Kevin. I would like to keep our private life private for now."

"I can assure you whatever you tell me won't be made public," Edie said. "How long have you, and Mr. Drake been seeing each other?"

Megan squirmed in her chair, took another sip of coffee, and said, "Six months, but I've known him for many years."

"Before you met Todd?"

"Yes. Kevin is a well-known builder in town. I'm a realtor. We travel in the same business, and social circles," Megan said.

"How did you meet Todd?"

"I wanted to grow my small brokerage firm. Kevin introduced me to Todd, who had just graduated from SMU, and wanted a career in real estate. Todd was a go-getter, charming, and smart as hell. Todd's energy, and connections contributed to our standing in Houston, and to our success."

"Did Todd know about your relationship with his father?" Edie asked.

Megan turned her head slightly to look directly at Edie. Silence filled the room.

Megan shook her head. Without lowering her gaze, she said, "Kevin's wife, Todd's mother, died two years ago. It was devastating for Todd. We decided not to tell him about us. We probably should have."

"I see. Let's move on then," Edie said. "Can you think of anyone who would want to kill Todd? Did he have enemies?"

Megan rubbed her forehead. "No, I don't know anyone. I think Todd had more people jealous of him than angry with him. He is, I mean he was a successful, savvy businessman. I don't think people wanted to kill him," she said, sighing deeply. "I think they wanted to be like him."

"Do you know about the parties Todd hosted that involved drug use?" Edie continued.

"I know about the parties Todd gave to meet people, and promote our business. Like I said, he was a go-getter," Megan replied. "I know nothing about drugs."

"Did you attend any of these parties?" Edie asked, watching closely for any sign of surprise, or shock from Megan. So far, she saw nothing.

"I stayed away. Todd and I had a good business relationship. I handled running the office, dealing with the agents, and smoothing out contract problems," Megan said, pausing to take another small sip of coffee.

"I serve on several charitable boards. I attend business luncheons, and political functions. Todd worked the real estate end by serving on the board of The Houston Association of Realtors, going on listing appointments, and holding open houses."

Megan glanced around the room before focusing on Edie. "Both of us had clients we worked with. Todd had more clients than I did. Sometimes we'd go to a luncheon together, or to a listing appointment together. The arrangement worked like a perfectly oiled machine. Until now."

"Did you hear of any personnel problems connected with Todd?" Edie said.

"I know Todd had a temper he let fly at some of the staff, and agents. You know he was born with a silver spoon in his mouth," she said, softening her tone before continuing. "He was spoiled. I heard things about his temper tantrums, but since our business wasn't affected, I basically ignored what I saw, and heard. I let Todd handle his own problems."

"You saw something? What did you see?" Edie asked.

"Several things, like Todd coming in the office with a hangover, and taking his misery out on the agents."

Edie picked up her pen and wrote, **Todd had a drinking problem?**

"I saw him raging at Billy Parsons, our assistant. Billy was in tears," Megan continued leaning slightly toward Edie. "That was something I couldn't ignore. I met privately with Todd and encouraged him to be more sensitive to Billy. He promised to try. That's all I could get him to do. Promise to be better."

"Did Todd have a significant other?"

"As far as I know he played around. I know several agents in town he dated, but none lasted long," Megan said. "How much longer will this questioning go on?"

Edie took a few moments looking over her notes. Megan crossed her arms over her chest, and waited.

"Did an agent, or anyone on your staff, leave your firm because of Todd's temper?" Edie asked, ignoring Megan's icy stare.

"Not that I know of. Agents leave real estate firms all the time. It's part of the business. As for our staff I can't think of any who left angry. In fact, few have left us."

Edie sat back watching Megan who never flinched.

"Okay, Megan. I believe that's all I have for now. Thank you for coming in."

"I hope you have asked me everything you wanted to know," Megan said lifting her body out of the chair.

"A few more things before you run out."

"There's more?"

"Don't leave town," Edie said. "Don't talk to the press. If you remember anything call me. Here's my card."

"I don't think I have forgotten anything, but if I think of something I'll call you," Megan said. She walked toward the door stopping to take a slim silver holder from her purse, and removed a card. "If you, or anyone you know, needs a realtor here's my card. So long, detective."

Megan lifted her head high, walked out of the room, leaving her coffee cup, and a line of admiring detectives behind.

Edie looked at the eye-catching card with Megan's stunning face on one side, and her office logo and phone number on the other. Gathering her notes, and the lipstick-stained cup, she paused on her way out to throw the slick card into the trash.

CHAPTER 6

"Miss Maxwell, your clients are here," Jackie announced over the office intercom.

Lara jumped up from her chair, grabbed her purse along with the client file, and hurried out to the reception room to meet with her buyers. Showing homes to buyers was an excellent way to forget that dreadful press conference, and her annoying run-in with Megan.

Besides, Lara always enjoyed showing property. She enjoyed getting to know her clients, their likes, dislikes, and their quirks. It wasn't unusual for Lara to become friends with her clients. Many times, their friendship extended past the closing date.

Buyers were her favorite people. Even so, there were times when she had the misfortune of getting stuck with disgruntled, unhappy buyers who took their frustrations out on each other while Lara drove them around town. Looking for a home can be stressful, especially when couples can't agree on what they want. Lara empathized with the unhappy ones up to a point. When they began screaming at each other, Lara's understanding attitude turned to indifference. Fortunately, there were only a few angry ones. Her clients today, Dick and Vanessa Clark, were an easygoing, enthusiastic couple who also liked each other.

"Hello Dick! Hi Vanessa," Lara said in her Miss Congeniality realtor voice.

Vanessa stood. "Good morning, Lara. I want to introduce you to my mother, Kate. She's visiting from Baton Rouge. I told her it's okay to come along with us."

"How nice to meet you, Kate," Lara said to the elderly woman who looked like a miniature Vanessa with her blue eyes, short brown hair, and pointy chin. "The more the merrier. Glad you can join us."

Dick rose to his full six-foot-three stature, and shook Lara's hand. "Thanks for being available today, Lara. We realize this is a bad time for you. We're sorry for your loss."

"Thank you. Working to help you find a house helps," she replied.

Megan entered the room waving slightly to Jackie before saying, "I'll be at HPD for an hour." She stopped when she saw Lara, and her clients.

"Megan, I'd like you to meet Dick and Vanessa Clark, and Vanessa's mother, Kate," Lara said. "This is my broker, Megan James."

Megan gave them her most brilliant smile before saying what a great pleasure it was to meet them, and how lucky they were to have Lara as their realtor, blah, blah, blah… a real estate broker's gooey, canned statement.

Vanessa, Dick and Kate took it all in, falling for Megan's bullshit hook, line, and sinker.

"Wow," Vanessa said after Megan left. "She belongs on the cover of *Vogue*. She's gorgeous, and so down to earth."

Lara grunted, took her car keys from her purse, and mumbled, "Yeah, she's terrific."

She opened her car doors for everyone to pile in.

Show time!

Backing out of her parking space, Lara turned right on Chimney Rock heading North, and began her real estate banter.

"The first house is in Yorkshire, and is 3,500 square feet, two-story, three beds, two baths with a pool," Lara began before being interrupted by Vanessa.

"Lara, I don't want to be a busybody or upset you. Can you talk about yesterday? It's all over the news. You poor thing. It must have been horrible."

She knew it was coming. No way for her to hide from the glare of the headlines. Vanessa's curiosity was understandable. After all they had the star witness in the car with them.

"It was heartbreaking, and horrible. Everything about yesterday is a blur. It was the worst day of my life."

Feeling a wave of nausea overtake her, Lara took a gulp from her water bottle. The sick feeling subsided. She decided to say no more hoping her audience of three had heard enough.

"What a terrible thing to go through," Dick said. "I hope you're safe."

There it is. That nagging fear.

Lara played brave by saying she felt safe. Bracing herself for more questions, she was delighted when Kate spoke up.

"I believe the weather here is as hot as Baton Rouge."

Lara wanted to hug Kate for deftly turning the conversation to the most benign topic of all, the weather.

Five minutes later she pulled into the drive of the first house. She unlocked the front door, and loudly called out, Realtor! This was a habit she adopted several years ago when she entered a house unannounced to find the owner in the shower. After the screaming subsided, she vowed to never enter a home without verbalizing her presence.

Lara had scheduled four home showings in the same West Houston area. As she followed the Clarks through each house her mind wandered. Try as she might she couldn't stop the image of Todd's limp, blood-soaked body from invading her thoughts. Fear crept in, haunting her as she walked through room after room. Who was evil enough to murder him? Was she the next victim? Her hands trembled, and she felt dizzy.

Concentrate on your job.

The first three homes didn't pique the Clark's interest. They were too small, too large or just not exactly right. By the time they entered the last house, Lara was hot, thirsty, and worried that her clients were getting discouraged.

Her concern melted away as soon as they entered the two-story Mediterranean style home in Lakes of Parkway. Dick and Vanessa immediately perked up.

"Oh my God," Vanessa said. "Look at this beautiful entrance. Wow! Look at the high ceilings."

Now they were enthusiastic, walking more slowly through each room, talking about where their furniture would go, pointing out fixtures, and flooring to each other. Lara walked with them answering their questions, knowing instinctively that this was the house for them.

When they entered the open kitchen, Dick and Vanessa beamed. With arms entwined they walked the area, touching the gold flecked granite counters. They stood against the kitchen island admiring the adjacent great room. They had found a home.

"I adore this kitchen," Vanessa said. "The six-burner gas stove alone would make a gourmand salivate. I want this house."

"Let's go talk about it over a cool drink," Dick said. "Can we call you later, Lara, with our decision?"

"Oh, of course, but just a gentle reminder. This is a seller's market," Lara said. "That means the sooner you decide the greater chance you won't be in a bidding war with another buyer. There's a great restaurant around the corner from the office where you can talk."

"We'll call you by tomorrow morning. Is that okay?" Vanessa asked.

Lara looked at her watch, saw it was four-thirty, and smiled. "That won't be a problem."

Lara opened the front door allowing her clients to go ahead into an intense wall of heat. She quickly ushered them to her car, started the ignition, turned the air conditioner on high, and reached into a cooler handing each person a bottle of water.

"Y'all sit in the car, and cool off. I'll make a quick call to the listing agent to make sure no other offers have hit her desk."

Lara walked a few feet from the car, and pulled her phone out.

"This is Jane Layton," said a pleasant voice.

"Jane, this is Lara Maxwell with Drake Properties. I'm showing your listing in Lakes of Parkway," she said. "The buyers may be interested in making an offer. Do you have any other offers coming in?"

"Not yet," Jane said. "Send me an offer, I'd love to work with you."

Lara hurried back to her car. "Good news. As of now, you won't be competing with other offers."

She paused to look for any reaction from her clients, and saw three beaming faces. For this moment all the fear, and sorrow that had been her constant companion evaporated.

CHAPTER 7

"You're back," Jackie said. "Did you find a house for your buyers?"

"I think I have a sale," Lara replied as she hurried past the reception desk.

"Well, aren't you hot," Jackie mumbled.

It was tempting for Lara, after hearing Jackie's retort, to retaliate with a sarcastic comeback. Instead, she continued to her office. She didn't have time to mess with weird Jackie today.

What a relief to be in her small, windowless, yet cozy office. Here she felt safe. How unreal, even eerie that only a day ago she never applied the word safe to her life, yet now she could think of nothing else but her safety.

Glancing at her phone she saw it was just five o'clock, plenty of time to work on a sales contract for her clients, Dick and Vanessa.

Lara realized she was doing what Megan had warned her about. She was becoming too fond of her clients. She tried to keep an emotional distance from buyers and sellers, but try as she might she became emotionally tied to the pleasant, positive ones. Only a hard-ass could resist people like the Clarks. Working with them after all the blood, and horror of yesterday was a lifesaver.

Before she began, Lara closed her eyes, took a deep breath. She continued breathing deeply several times to clear her mind, and soothe her jangled nerves. She was interrupted by the strident ring of her cell phone, ending her meditative trance with a jolt.

"Hi, Lara," said Sonya. "How's your day going?

"I'm putting together an offer on that house in Lakes of Parkway. Where are you?"

"I just left my listing appointment in the Woodlands. I thought maybe you could meet me at Carrabba's around seven for dinner."

"Count me in!" Lara said. "See you then."

Lara clapped her hands. Not only did she love being with Sonya, but she also didn't have to eat dinner alone tonight. She honestly had been dreading being alone after yesterday's horror. What she needed was someone to talk to, and Sonya fit the bill. She turned to her computer, and began filling out the contract form. In a half hour she finished the offer, and began tackling her emails. She was halfway through when Jackie buzzed her desk phone.

"You have a call on line two."

Lara pushed the blinking button, "This is Lara."

"Hello Lara, this is Detective Ross."

Lara's heart rate quickened. She closed her eyes. *Shit!*

"Hello, detective," she said, trying to sound friendly. "I didn't expect to hear from you so soon."

"I'd like you to come to my office tomorrow for a more extended interview than we had yesterday," Edie said. "What's a good time for you to come in?"

Lara's mind reeled in confusion as she mentally went over her schedule.

"Well, I've got the Tuesday morning sales meeting. After that I'll probably meet with my buyers to sign an offer," Lara stammered. "I might be able to come to your office after lunch. How long will it take?"

"It shouldn't take longer than an hour," Edie said.

"An hour? I told you all I know yesterday. I, uh, I have a business to run."

"Yesterday you were in shock. I normally talk to witnesses the day after the crime was committed so I'm actually giving you an extra day," Edie said. "I'll see you at eleven-thirty tomorrow morning. Come to our headquarters at 1200 Travis, and ask for me."

The line went dead. "Hello, Edie? Well, dammit to hell!" Lara said to the office walls. "What nerve!"

Lara wrote the time and place on a piece of yellow sticky note, and slapped it on her computer screen. *Relax,* she told herself as she put her fingers back on the keyboard, but try as she might she kept coming back to her conversation with that rude detective.

Why do I have to go downtown? Am I a suspect?

Anxiety rushed through her body. Feeling her cheeks flush she sat back, and fanned herself with a couple sheets of paper when a knock came on her door.

"Yes, come in," she barked.

"Are you busy?" Billy Parsons asked.

"Not too busy for you, Billy. Have a seat," she said. Billy was one of her favorite people in the office. He made her laugh, and forget her problems. He was just the person to lift her out of her agitated state.

Billy took the chair across from Lara clasping his hands in his lap. His blonde, boyish good looks, and wit endeared him to all the agents. Well, almost all. Sonya did her best to avoid him.

Lara knew how hard he worked as Megan and Todd's assistant while always keeping his affable manner. Right now, he seemed to have lost his jovial persona. His sweet, soft face was harder looking. Dark circles emphasized his blue eyes, and he seemed paler than usual. His right leg bounced. Lara felt her chest tighten.

"Billy, are you sick?" she asked.

"Heavens no," he exclaimed, "Unless you consider a hangover as being sick."

"Rough night last night, huh?" Lara said.

Billy leaned over gazing intently into Lara's eyes.

"I can't sleep. I'm so upset, and angry over Todd's murder."

"So angry you decided to kill a pint of bourbon?"

"Clever girl," Billy said. "Yes, that angry. Todd meant a great deal to me. I'm heartbroken."

"I always thought you had a crush on him, Billy. I know he was mean to you. Heartbroken seems a little overboard."

Billy took a deep breath, rubbed his forehead, and looked up at the ceiling. "Okay, he was mean. There were times though when he was actually helpful. You may not know this, but he introduced me to Houston's movers, and shakers. He knew I wanted to be more than his assistant."

"That's right! I forgot. You're a licensed realtor."

"I don't want to be Megan's lackey forever," Billy replied rising from his chair. He took a few steps to peer out into the work area. Satisfied no one was around, he closed the door, and stood in front of Lara's desk.

"You've always been respectful to gay little me when others in this office have not. I trust you, and have to confide in someone."

Oh shit. Is he going to confess to murdering Todd?

"What's going on?" she said.

Billy's face turned red as tears welled in his eyes. He began pacing, wringing his hands. Lara braced herself for whatever Billy was going to say.

"This is hard to admit, so bear with me," he began. "Todd told me he could hook me up with a couple of guys who would be good contacts, you know, someone who could help me get started in real estate. These men were in top positions with several oil companies. The gay ones were securely locked in their office closets but came out at local bars where they felt safe. I had a big chance to be their go-to realtor."

Billy took a deep breath before continuing. "These so-called respectable businessmen, gay and straight, were involved in sex parties hosted by, get this, Todd."

Lara sucked in a deep breath. "Sex parties? What? I've never heard of this. Are you sure?"

This must be one of his jokes!

"You're one of the few who didn't know. Todd wanted to protect you," Billy said. "These parties were all Todd's idea, and a brilliant one at that. He'd invite newly hired men in oil and technology companies to his upscale parties. He also invited beautiful, willing women. Those high-salaried tech nerds were so grateful that most hired Todd as their realtor."

Lara sat in stunned silence watching Billy pace while he poured out a story she was having a hard time believing.

"Sex party? Are we talking orgies? Does that even happen?"

Billy rolled his eyes. "For heaven's sake Lara, grow up. Of course, they're orgies. Yes, it does happen."

Lara's face reddened. She didn't consider herself a prude, but she shied away when Billy talked about his sexual escapades. He had funny stories, but there were times he gave too much information. Now he's talking about orgies. What next? Did she dare ask? Her curiosity got the best of her.

"How many people are we talking about?"

"Think of all the major, and minor oil and technology companies in Houston. Then multiply that by all the new hires, and you're talking tons of people, a few women, mostly men. Todd shrewdly lured people from pretty much every profession including real estate to his parties. He told them it was an opportunity to make business, and money connections. Think of this as a sexual meet and greet."

Lara studied Billy who seemed to enjoy telling yet another one of his lurid tales. This time instead of being bored she listened in rapt attention.

"Go on."

"Sit back. I'll paint you a picture," Billy said warming to his audience of one. "Now, mind you, I didn't go to the straight parties. I was busy entertaining at the gay events. One time my party didn't happen so I went to Todd's soiree out of curiosity."

Lara leaned back intent on every word.

"Most of the parties were held at that new hotel downtown that starts with a Z, Zooey? No! *Hotel Zoie.*"

Lara laughed, thinking Billy could even make name recall entertaining.

"Todd had rented the banquet room with an awe-inspiring view of downtown Houston. Very sexy! Todd would stand at the entry sipping bourbon with water while greeting everyone. The men were all young techie new hires straight out of grad school. Their incomes gave them an automatic invitation. They came alone for one thing, and one thing only, available, hot women."

"What about the techie women?" Lara asked.

"They were actually not bad," Billy replied. "From what I saw they enjoyed talking to everyone, including the men. They weren't drunk, or disorderly like the men could be."

"Who was there? Anyone I know?"

Billy took a sip from a bottle of water Lara had given him.

"I think you'd know several of the women," Billy smiled. "Todd had a knack for inviting great looking women. A few of them confessed to me they wanted it all, a lover, a sugar daddy, and if they were lucky, a husband. Others told me they were curious, or hoping to make a good business connection."

I'm thinking sex pawns, not business women, Lara mused.

"This was the place to screw money, and power," Billy said. "The people Todd invited were in professions vital to new hires, like personal shoppers, physical trainers, and of course, real estate."

Real estate! The most important service for anyone new to town.

Lara was beginning to understand how Todd got so many new high-end buyers. In the past months she noticed several agents who were struggling had suddenly found moneyed clients. Her mind whirled with questions, but Billy was on a roll. He loosened a couple of buttons on his shirt, pulled it tightly around his chest, and strutted, stretching to look taller than his actual five-foot-seven. Lara thought he looked like a show girl with his blonde curls bouncing around his ears.

"The clothes these women wore! Most were in short, tight-fitting dresses with plunging necklines." He stopped strutting, dismissively waving his hand as he continued. "The men were such nerds. They would stand around drink in hand, wearing brand-new jeans, and try-ing to look like Texas cowboys while gawking at the women." Billy mimed their expressions, his eyes and mouth opened extra wide. Lara laughed at his performance.

"It was funny, but pathetic. I'll bet you anything not one of them had a date in college," he continued. "The music was sexy too. Todd hired a three-piece band that played slow, bluesy music. Everyone, even if they weren't good dancers, got out on the dance floor."

Billy swayed his body as if having sex while dancing. Lara clapped. After all, Billy was a good dancer.

Billy bowed, and continued. "On the other side of this huge room was a bar. Oh, that bartender!" he said as he rolled his eyes heavenward. "Alex the Italian stud. His black pants fit every muscle. The cherry on top was his form fitting black vest over a white shirt open to the top of the buttoned vest," Billy said as he walked around pretending to model tight pants, and a low-cut vest. "Whatta hunk!"

Lara found herself both horrified, and fascinated with this story of debauchery. Billy was entertaining, and actually, a pretty good actor.

"The food was wonderful. Picture a long table of scrumptious party food, caviar with Crème Fraiche tarts, lobster toasts with avocado, and bacon-wrapped scallops."

"Ooh, I love lobster toast!" Lara said.

"At the end of that table was an array of party drugs, Molly and Ecstasy, some joints, and for the intrepid few, bags of blow," Billy continued. "The drugs were there to loosen everyone up. Before I left, I saw a group of five or six together on the couch in a cuddle puddle."

"A what?" Lara was having such a good time that the term almost got past her.

What in the world was he talking about?

"Cuddle puddle. That's where people gather in a group touching, and caressing each other. I also saw several couples go to rooms."

"Wow!" Lara said trying to get a grip on everything. "Unbelievable. By the way, you should be on stage, Billy."

Billy smiled. "The nouveau riche think their brains, income, and degrees make them entitled. They are arrogant, and really believe that since they have money they can have any woman, or man they want."

Lara shook her head. "I suppose money makes people sexy, and ir-resistible. Was Todd involved in drugs?"

"I'm not sure. I only saw him drink heavily," Billy said. "I know he was into sex. I saw him on the couch with a woman straddling his lap. Should I go on?"

"Don't!" Lara's hand went up. "I get the picture."

"I remember Todd told me he would never ask you to the parties. I guess he wanted to keep you to himself," Billy said with a sneer.

Lara's heart skipped. *He knows.* She decided to ignore his last state-ment.

"Where did the drugs come from?"

"Alex. He and Todd planned all this together. They brought me in as the party organizer. It was all so seductive. I met lots of men. Todd got all the real estate business. Alex got the drug business."

Billy fanned his hands to each side of his face, then said with a weak smile, "Who could ask for more?"

"Sounds like you were riding high. Did you get a cut?" Lara asked.

"I made some extra money for my time organizing the parties. I enjoyed the perks of meeting people in high places, and taking as many drugs as I wanted. When you figure how much Todd paid Alex for the drugs, plus how much he made in home sales I wasn't compensated nearly enough. What else is new?" Billy shrugged his shoulders.

"Business was actually conducted at these parties," he continued. "Connections were made. Why do you think Drake Properties has so many high-end clients? Why do you think Drake is number one in sales in Houston?"

"I feel so, so dumb," Lara said. "I thought we were successful be-cause we worked so hard."

"You think everyone is like you, Lara. That's just not the real world."

Lara sighed. Billy was probably correct. He could be blunt to the point of being rude, but he also had a surprising insight into the people around him.

"Billy, tell me you didn't kill Todd."

"Are you fuckin' kidding? He was pretty close to the bottom of my list of people to kill," Billy replied. "Seriously, you know me, Lara. I'm afraid of my own shadow. Todd actually helped me out of a brief financial bind. Nobody, and I mean *nobody* would kill off a cash cow like Todd was for me." Billy slouched further down into his chair. "Besides, I have a more serious problem. I don't think I can go through a day now without popping a pill. I'm afraid I'm addicted. I'm scared."

Lara got up, and took a chair next to Billy. She held his hands while he sobbed. "I'm sorry to dump all this on you."

"Don't worry. It's okay. What scares you?"

"I'm so messed up. My addiction scares me. I've become afraid of everything, and everyone. Even Megan scares the shit out of me," he said with a chuckle.

"Join the group," she said. "I want to make sure you're okay, and the only thing I can think of is my typical knee jerk reaction, a good therapist. When my parents died, I found a wonderful therapist who also works with addicts. Her card is in my desk drawer somewhere."

"Spare me. I've been through therapy before. I actually went to a therapist who said she could help me not want to be gay. Can you imagine? The phony ass tried to hypnotize me out of liking men, and into wanting women. Like I could change what I've always been. What a crock of shit. Therapy is not for me."

Undeterred, Lara went to her desk, and began rifling through her top drawer.

"Just in case you change your mind, I found it!" Lara said slipping the card into Billy's shirt pocket.

"I'll think about it," Billy said. "I've got to go. I'm supposed to be taking contracts to title companies. Thanks for being here." He gave Lara a quick hug, grabbed more tissues, said a mumbled goodbye, and walked out the door.

Lara plopped down in her chair gazing across the room at her favorite Claude Monet print, *Garden Path at Giverny*. She had deliberately hung the painting to remind her that there was beauty in the world.

She had replaced anxiety with despair. What would happen to Billy? Were drugs the reason for Todd's killing? Try as she might it was hard to digest all that Billy had told her. It was as if he'd pulled up a large rock, and showed her the dirty underside. She thought Todd was a jerk, but now she knew for sure what a sexist prick he was.

She shook her head, sighed, and stared at the painting wishing she was walking toward the distant light on the path, surrounded by flowers, and overhanging trees.

Peace along a lighted path.

CHAPTER 8

Lara was glad she'd made reservations at *Carrabba's* because tonight it was super crowded. The hostess showed her to a corner booth in the bar area. She sat back against the cushion, breathing in the aromas of marinara sauce, garlic, and fresh baked focaccia. Happy hour was over, but the bar was still crowded with diners at several tables. She saw a group of people who were probably her age gathered at the dimly lit bar, laughing. Was it just a day ago she was as carefree?

Out of the corner of her eye she saw a tall blonde woman part the crowd, leaving men gawking in her wake. Sonya lit up the room with her brilliant smile looking at least ten years younger than the thirty-something group at the bar. Lara shook her head thinking how nice it must be to have great genes.

"Hey girl," Sonya said. "Have you ordered yet?"

Before Lara could answer a waiter appeared to take their drink orders. She ordered a cosmopolitan, her favorite summer drink. Sonya ordered a dry martini with extra olives, her favorite year-long drink.

"Tell me about your day, Sonya."

"My day has been brutal," Sonya replied. "I'm totally exhausti-pated."

"You're what?"

"Exhaustipated. Too tired to give a shit."

Lara broke out in a hearty laugh.

"Sonya, you have a way with words," she said. "What is it you don't give a shit about?"

"I don't know, real estate, clients, maybe everything. I've had a crappy day," Sonya replied. "This morning I showed a house in The Woodlands. All was going well until we went into the prime bedroom, and found the owners in bed."

"What? Were they doing it?"

"No. I was extremely relieved that they had finished," Sonya said. "They acted like they didn't know I was coming even though I'd made an appointment. When I entered the house, I announced my presence. Obviously, they were too busy to hear me. I quickly ushered the buyers, and by the way, their four-year-old son, out of the bedroom. I've never had that happen before. I guess there's a first time for everything."

Lara shook her head. "What did you say to them?"

"I made a feeble apology. Something like, excuse me for interrupting. What I really wanted to say was, couldn't you have waited?"

Lara laughed. "If only we could say what we really think."

"We wouldn't be realtors if we did. Instead, I apologized to the buyers for the seller's behavior," Sonya shrugged. "Go figure. Someday I'm going to stop apologizing for others. Anyway, long story short, I quickly ushered the buyers out of the house. What else could I have done? Help the owners dress, and make the bed?"

Lara smiled as the waiter brought their drinks. Taking her glass by the stem she raised it toward Sonya. "To real estate."

The waiter returned. They ordered dinner, and another round of drinks,

"This afternoon Billy was in my office with a whopper of a story," Lara said.

"That's typical Billy. He always has some wild-ass story geared to shock as many as possible."

"This one is hold-on-to-your-seat wild," Lara said. "According to him, Todd's way of getting all those high-end clients was by hosting sex parties. I was flabbergasted. Have you ever heard of these parties?"

Sonya looked around the bar, tapped her fingers on the table, then took a sip of her martini. "I've heard something about them. I don't get into idle gossip, Lara."

"I don't think this is idle gossip. I believe everything he said. Well, almost everything."

"Lara, sometimes you can be so gullible."

The waiter brought their food. Lara picked at her lasagna. She felt hurt by Sonya's remark. Why wasn't her friend shocked? She seemed almost bored by what Lara thought was a pretty stunning revelation.

"I'm not gullible this time, Sonya. Anyway, apparently drugs were available at these parties. Billy told me he saw drugs, and drug use."

"I pay little attention to what Billy says. I'd suggest you do the same."

Lara knew that Sonya never really liked Billy the way she did. Maybe Sonya was sincerely not interested in anything Billy had to say. But still, why was she so evasive? Lara dropped the subject. For now.

Midway through the meal Sonya put her fork down, cleared her throat and said, "Lara, I know you're upset about Todd's murder, and who wouldn't be after what you've been through, but you seem a little off kilter. I think something else is bothering you."

"Something else besides sex parties, and drug addiction?" Lara replied. Taking another sip from her drink she pushed her plate aside. "You know me too well. That woman detective called. She wants to see me after tomorrow's sales meeting."

"Don't think she's picking on you," Sonya said. "On my way here, I called Jackie to check in. She told me Megan had an interview with the detective today. Wouldn't you love to have been a fly on the wall for that interview?"

Lara sat back smiling at the thought. "I'm picturing sleek, elegant Megan being interviewed by a drab detective. It is amusing. I'm willing to bet Megan chewed that detective up, then spit her out."

"I'm not sure I'd take that bet," Sonya said. "You have to be a pretty tough cookie to become a detective in a big city police department. Anyway, I think the detective is interviewing everyone in the office. No one is getting away from scrutiny."

Lara wrapped her arms around her waist. "Sonya, is it possible that Todd's murderer is someone in our office?"

"Anything is possible. You never know what evil lurks in people's hearts. How well do you think you know everyone in the office?"

"After hearing Billy's tale, not that well," Lara said.

The waiter interrupted to clean off the table. Lara wiped a few crumbs from her lap, and continued, "It's hard for me to believe Todd was murdered. I can't escape this nightmare," she said. "I can't get the image of Todd's body in a pool of blood out of my head. Knowing the murderer was in the house during the time I was getting those signs, scares the shit out of me. What if the killer thinks I know something, and wants to shut me up?"

Sonya reached over, and patted Lara's hand. "This must be awful for you. If I'm shaken by Todd's murder, I can only imagine how upset you must be. I'll help you as best I can to get through this."

Lara fidgeted with her cocktail napkin trying to gather her thoughts.

"I don't know what I'd do without you. You're my rock, Sonya. To-day I literally pushed myself to put one foot in front of the other, to show homes, and be pleasant to my clients. I'm in pain, real physical pain over finding Todd murdered. I actually saw chunks of Todd's brain on the carpet! I can't think straight. I'm on the verge of tears all the time." Lara put her head in her hands. "I don't feel safe anymore. Today I was constantly looking over my shoulder."

"You're on a tightrope, and need some sleep. Come stay with me for a couple of nights," Sonya said.

"Thanks, but I'm looking forward to going home, and being alone. If I get jittery, I'll come to your house," Lara said. She looked across the table at her friend, and took a gulp of her drink before continuing. "I can tell you what scares me more than a crazed murderer. I'm terri-fied to talk with that detective. I'm afraid she might put me in jail. I've just got to tell you something no one knows, and eventually the police will find out."

Sonya sat back as her hand flew to her chest. "Seriously? You'd bet-ter not tell me you shot Todd."

"I didn't. Instead, I fucked him. In fact, I fucked him three times, and now I'm so fucked!"

Sonya sat stunned. "Well, you slut!" she said with a chuckle. "I'm sorry honey, very insensitive of me. What do you think you're going to jail for, felonious fucking?"

"Very funny, Sonya. I'm thinking suspicion of murder." Lara gently blew her nose.

"Think about this. The police don't put people in jail for suspicion. They need solid evidence. Calm down girl," Sonya said.

"I'll try," Lara replied. "My fling with Todd was just three months ago. Now he's murdered. You don't think I'd be the number one suspect if they knew?"

"I guess you have a point. I'm not up on police work, but I imagine having an affair with the victim doesn't automatically make you the killer. Maybe a suspect. Hell, I don't know," Sonya said. "So, what's this about you and Todd? What were you thinking?"

"There was a time when I thought he was rather sexy. You have to admit he was pretty cute."

"Yeah, cute in a sleazy way. I never thought of him as being bed worthy," Sonya said. "I know how easy it is to fall for a jerk. None of us are immune."

Lara put her chin on her hand thinking how lucky she was to have someone to talk to who would listen, not judge. "It all happened when I was at the office working late. Todd was there. I'm sure you know Megan keeps wine, and liquor in a cabinet. I think she hits the bottle a lot. Anyway, we drank some wine, talked business, and one thing led to another."

"It happened in Todd's office?" Sonya asked.

"On his couch. A week after that we met for dinner, and it happened again at his townhouse."

"Was that it?" Sonya asked.

"Sorry to say it wasn't. One more. Afterwards I realized Todd was getting possessive, and I wasn't enjoying, uh, being with him," Lara demurred. "This was around the time David and I got together."

Lara felt her cheeks redden, and her skin tingle. She always hated telling anything personal. Especially now. Everything about Todd gave her a guilt complex. What had she ever been thinking?

"Anyway, I told Todd we had to get back on a business level," she continued. "He reluctantly agreed, but kept after me to help him with open houses. He'd call, and say he needed me to go with him on listing appointments. Each time I told him I was busy. Yesterday was the first time I agreed to help. Obviously, that was a bad decision. All day I was angry more with myself than Todd. After the open house I was determined to stop being a guilt-ridden flunky, and tell him to fuck off."

Lara sipped her drink, and continued. "So here I am probably a suspect for murder. Once the police find out I'll become the prime suspect. You know, the jilted woman kills her lover, or lover killed in a jealous rage. There are so many scenarios they can come up with, none of which are true."

"You need to tell the detective exactly what you just told me," Sonya said. "We always tell our clients to disclose everything. Now it's your turn. Hell, Lara we've all screwed the wrong man. That doesn't mean we'd murder them. Although if I knew what I know today I probably would have murdered my late husband."

Lara softly laughed. Sonya had been married to an attorney who died of a heart attack while running in the Bayou City Classic Fun Run. She was a teacher at the time with a young daughter. Her grief turned to rage when she found out her dearly departed hubby had left her with a large gambling debt. Sonya's savings were gutted. She quit teaching, and went into real estate. Soon after, her mother moved in providing extra help with finances, and child rearing ensuring Sonya would not lose her house, or her mind.

"There are men in our life we'd love to murder. By the grace of God, we just dump them," Lara said.

"That's funny because there were several men you chose who I thought you should have shot," Sonya said. "Todd isn't the only asshole you've been with."

Well, there it was! Another reality check. Lara was quite aware she had made hideous choices in men in the past. There was Stan who worked in public relations for the Astros, and loved the women, and the men. Then there was Chad, an accountant who drank himself out of her life, and into AA. She knew Todd was an ass before finding out about the orgies. Now David, an engineer with Shell Oil who was showing an ugly, hateful side. She was realizing that wishing for a good outcome doesn't make it true.

"All the men in my past, and present life, except Todd, I met in a bar. I think I'll swear off going to bars."

"Let's don't go overboard here," Sonya said.

"If I can just get through this miserable time, I'll try to figure out my problem with men. Right now, I'm an emotional mess."

Lara fidgeted with a cocktail napkin then leaned closer to Sonya. "I think Billy knows about Todd and me."

"Holy shit! I hope not. Billy's a loose cannon. You really need to let the police know before they find out from Billy, or someone else he's told."

"I'm confused, tired, and a little tipsy. I think I'd better call it a night."

"Okay, but please consider telling the detective about Todd and you," Sonya said. "Wait here. I'll get the check."

Lara watched her talk to the waiter along with several men before returning to the booth.

"Did I see you give a couple of those men your business card?" Lara asked.

"They recognized me from my newspaper ad," Sonya said with a smile. "They may need a realtor."

Lara rolled her eyes. "Of course, they will."

As they left the restaurant, Sonya's splashy newspaper ads with her face plastered above her currently listed homes, flashed before Lara's eyes. She had to give it to Sonya, she knew how to market. Lara made a mental note to check out the cost of a small ad.

"Remember to call me if you need somewhere to stay," Sonya said hugging Lara goodbye.

Lara got into her car turning right on Voss toward the freeway. She took a deep breath, and turned on her favorite soft jazz CD. She adjusted her rearview mirror, and noticed a car following much too close.

Get off my butt, she thought as she merged on the freeway.

The music drifted around her as she glanced at her rearview mirror, and saw what she thought was the same car still close behind. She moved over to the right lane, then took her exit. Again, she looked in the mirror. Again, the same dark sedan was behind her.

Calm down. It may be a coincidence.

She turned left into her condo complex parking lot. She drove to her assigned slot. Turning her head toward the street she saw the sedan slowly pass by again. This time she could see the driver's profile in the dark car. She couldn't determine if it was a man or a woman. The driver had shoulder length hair, and a somewhat familiar profile.

Son of a bitch! Do I know this person?

Lara grabbed her cell phone, and called David, who lived three blocks from her.

"David, are you in bed now?"

"Not yet. What's going on?"

"I'm outside my place. I think someone is following me," Lara replied.

Before she could say more David told her to stay put, lock the car doors, and wait for him.

Lara slumped down in the car seat, peering over the lip of the door, and out the window. A car drove by slowly. The same car. Lara scrunched down further until the sedan drove out of sight. Seconds later she saw a car speed up to her parking slot.

David!

Lara opened the car door and flew smack into David's arms.

"What took you so long?"

CHAPTER 9

Edie

Edie trudged through the hot humid air, and quickly got into her car. She turned the A/C on high moving the side vents toward her. On days like this, when the heat index was predicted to be 102 degrees, Edie fantasized about life as a detective in Hawaii, or California. Cities similar to Oahu and San Diego. Cool ocean breezes. Paradise!

A horn blast yanked her back to reality. Thanks to her reverie she'd slowed down to a little below the speed limit, enough to make any red-blooded Houstonian furious.

As she sped up, she thought, *That asshole would shit if he knew he was honking at a police detective. I'd love to see his face if I pulled him over.*

The cold air gliding over her face mellowed her response. She allowed the irate honker to pass while he mouthed obscenities behind a rolled-up window.

After finding a parking spot she dragged herself into the delightfully air-conditioned squad room. She passed a cluster of detectives, poured herself a cup of coffee, then walked directly into her office. Taking a tissue from a side desk drawer, Edie wiped the sweat from her forehead, then pulled out a small hand mirror to check her makeup.

A loud knock on her door made her jump.

"Yes, come in," she said irritably.

"Good morning," Captain Henry said. "How's the Drake case going?"

"Good morning," Edie said shoving the mirror back in the drawer. "Ron and I are still working on the list of interviewees. I've been thinking about how careful we need to be with everyone we interview. Todd had a lot of prestige in the community. His co-broker, Megan James is a real estate rock star in Houston."

"After meeting her in person yesterday I'm thinking that woman would be a rock star in any city," Captain Henry said. "She's beautiful. Is she under suspicion?"

"C'mon Captain. You know as well as I do that everyone who knew the victim is a suspect," Edie said. "I'm concerned that when Todd's drug-laced sex parties come to light it could ruin Megan along with the realtors in her firm."

Captain Henry sighed. "That's what happens in sensational murder cases like this one. All the more reason to wrap this up soon with as little media coverage as possible."

Edie leaned back in her chair. "I've been thinking about that narc detective, Buzz Cline, and his suggestion to ask Lara Maxwell to be an informant. She's coming in today before noon. I'm considering asking her to be our eyes and ears at Drake Properties."

"Isn't she a suspect?"

"I'm not crossing her off the suspect list yet," Edie replied. "She could be the shooter. I'm just thinking out loud. I'll know more after the interview."

"Are you talking to anyone else this morning?"

"Jackie Long, the office manager at Drake Properties will be here any minute now," Edie replied. "She insisted on coming in early before the office sales meeting. I'm instantly suspicious of someone who squeezes a police interview into their own schedule. Makes me think she's giving herself an exit."

"I trust you to get everything you need, no matter how much time she gives you," Captain Henry said. "Keep me posted."

He turned to leave, then looked back over his shoulder. "Oh, and as far as Ms. Maxwell goes, go with your gut feeling."

Five minutes later the squad room secretary buzzed Edie. "Ms. Long is here."

"Please send her in," Edie said

Jackie silently stood framed in the doorway of Edie's office, impeccably dressed in a creamy linen suit.

"Hello Ms. Long, I'm detective Edie Ross. Would you like some coffee before we start?"

Jackie smiled faintly. "You can call me Jackie, and I'd prefer water."

Edie took a bottle of water from the squad room refrigerator. She poured herself more coffee, then showed Jackie into the small interview room.

"I know you're pressed for time this morning so we'll make this quick," Edie began.

Jackie smiled shyly as she uncapped the water bottle, taking a large gulp.

"Tuesday is our sales meeting. I'm responsible for setting up the conference room," she said. "Todd used to help by picking up the food, but now that he's not here."

"This is an initial interview. I have a few basic questions. You can leave anytime. You can refuse to answer any question I ask. Keep in mind this is not the time to lie. Do you understand?"

Jackie nodded.

"How long have you worked at Drake Properties?"

"Three years," Jackie replied. "I moved from Corpus Christi."

"What did you do in Corpus?"

Color rose to Jackie's face as her eyes darted around the room. "I worked for an accounting firm. I have a degree in accounting."

"What is the name of the firm? Why did you move to Houston?"

Jackie shifted in her chair. "Detective, I want to answer all your questions, but I fail to see what this has to do with Todd's murder."

"The background of everyone who was associated with the victim helps us find the killer," Edie said. "Relax, it's just a normal interview question."

"Okay. My job was with Franklin Accounting on Ocean Drive in Corpus. I left because I was bored, and wanted to live in a bigger city."

Edie quickly made a mental note to check with Franklin Accounting.

"What is your position with Drake?" Edie continued.

"I'm the office manager."

"Where were you Sunday between one and four in the afternoon?" Edie asked.

Jackie sat up straight. Beads of sweat collected on her upper lip. She smoothed back her sandy brown hair. Tears welled up in her eyes, and streamed down her cheeks.

Edie moved a box of tissue from the corner of the metal desk toward Jackie. After years of interviewing suspects, she knew tears could be a sign of fear, remorse, or a way to get out of telling the truth.

"This is so surreal," Jackie said patting her eyes with the tissue. "I'm a private person. I have to ask you to keep this secret for me."

"Nothing you say here will be made public."

Jackie looked pleadingly at Edie, and sighed heavily. "I was with Alex Ricci."

"Alex Ricci, the bartender at *Ceres*?" Edie asked.

How did this woman get involved with a suspected drug dealer?

"Yes."

"Where were you and Ricci?"

"We spent the day at my townhouse in West University," Jackie replied. "We didn't leave."

"Why was your relationship with Alex a secret?"

"Because he does, I mean did business with Todd. I didn't want Todd, or anyone to know about our relationship. That's a moot point now," Jackie sniffed. "I still don't want people in the office to know."

"Are you aware of the type of business Alex did with Todd?"

"Yes. He tended bar at parties Todd hosted," Jackie replied.

"Is that where you met Alex?"

"I met Alex at the office. He came to see Todd. I've never been to Todd's parties," Jackie replied, smoothing a wrinkle from her skirt. Her head rose, and her eyes darted from Edie to the far wall, then back to Edie.

She's lying.

"There were drugs at those parties, Jackie. Did Alex supply the drugs?" Edie deadpanned.

Jackie's her eyes blazed with anger, and indignation.

"Not only no, but hell no," she said. "Alex is the bartender at *Ceres*. He moonlighted at Todd's parties because he liked Todd, and he needed the extra money. He doesn't take drugs or deal drugs!"

Jackie rubbed the back of her neck, then put her hand around the bottle taking another sip of water. She looked at the small wall clock across the room, and sighed loudly. "I'm going to have to leave soon."

Edie watched Jackie squirm in her chair while her eyes scanned the room resting on the door.

That question certainly perked her up. She's acting like a trapped animal.

"I have a few more questions. Did you like working for Todd?"

"He was a good boss. I know he was hard on the agents," Jackie replied. "He was a professional, and a bit of a taskmaster, but I liked him."

"Was he hard on you, Jackie?"

"Not really. Todd wanted a smooth-running brokerage. I think I contributed to a successful, well-run office. I'm responsible for all the contractual details combined with the daily operations. Actually Todd, Megan, and I worked well together."

"Can you think of anyone who didn't work well with Todd, someone angry enough kill him?" Edie said.

Jackie put one shaky finger in her mouth, and bit on her manicured nail.

"I can't think of anyone right now. Maybe Billy? Todd gave him a rough time," Jackie said.

Edie put her chin in her hand ruminating on how Billy Parson's name seemed to come up in every interview.

"I shouldn't have said Billy," Jackie said, as if reading Edie's mind. "I don't think he's capable of murder. That's such an incredibly insane act. I really can't think of anyone who'd kill Todd."

"So, why did Billy come to mind?"

"I don't know why," Jackie sighed. "He was the first one who popped into my mind. Maybe because Todd was mean to Billy. He'd yell at the poor guy in front of the agents. If Todd had treated me that way, I'd have wanted to kill him."

"Did he yell at others in the office?" Edie asked.

"There were times Todd's anger was directed at agents. He had a bad habit of telling agents off in front of whoever was around. He really should have taken the offending person into his office, and closed the door," Jackie said. "Hell, I guess all the agents in the office could be suspect."

Jackie bit the side of her lip. "Except for one agent, Lara Maxwell. Todd never, I mean *never*, said a cross word to her."

"Why do you think that was?"

"I don't have experience working in any other real estate office," Jackie said. "But from what I understand every office has at least one darling that no one messes with. Come to think of it we have two, Ginger McRae who is a major top producer, and Lara. I think Todd and Megan were more afraid of Ginger."

"Afraid? Why?" Edie asked.

"It's all about money. Top producers bring the broker major business with major money," Jackie said. "Ginger is a big money maker, and a prima-donna. Todd and Megan have always walked on eggshells around her. Can you imagine if one of them ever raised their voice to her? Why she'd be out the door taking her business to another broker who'd welcome her with open arms. Now, that's power. Money talks, and shit walks."

"Do you like Lara?" Edie asked, sensing Jackie's annoyance whenever she said Lara's name.

"Not particularly," Jackie said. "Little miss perfect. All the agents think she's so wonderful. Well, I don't. She's merciless, that one."

Jackie fidgeted in her chair, rubbing her hands together while furtively glancing at the wall clock. "I've really got to go now, detective."

"You can go," Edie said. "Here's my card. If you think of something, call me."

Jackie rose from her chair, and grimly walked toward the door.

"You forgot your water," Edie said as she gave the bottle to Jackie. "And by the way, stay in town."

Jackie pursed her lips. "Is that an order?"

"It's a strong suggestion at least until we get this investigation wrapped up," Edie said. "You wouldn't want us to come looking for you."

After Jackie bolted from the room, Edie sat back looking over her notes. Jackie was a puzzle. How did this prim, nervous, plain woman wind up with someone like Alex, a handsome bartender, and suspected drug dealer? Maybe the psychological idea of *opposites attract* applied here.

The door opened, and Captain Henry stuck his head in. "Hey, Edie. If you're finished, Detective Lund needs the room."

Edie gathered up her notes before returning to her office. She opened the thin file from the Medical Examiner's office, re-reading Todd's autopsy report. Two shots fired. One in the head, and one in the chest close to the heart. The shot to the head killed him instantly. The shot to the heart seemed unnecessary. Or was it? One fatal shot to the head is enough for an assassin. Another in the heart shows passion, rage. The murderer was deliberate, and obviously a good shot. She made a note to see who at Drake Properties had a license to carry.

Edie got up from her desk and paced the room. She heard raucous laughter from the squad room, and closed her door. A quiet office aids concentration. Edie needed to focus on the one thing that continued to nag at her. The bullet to the heart was perplexing. If this murder was a crime of passion, then who had such passion? Maybe the second shot was to his head. If that were true, then why? Todd's private life was a puzzle yet to be solved. She returned to her desk, took out her notebook, and began writing. Who was he sexually involved with? Who did he socialize with? Was his social life completely wrapped up in his parties?

Edie looked at the wall clock. She had half an hour left before her interview with Lara. Her mind raced in all confusing directions. Alex and drugs, Todd's anger, Jackie screwing Alex, Billy, and the rest of the over-worked, over-wrought people at Drake Properties. Megan, the cool, efficient, perhaps heartless, businesswoman.

Edie opened the desk drawer where she kept a comfortable pair of walking shoes. "I'm getting out of here," she said to the walls. She quickly laced her shoes, turned out the light, and closed the door behind her. Without saying a word to anyone she briskly walked out of the building.

One lap around the block before tackling the next Looney Tune.

CHAPTER 10

Jackie

What did that detective mean about not leaving town? Would they really hunt me down?

Jackie ignored the warning, and the nausea that overcame her. She snatched her water from the table, pulled her shoulders back, and stormed out of the interrogation room. Her heart was beating so fast that she ran into a desk, stumbled, then righted herself.

Be careful. Don't panic.

The morning sun brought sweat to Jackie's face. She wiped the moisture away. Was she crying? Yes. Fear always made her cry. The detective's parting shot about not leaving town struck a familiar fear. It seemed she was always running from something, or someone. Her hometown, her past. Now she was running from that detective. When would it end?

This morning, she parked several blocks away from HPD headquarters for exercise. Now the heat, humidity, and her pounding heart made the walk torturous. She slowed down to control her anxiety. The slower pace calmed her. Her thoughts of Alex, and the police knowing about the two of them, whirled about in her head. Alex would be upset with her for telling. Maybe if she bought him that blazer he saw at Neiman's. Expensive presents and sex calmed him down.

What have I gotten myself into?

Her chest tightened. She stopped to take a deep breath. What would her father think of her? He always said, 'You can't buy love.' He was wrong. You could buy anything including sex, and pretend it is love.

What would Megan and the agents think if they knew about Alex? Sonya would understand. Megan wouldn't care. All the beautiful, privileged women would be shocked. Every one of them would be impressed if they knew she was sleeping with handsome Alex. They might even have respect for her, become her friends.

Silly woman. That won't happen. You've always been on the outside looking in.

Over the years she had tried to erase the memory of standing on the playground watching the other girls playing games. They had rarely asked her to play. She had envied them, longed to be one of them. But that was not meant to be. They were prettier, and not as tall, or as klutzy as she. She could still hear their taunts followed by laughter. "Klutzy, plain Jane-Jackie. Hey giraffe, how's the weather up there?" She had nowhere to hide, no one to protect her.

To hell with them. She'd keep her dirty little secret, and Alex.

Now if the police would just leave her alone.

CHAPTER 11

Lara stretched, pulling at the sheets. She looked over at David who stirred, rolled over, and slung a long leg over her hips.

"Good morning," Lara purred. David reached under the sheet and began massaging her inner thigh. Lara moaned, and turned. "I'm sorry baby. I've got to get to the office early."

One last lingering, deep kiss. Lara pulled the sheet back, and put her slippers on before padding to the kitchen to make coffee.

David followed wrapping his arms around her waist while kissing her neck.

"Stop it, and get some clothes on," Lara laughed.

"If you insist," David said returning to the bedroom.

Lara watched him leave. David didn't just walk like a normal male. He strolled, like an imperious lion on the savannah.

If only I had met David before my time with Todd.

She met David right after she stopped seeing Todd, but for some reason she felt guilty. The guilt came from keeping Todd a secret. Maybe she should just go ahead, and tell him about Todd. Then what? How could she explain the unexplainable? Better keep quiet, and hope her past would remain in the past.

Lara shook her head trying to stop thinking, and instead focus on fixing some breakfast. Finding a couple of day-old cinnamon rolls, and half a cantaloupe in the refrigerator, she put them on the table in case David was hungry. There was little time to cook, and she hadn't been to the grocery store in a week.

When David returned, he was dressed, and shaved. He looked at the table with unmasked disgust. "What is this shit, Lara? I see you didn't go to any trouble for me."

Lara laughed, and then realized by the scowl on David's face that he was not kidding. He was dead serious.

"I'll grab a breakfast taco on my way to work," he said. "Don't forget, I'm going to a meeting in New Orleans. I'll see you when I get back."

Without another word, David walked out.

"I'll be damned," Lara said to the kitchen wall. "He's in a snit over food." The familiar feeling of dread came over her. The dread she felt when her past lovers showed their ugly side. The dread before the unraveling of a relationship.

She looked at the clock. *I don't have time to think about this!*

She put what she thought was an adequate breakfast back in the refrigerator, then hurried to get dressed.

Lara was glad she was the first one in the office because she accomplished more when no one was around to distract her. After making a pot of coffee she settled in at her desk, staring at the computer screen. Her thoughts drifted to David. What had made him turn so cold, and angry? Was her failure to whip up a gourmet breakfast that upsetting? Men could be such pains in the ass. Pain in the ass or not, at least David had come to her aid last night. Someone had definitely been following her. The driver's shadowy image behind the wheel of the car turned her stomach.

Why would anyone follow me? Was it a man or a woman? Enough!

Lara rubbed her forehead. She looked at the blank computer screen, and willed herself to concentrate. After taking a long drink of coffee she dove in, and finished going over the Clark's offer making sure all necessary blanks had been filled in. Then she tackled her emails. The office was quiet, too quiet. Like a tomb. Out of the corner of her eye, she saw a figure go past her door. Her heart skipped a beat. She got up from her desk, and walked down the hall. She stopped at Todd's office. The door was open. She stuck her head in.

"Lara!" Jackie exclaimed before jumping up from Todd's couch.

"Jackie, for God's sake how long have you been here?"

"Not long," she said. "You were busy so I didn't bother to say hello."

"I wish to hell you had. I think the scare took five years off my life."

Jackie tried to walk out, but Lara stood in the doorway. "What are you doing in here?"

Flustered, Jackie pulled at her perfectly pressed skirt, and said, "I just wanted to sit in Todd's office. I don't know why. Besides, I'm the office manager. I can be in anyone's office."

Lara leaned against the doorframe. She scratched her one accessible flea bite, and watched as Jackie fidgeted with a piece of paper on Todd's desk. She knew very little about Jackie except that she had lived in Corpus Christi before coming to Houston. Lara guessed that her age was between forty, and fifty-years-old. She was slim and always business-like, starched, and perfectly pressed. Even her hair was starched. She once bragged to an envious Lara that she rarely combed, or styled her hair. Instead, she had a standing weekly appointment with one of Houston's premier hair stylists.

The one quirk that made Jackie somewhat lovable was her habit of writing malapropisms in her inter-office emails. Sonya and Lara kept a secret file of "Jackie-isms." Lara's favorite was sent when Megan had been sick.

Megan won't be at the meeting today as she is feeling squeazy.

Jackie didn't look so starched now. Her hair was messy, smudged mascara rimmed her eyes, and her skin was paler than usual.

"I had an interview with the police this morning," Jackie said.

"Why so early?"

"It started at six-thirty because I had to get back here to set up for the meeting. I was interviewed by Detective Ross. She wanted to know how well I knew Todd, where I was Sunday, things like that. I just can't believe Todd's gone," she said looking beyond Lara's shoulder.

Jackie took a long, deep breath. "If you'll excuse me, I've got to get ready for the sales meeting," she said edging her way past Lara. "We'll talk later."

Strange woman

Lara turned out the light in Todd's office and closed the door.

Before the meeting, Dick and Vanessa Clark arrived to sign their offer. When they left Lara emailed it to the listing agent, then grabbed a cup of coffee before joining the other agents for the sales meeting.

The conference room was full. Agents sat at the center table, and in chairs placed along the wall. Lara stopped at the buffet where muffins, sweet rolls, and fresh fruit were displayed. She took a muffin before sitting between Sonya and Chaya Getz.

Lara remembered liking Chaya the first time she met her. Chaya's wit, and wisdom had helped Lara through many a tough transaction. Her office door was always open. Unlike Lara, Chaya seemed to thrive on people coming into her office with the latest gossip.

Chaya had grown up in Meyerland, a community nestled in the heart of Houston. Her family regularly attended a synagogue. Chaya's loving presence at Shivas made her the darling of widows, and widowers who eagerly ask her to list their homes when the grieving period was over. Each of Chaya's new listings ignited a burning question in the office, "Who died?"

"I'm glad you're here," Chaya said as she gave Lara a quick hug.

"Thanks. I think I'd go out of my mind if I didn't have my work."

Lara looked around the table seeing the usual people, mostly women, all dressed impeccably per Megan's dress code; jackets for men and women, no jeans, no tats showing, and name tags prominently displayed.

Which one of these people could be capable of murder?

Lara saw Billy enter the room. He immediately took a seat without talking to, or looking at anyone. She would have considered Billy a suspect until yesterday. Now she thought Billy too fragile to murder anyone. But hadn't she read somewhere that drug addicts could be incredibly strong when angry? She pushed the thought out of her mind. Billy wasn't evil, or desperate enough to murder.

Her gaze rested on the newest agent, Jason Morris, an ex-Marine who had served in Afghanistan.

He's been to war. He's possibly killed.

She always regarded him as the most stable agent in the office. Lara inwardly chuckled remembering when they first met. She asked if he liked his new job. "Real estate is the toughest job I've ever had," he replied.

Really? Real estate is tougher than dodging land mines in Afghanistan? On second thought, that could be true. There were days she'd rather dodge land mines than drive assholes around town. No, it isn't Jason. He's only been in real estate for six months. Definitely not long enough to want to chew up the carpet, and kill your broker.

Lara was brought out of her dark musings when Sonya handed her a folded note.

Which one of these crazies do you think did it?

She looked at Sonya, shrugged her shoulders, then took a pen, and scribbled: **Miss Marple, in the bedroom, with a gun,** then passed it back to Sonya.

"Good morning, everyone," said Megan. "There's plenty of food left. Please get more. This will be a short meeting as we are all in shock over losing Todd."

The Tuesday office sales meetings at Drake Properties were always well attended. This was the weekly group therapy session. Megan began each meeting bringing everyone up to date on the new listings, and sales totals. The rest of the meeting consisted of Megan encouraging agents to discuss transaction, property, and client problems. These lively discussions were a way to facilitate cohesiveness, and problem solving among the agents.

Megan always began each meeting with a positive message. Today the message was boldly written on a poster.

"NO ONE EVER TOLD ME THAT GRIEF FELT SO LIKE FEAR"-C.S. Lewis.

"I chose this quote today because we are grieving our loss," Megan said. "I've talked with many of you who are fearful of basically doing your job as a realtor. We are all vulnerable to crime. I thought we'd take today to talk about our sorrow, and fears."

She turned to Lara. "I know you aren't prepared Lara, and your emotions are raw, but would you mind telling everyone what happened Sunday?"

Lara was taken aback. She truly detested speaking in front of any group of people. She looked around the room, and saw the agents smiling at her, a few with tears in their eyes. She stood in front of the group, and began.

"It was just a normal open house with Todd the star, and me the worker bee," she began. Most of the group grinned and nodded.

"I left Todd to pick up the directional signs. When I returned to the house, I found him on the bedroom floor," Lara choked back a sob. "Everything after that is a blur with police everywhere. The medical examiner cordoned off the bedroom while the detective talked to me. It wasn't long before the owners came in, and all hell broke loose. It was not a pretty scene."

Chaya raised her hand. "What a nightmare for you, Lara. None of us can even imagine how awful it must have been," Chaya said. "Those homeowners must be beside themselves."

"I'm heartbroken for Lara, and all of us," said Ginger McRae. As a top producer, and office maven, Ginger considered herself the agent's spokesperson. "We need to know where to go from here."

To Lara's relief, Megan took over. "Apparently everyone in the office is going to be questioned by the police," she said. "No one is under suspicion, or everyone is under suspicion. Who knows? The only thing for us to do is cooperate. Meanwhile, please be extra careful when showing property, and when holding a house open. Keep your eyes open, and trust your gut instinct."

"I remember having the feeling that something was wrong," said Lara. "It was as if something was off. It was eerie."

Jason rose from his chair.

"I think we've all had that feeling," he said. Several agents nodded in agreement.

"I'm thinking we need to buddy up for a while," he continued. "We should never go to an open house or show a vacant home without another agent with us."

Sonya raised her hand. "Will you be my buddy?" The room exploded with laughter. Jason smiled, and winked at Sonya before taking his seat.

"Jason is absolutely correct," Megan said. "I strongly suggest that to be extra cautious in this big city, two agents go to show an empty house. I want all of you to know that if you need me for anything I'm here. The sensational aspect of Todd's murder will be a challenge, but together we will come out on top."

Megan shuffled through her meeting notes. "I don't see any reason to continue. I'll send an email letting everyone know the details of Todd's funeral. I want all of you to know how valuable, and dear you are to me. Please be safe."

The agents slowly filed out of the meeting. Some shook Megan's hand, others were bold enough to give her a slight hug. Lara took another muffin, and poured herself more coffee.

"Lara," Megan called. "Don't go. Come into my office."

Lara reluctantly put the muffin back, kept the coffee, and followed Megan into her office.

"Mr. and Mrs. Bard, the owners of the house on Crestline, are coming in to talk with us now," said Megan.

"That's just great," Lara said. "I hope they've calmed down. I think they blame me for Todd's murder."

Jackie knocked on Megan's door, and ushered in Jack and Melanie Bard who both looked ashen faced, and grim.

"Please sit down," Megan said pointing to two chairs next to Lara.

"Thank you, Ms. James," Jack said as he helped his wife to her seat, then took his. "Hello Lara."

Lara nodded warily.

"We need to talk to you about our house," Jack said. "I know it's a bad time, but it's better to get this out now."

Megan folded her hands placing them on top of her desk. "This is a terrible, confusing time for all of us. I want you to know Drake Properties is behind you," Megan began. "We are dedicated to selling your home. In fact, I will take the listing, and work with you personally if you'd like."

"You know we have to be in Cincinnati in less than a month. That's when I start my new job," Jack said.

"I'm aware of your time crunch," Megan said. "Will your company help with housing?"

"Yes, but that's not the point."

Megan sat back, smiled, and said, "What is the point, Jack?"

"We both feel the time has come for a change," Jack said as he looked at Melanie, who was staring at the wall behind him. "We think the best thing is to find another real estate company. We think our house will never sell with a Drake Properties sign in the yard, screaming to all that Todd was murdered there."

"Buyers come to Houston from all over the country, and the world," Lara said. "Not everyone will associate your home with murder."

"We just want to sell as quickly as possible, and right now is the best time to put the house on the market with another broker," Melanie said. "I want to get out of Houston as fast as possible. Will you just cancel the listing agreement now?"

"Of course," Megan said as she turned to her computer, pulling up the Termination of Listing form.

Lara watched Melanie nervously pull her hair back behind her ears. She wondered why Melanie avoided looking at her. Instead, she darted her eyes around the room never fixing on one person, including her husband.

"Melanie, I sincerely want your home to sell," Lara said.

"I do too," Melanie said looking past Lara. "I need to get away from Houston."

By the time the Bards left the office with listing termination in hand, Lara had the beginnings of a bitch of a headache. After taking two aspirin she settled back in her chair, and closed her eyes. The phone buzzed. She jumped up, and grabbed the receiver. "Yes."

"This is Jackie, Lara. Remember, you have an appointment with the police detective in half an hour."

"Crap!" She jumped up, grabbed her purse, then dashed out of her office, her head, and heart pounding.

CHAPTER 12

Lara drove through Memorial Park cautiously watching the speedometer.

That's all I need. A speeding ticket while on my way to the police department as a suspect in a murder case.

She found a parking slot half a block from the gray, ominous Houston Police Department Headquarters building. Many times, she had driven past this edifice wondering if the interior was like what she saw on her favorite cop shows. After briefly scanning the first floor, she concluded it was like every other government building she'd been in. Drab and dull.

After she signed in, a uniformed officer led her to Edie's third floor office. To Lara's surprise, Edie's office was cheery compared to the gray monotony of her surroundings. The detective's desk was adorned with photos of smiling children in brightly colored frames alongside a large red vase that contained a brightly colored arrangement of fresh flowers. On the wall behind the desk hung a family portrait showing Edie looking radiant beside her mustachioed, good-looking husband. The children, a boy and a girl, both looked delightfully impish.

"You have a beautiful family, detective," Lara said.

"Thanks," Edie replied. "They are a handful, but worth any aggravation. How are you doing today, Lara?"

"I'm okay. I'm still shocked and bewildered by Todd's death."

"That's completely understandable. Why don't we go into another room and talk about it?"

Lara followed Edie through the swarm of male detectives who were mulling around pretending to be busy as they eyed her. As they passed the coffee urn Edie offered Lara a cup which she eagerly accepted.

The two women entered a small, starkly furnished room with light blue walls, and two blue metal chairs beside a table with a computer on top. Edie motioned Lara to take a seat.

Lara pulled the chair away from the table creating a loud scraping sound that jarred her already jangled nerves.

"Shit!" she said. "Can't the city afford an extra ten dollars to put felt pads on the legs of these chairs?"

Edie scraped her chair back before sitting. "I'll ask my superiors to get on that right away."

Lara saw the tape recorder next to Edie. "Are you going to tape what I say?"

"I am, with your permission."

"Alright," Lara said as she nervously picked at the sleeve of her blouse. "I hope this doesn't take long. I have clients…"

"I know you're busy, Lara, and I'll try to make this as short as possible," Edie said. "By the way, is it okay if I call you Lara?"

"Of course, it is," Lara replied.

"Are you comfortable?" Edie asked.

"About as comfortable as anyone could be sitting in this hard ass chair."

"Yeah, there's not a lot of comfort here," Edie said. "This is not a living room chat. This is an interrogation room. Can we begin?"

Lara looked directly at Edie and shrugged. "That's why I'm here. Bring it on."

• • •

At Edie's request, her partner Ron Yates sat in the darkened observation room listening intently to Lara. He initially thought Lara was a smart-ass, but the more he watched the more he was convinced she was a distraught woman whose life had been upended. He chuckled at the thought of how tough it was to concentrate on anything other than the fact that she was drop-dead gorgeous.

Ron's job was to look for any signs of guilt or lying. He pulled the chair closer to the two-way window, and took out a writing pad to record his impressions. On the top of the page he wrote, FOCUS.

•   •   •

"Have you had time to think about what went on before Todd was shot?" Edie asked.

"I have," Lara said, holding her cup tightly to steady her trembling hands. She saw Edie glance at her hands. "Obviously I'm very nervous. I've never been in this position before." Looking around the stark room she added, "Or in a police interrogation room."

"Few people have. Relax, and we'll just talk," Edie said in her best, I'm your trusted confidant voice. "When we talked the day of the murder, you said you felt someone was in the house. You also said you heard a noise, like something falling on the second floor. Can you elaborate?"

"I can't explain it, but I was unnerved all day. I just thought I was pre-menstrual."

"Can you give me a better idea of what unnerved you?" Edie asked.

"It began when I first got into the house. I was hot, and irritable from pounding signs in the ground. I had the eeriest feeling someone was in the house. I checked the doors. They were all locked. I blew it off as empty house jitters."

Lara slapped her hand on the tabletop. "That's it! Maybe someone was hiding in the house the entire time. But how could that be? I went through every room turning on lights. I would have known."

"Anything is possible when someone is intent on murder," Edie replied. "Did you walk outside to see if anyone was there?"

"No, I didn't. I had just come in from the heat, and was sweating like a pig," Lara said with a slight chuckle. "Going back outside didn't even occur to me, but I looked out the front window, and there were no cars in the street."

"More than likely the shooter came in during the open house, or after you left," Edie said while looking at her notes. "Was there anyone you met who seemed suspicious, or acted in an unusual way?"

Lara shook her head trying to visualize the people who came through the house. "Detective, I've been holding houses open for several years. I'm well aware of how vulnerable agents are. I've learned to be cautious. I can't think of one person who set off my inner alarm."

"Was there anything else that may have upset you?"

"I think Todd's late arrival may have been part of my unease," Lara said. "He's never on time, but this time he was later than normal. He came in maybe ten minutes before the open house was scheduled to begin."

"Why do you think he was so late?" Edie asked.

"Your guess is as good as mine. He was so self-confident, and superior acting that it was almost impossible to read him," Lara said.

I wasn't his keeper.

"Was he acting differently? Was he agitated?"

Laura shook her head. "I don't believe I've ever seen him nervous."

"How well did you know Todd?" Edie asked "Did you know his friends, his family, anyone he was intimate with. His lovers?"

Lara's stomach knotted. *Lovers!*

"I met his father when he came to the office to take Todd to lunch. He's Kevin Drake, the builder. Perhaps you've heard of him?"

"I've actually been through his homes when I was looking to buy, but never met him," Edie said. "What about Todd's friends?"

"He had several boyhood friends who went to SMU with him. His father probably knows more about them," Lara said.

"Did he have any girlfriends, or maybe a significant other?"

Lara looked down at her lap wondering when this interrogation would end. She never knew a thing about Todd's personal life. Her moments of lust with Todd were private and needed to remain so. Todd's sex parties were up to Billy to disclose.

Say as little as possible. Leave with your dignity intact.

After taking a swig of the now lukewarm coffee, she sighed deeply. "I've never been Todd's social director. All I know is office scuttlebutt. Apparently, he dated some clients. Especially women in the River Oaks set," Lara said, referring to the priciest neighborhood in Houston. "He was high-end all the way."

"Write the names of women he dated on this pad," Edie said passing a legal pad, and pen over to Lara.

Lara quickly scribbled the few names she could remember, calmly put the pen down, and pushed it over to Edie.

Edie leaned in closer to Lara. "I want to remind you that this is a murder investigation. Anything you know or think you know needs to be said."

"I understand," said Lara waving her hand toward the ceiling corner. "I know there's a camera in the corner, and detectives watching us behind that mirror." She pointed at the mirror on the far wall. "This whole damn thing is getting on my last raw nerve."

"You need to be straight with me, Lara. If you're withholding anything, you'll be here longer than you want to be."

Lara looked around the barren room wondering if she could trust Edie. What choice did she have? Either open up, or be in this hell for who knows how long. She would answer Edie's questions with caution. Anything to get out of here.

"On Sunday, you told me Todd was cruel to people," Edie continued. "Will you be more specific?"

Sighing deeply, Lara began, "I'll do my best. I want you to understand how much Todd enjoyed his role as broker of Drake Properties. He reveled in his extensive knowledge of the real estate market. He was a real estate super star. He was cold and calculating in business. He was handsome, charming, and adored by his clients. They all felt they were his friends. He was witty. He told wonderful jokes. When he was in his charming persona, everyone wanted to be around him," she said, hoping she'd clearly described Todd's positive side.

She sat back taking another sip of the now cold coffee. She screwed her nose up. "I can't stand cold coffee."

Edie sat quietly without comment.

"I guess I'll drink it cold," Lara grimaced before continuing. "When he was in the office, he was a different person. He was mean as hell. The type of person no one wanted to be around. A Jekyll and Hyde personality. He demanded professionalism from the agents. If someone didn't perform to his standards, he would scream in a rage at the offending agent. He was also horrible to his assistant, Billy Parsons."

"I've heard that from several I've interviewed," Edie said. "Can you give me an example?"

Lara thought for a minute before responding. "Billy is a licensed agent but doesn't have the client base to keep him solvent. He is in a salaried position as assistant to Todd and Megan. Because he is licensed, he can hold open houses, get signatures on contracts, and perform all the menial tasks, which leaves his bosses free to bring in more business. He's gay, witty, and somewhat effeminate, which drove Todd nuts."

Lara rubbed her forehead. She felt another headache coming on. Breathing deeply, she willed herself to calm down. "Todd would yell at Billy, 'cut the gay boy crap, and concentrate on your work.' The poor guy would run all over town doing Todd's bidding. I don't know why he has stayed at Drake. More than likely his salary kept him around. Todd and Megan pay their employees well."

"Could he possibly have been in love with Todd?"

"Funny you should pick up on that," Lara said. "There were several agents who thought so. Who knows? The only thing I'm sure of was everyone in the office feared Todd's wrath."

"Were you afraid of him, Lara?"

"No, not afraid," she answered, then sat back trying to sort out exactly what her attitude was toward Todd. "I'd say I was wary and watchful. He was an asshole, that's for sure. He could explode without warning. Then there were the good days when he could make everyone in the office laugh. He was a terrific broker who backed up the agents whenever he was needed."

"Did Todd ever explode at you?"

"No, not really. I guess you could say he would snap at me if I missed even a minute detail in a contract, but never explode," Lara replied.

"Why do you think he never berated you in front of the others?"

Lara smiled. "Because I did nothing wrong."

Edie tried unsuccessfully to suppress a chuckle. "That's a good one. Is there another reason you can think of?"

Be careful

"I don't know," Lara said. "Maybe because I always laughed at his jokes, and I'm a tight-ass with contract details."

"Do you know of anyone in the office who had a burning hatred for Todd?" Edie asked. "It sounds like he was impossible to be around."

"Real estate offices have revolving doors. Agents come and go with relative ease. That's the beauty of this business," Lara said. "Pretend you're an agent with Drake and you can't tolerate Todd. There are many brokerage firms in Houston waiting to welcome you to their office. That was the case for some agents who couldn't stand Todd. They left."

"Do you know anyone who may have carried a grudge against him?" Edie asked.

"Hmm, I'll have to think about that. No one comes to mind," Lara said. "I hate to interrupt this conversation, but I've got to pee."

"I'll show you where the bathroom is."

Edie deposited Lara at the nearest bathroom. Instead of returning to the interview room, she knocked on Captain Henry's office door.

"Come in Edie. How's the interview with the redhead going?"

"She's a nervous wreck," Edie said. "That room is really intimidating to her. I think she's hiding something."

"Do you still think she's a viable suspect? If not, do you think she would be a good informant?"

"I'm pretty sure she's not our killer. Asking her to inform on her fellow agents may be a challenge, but we could sure use the information," Edie said. "By the way, she's eager to get out of here. I think she'd open up more if she weren't in the squad room. It's twelve-thirty. I want to continue this interview at *Ana's*. Do I have your approval?"

"It's not exactly by the book, but whatever you think will work, you need to do. Be sure to take the recorder, and yes, the department will pick up the lunch tab," Captain Henry said with a dismissive wave.

Edie returned to the interrogation room. Lara sat rigidly drumming her fingers on the metal desk.

"It's lunch time. Lara. I'm hungry. Are you?" asked Edie.

"Not particularly, but I should eat something," she replied.

"I'll tell you what. Grab your bag, and we'll continue this at *Ana's*," Edie said smiling. "Hope you like Mexican food."

"Crazy about it!" Lara said feeling her entire body relax.

Alright! I made it without throwing up my coffee, or spilling the beans.

She bounced out of the chair, grabbed her purse, and trying not to break into a run, followed Edie out of the room.

CHAPTER 13

Ana's was always crowded at lunch, and today was no exception. As soon as Lara entered the restaurant, the hostess escorted her to a corner booth. She slid in across from Edie.

"You must rate," Lara said. "How'd you get seated so soon?"

She decided to not push the detective for an answer, and ignore Edie's mischievous grin. More than likely, Edie pulled out her badge to get this quiet booth. It must be nice to have that kind of power.

After the waiter took their order, Lara, always the chatty realtor, broke the silence.

"So, tell me about you, Edie. You have such an interesting job. I deal with normal whackos in my job, but you deal with fucking evil crazies in yours. How do you handle it day after day?" Lara abruptly put her hand over her mouth. "Geez I'm sorry for being vulgar. I meant, evil crazies."

Edie smiled. "That's okay. Be yourself. I will not be overcome with the vapors because you say fuck."

"Oh, that's funny," Lara said. "I know you've heard it all. I just don't want you to get a bad impression of me."

"No worries," Edie said. "So now you're interviewing me?"

"No," she replied with a smile. "I'm honestly interested in your work, and how you handle the constant parade of nut jobs. Besides, maybe I can pick up some pointers."

"It was hard going when I first came on the force, but over the years I've learned how to deal with the stress," Edie said. "I suppose after years of working homicide I've become inured to the craziness. It comes with the job."

"I understand. I'll bet I could match crazies with you. The only difference is my crazies don't go around killing people."

Edie gave out a hearty laugh. "You have a point there." She took the small tape recorder from her purse.

"We need to continue where we left off," she said. "Same rules apply as if we were still in the interrogation room."

"So, you brought the tape recorder?"

"I apologize if it makes you uncomfortable, but like I said before, it is a necessary tool for the investigation."

"Oh, that's okay. I'm feeling better just being here. Tape away," Lara said as the waiter quietly gave them their plates of food.

"Lara, I have a gut feeling you know something that you're not telling me," Edie began.

"I can't think of anything," Lara said. "I will tell you I think I'm being followed."

Edie's head jerked up. "What? What makes you think that?"

"Last night I went to dinner with my working partner, Sonya Brown. After I left the restaurant, I was convinced a car followed me home. In fact, I was so certain that I called a male friend to come stay with me."

"Did you get a look at the person driving the car?"

"I got a brief look. It was dark, yet I could see that the driver had shoulder length hair. I couldn't tell if it was a man or a woman," Lara said. "David, my friend, is out of town today. I'm thinking of staying with Sonya until he returns."

"That might not be a bad idea." Edie said. "Here's what I want you to do. Call me anytime you think you're being followed, or think you may be in danger," Edie said as she tore a sheet from her notebook. "Here are my cell phone and home numbers. Put them in your phone. Don't worry about disturbing me."

Lara's stomach did a back flip. Could the murderer be stalking her, waiting to kill her? "You're scaring me, detective."

"I don't mean to scare you. I want to assure you that you have protection if you need it," Edie said. "Lara, I need ask if you had more than a working relationship with Todd."

Lara felt her heart drop. Here it was. The dreaded question.

"Yes."

"Tell me about it," Edie said.

Lara desperately tried to unscramble her brain. She suddenly realized Edie had lured her into a false feeling of security. She was trapped.

Lara sat back against the cushioned seat. *Choose your words wisely.*

"Do you need to tape this?" she asked. "It's not like I'm confessing to murder. I'm telling you about a personal indiscretion."

"Yes, I have to record this. If it makes you feel better, I keep tapes of interviews confidential," Edie said. "Taping an interview helps me keep track of who said what in an investigation. I know it's hard, but you need to trust me on this."

Lara took the napkin from her lap, wiped the tears from her eyes, and said, "I'm taking a big leap of faith with you."

She sat up straighter, took a long deep breath, and began. "It was several months ago. I went to this bizarre listing appointment, where I expected the wife to be at home with her husband, but no, it was just the husband. I think he was on drugs because he was agitated. He kept jumping up off the couch, going to the bathroom, and returning more hyped. He asked if I wanted a drink, and I said no. He drank, or should I say gulped bourbon like crazy. I realized he would not sign anything. I made a lame excuse and fled like hell!"

"Good decision," Edie said.

"I was rattled, and went to the office to see if Sonya was still there. She wasn't, Todd was. Like I told you before, he could be very supportive."

Lara scratched her palm, and then rubbed both hands together. "We started talking about my nerve-wracking listing appointment. Megan always kept wine in the office, and Todd opened a bottle. We talked, or should I say he talked, I drank. Well one thing led to another. Oh shit! I'm so embarrassed," she said shaking her head. "I never meant to get sexually involved with Todd. I guess I was flattered he found me attractive. Hell, I don't know."

Lara rubbed the back of her neck. She glanced over at the blinking red light on the tape recorder, and continued. "I soon regretted my foolish indiscretion. I told him we needed to stop seeing each other. He kept after me to meet him. I gave in, and helped him with the open house. Now he's dead. I just feel guilty, and pretty slutty."

"Guilty? Lara, I have to ask you. Did you kill Todd?"

Lara's fork dropped. Her hand went to her open mouth as she stared wide-eyed at Edie. After a few seconds she exclaimed, "Not only no, but hell no! I can barely kill a roach."

"Okay, let's get back to your time with Todd," Edie said. "So, it wasn't just a one-night stand?"

"No. I guess you could call it a three-night-stand. I've heard things usually happen in threes, quite the unlucky number. I didn't kill him!" Lara replied, feeling the anxiety rise in her chest.

"What about your friend, David. Does he know about this?" asked Edie.

"No. I'm still lugging that guilt around," Lara said. "The only one who knows besides you is Sonya. I told her last night at dinner. Are you sure this doesn't make me the main suspect? You can tell me. I can handle it."

"Everyone's a suspect until we find the shooter," Edie replied. "Personally, I don't think you're the killer. You can relax. One more question. Were you ever aware of Todd taking or selling drugs?"

Lara's eyes widened, and her heart skipped a beat.

"What? No, I'm not. He was a heavy drinker. I'm sure he never took drugs. But Todd dealing drugs? I don't think so."

"I guess it would surprise you that over the past year HPD Narcotics Division has been investigating Todd for possible dealing?"

Lara looked at Edie in disbelief.

"What if I told you the narcotics detectives were close to arresting Todd before he was murdered?"

Lara's mind raced. "You're talking about the parties, aren't you?"

"I am," Edie said, her face twisting into a scowl. "How do you know about the parties? Did you go?"

Now I've done it! Engaged mouth before brain.

"Billy Parsons told me yesterday," Lara sighed. "I didn't go. I wasn't invited. Apparently, I'm the only one who didn't know about the parties. I almost forgot. I'm pretty sure Billy knows about my fling with Todd. He never came right out and said he knew, but I could tell by the shitty way he acted when I wondered out loud why Todd never invited me to his parties."

"What did he say?"

"Todd wanted to keep me to himself, or something like that. I got the distinct impression he knows. Maybe Todd told him? I don't know," she replied.

Lara dipped her fork in the salad, and then put it down. She looked around the noisy restaurant wondering how she ever got into this position. This was not a friendly business lunch. This felt like a brutal blood-letting. Now that she thought back to her first time with Todd, he didn't seem surprised when she told him about her strange listing appointment, and the homeowner's erratic behavior probably fueled by drug use. Could it be that the drugged homeowner was one of Todd's party goers? He definitely fit the bill, young, somewhat nerdy, and new in town.

Lara watched Edie push her plate aside, and reach over to turn the tape recorder off. Relief flooded over her. The interview was over, and maybe she was off the hook.

"Lara, I believe you never knew about the parties. I also think you are in a unique position to help in this investigation."

"Help? I thought you were going to arrest me for suspicion of murder. Now you want my help? I'm all ears!"

"My supervisor and I think you would make a valuable, for lack of a better word, informant."

Lara sat back looking at Edie in stunned silence.

"Just hear me out before saying anything," Edie continued. "It's clear to me you are well liked by Megan, and the agents in your office.

I wonder if you would consider reporting back to me if you hear or see anything suspicious."

"I don't have a lot of confidence in my awareness. It seems for the past couple of years I've been blissfully unaware of what's going on around me. Remember I'm the one who was kept in the dark about the parties."

"Don't be too hard on yourself," Edie said. "You can be vital in helping to solve this case."

"Does that mean I'd be a snitch?"

"More like a confidential informant," Edie replied.

"Do I have to wear a wire?"

"I think you watch too much TV," Edie laughed. "No wire. I just want you to be my eyes, and ears at Drake Properties."

Lara sat back. She played with her uneaten salad, and considered what it would mean to spy on her fellow agents. The thought was distasteful, yet somewhat exciting. Could she do this? Why would she? She was being thrown into an unknown universe of murder, drugs, and God knows what else. Was it possible that less than a week ago she was bopping along having a pretty boring, safe life? She had to think. Nothing in her past prepared her for this moment. She liked Edie. She wanted to help the detective get the scum bag who killed Todd. She realized fear was holding her back.

"To be honest with you, Edie, I feel like I'm in danger now. I wonder if being an informant would put me in more danger. Now I'm worried about drug lords hunting me down. In fact, I'm truly scared shitless that the person who's following me is going to get me."

"I'm not going to bullshit you. It is possible you could be in danger," Edie said. "It is also possible you're in danger now. I don't like the idea that you're being followed. I'm thinking you need protection. One way or the other you'll be safe."

"If I get to a point where I just can't do it anymore can I stop?"

"Yes. In fact, you can back out anytime. We aren't asking you to be a detective. We aren't asking you to risk your life. All we want is for you to listen. If you hear anything let me know. I'll decide if it's important," Edie said. "I don't want you to sneak around and spy on your co-workers. I want you to use your intuitive instincts, and people skills. I think your co-workers feel comfortable with you."

"If I decide to do this, can I tell Sonya?"

"Good question. No one must know. I realize how hard it will be to keep quiet, but it's of the utmost importance. This will be between you, me, my partner, Ron Yates, and my superior, Captain Henry. I will be your main contact with my partner as backup."

Lara sighed. "Okay. I'll do it," she said. "When do I start?"

"As soon as possible, today if you can."

"Whoa! Okay, okay," Lara said. Taking a deep breath, she smiled at Edie. "I've got to be brave. I can do this."

"I know you can, Lara. We'll start off slow," Edie said. "Right now, I just need you to be present in the office, and listening to what's going on. Call me if you hear anything suspicious or revealing."

Lara took another deep breath, smiled at Edie, and then forcefully stuck her hand out in agreement.

CHAPTER 14

What have I done?

Lara drove away from Ana's in a daze. Could she really help the police, or would she make things worse? Uncertainty surrounded her. She needed time alone. She felt sick. Her entire body ached as a wave of exhaustion swept over her. All she wanted to do was go home to curl up, and sleep.

Pulling into the first gas station she saw, she took out her cell phone, and called the office.

"Good afternoon, Drake Properties. How may I direct your call?"

"Jackie, this is Lara. I won't be in the office the rest of the day. Please send any calls to my voicemail."

"What happened, Lara? Are you okay?"

"I'm getting a migraine," Lara fibbed. "The heat and lack of sleep has gotten to me."

"I'll take care of your calls. Get some rest," Jackie said.

On the way home she stopped at her favorite grocery store, Central Market. Her neck muscles relaxed as she stepped from the oppressive heat into the softly lit, perfectly air-conditioned store. She considered this market more like an extension of home, warm and welcoming.

Normally she would stroll down the aisles. Today she was in a hurry. No time to shop around, or pick out a fresh floral bouquet. She went straight to the fish market, where she chose a small salmon filet, then hurried over to the produce section. She tossed a tomato and a head of lettuce into her basket. She saw lemons neatly stacked in an open bin. She absent-mindedly grabbed one, triggering an avalanche of lemons thudding to the floor. Horrified, she put her hands out to unsuccessfully stop the flow. The terrazzo tiled floor was blanketed with yellow fruit.

"Shit!" she exclaimed.

Several shoppers walked by completely ignoring her dilemma. A few laughed.

Mortified, Lara left the hand basket on the floor, carefully stepped over the lemons, and stomped directly to the ice cream section. She found a half gallon of Blue Bell Cookies and Cream, paid the cashier, and fled to the parking lot. Slamming the car door, she sped out of the lot with her ice cream dinner.

By the time she reached her condo the sky had darkened, and a light drizzle started to fall. She had barely made it inside when the drizzle turned into a torrential rain. She put the ice cream in the freezer, and began shedding clothes on the way to the bedroom.

What a relief to be wrapped in a warm chenille robe. She curled up on the couch with a bowl of cookies and cream. She listlessly spooned at the ice cream while listening to the rain pound the roof, and fell asleep. When she woke the rain had stopped. Darkness was setting in.

Lara stretched and yawned, then glanced at the bowl of soggy cookie bits floating in the melted, uneaten ice cream. She took the bowl to the kitchen, and threw out the un-appetizing contents. Clutching the robe around her body she made a cup of steaming green tea before returning to her curled-up position on the couch. The rain picked up again coming down in a steady, gentle shower. The sound of rain always had a calming effect on her.

But, try as she might, Lara could not get her head around the day's events. She'd never been on first name terms with a detective, let alone interrogated by one. On top of everything she had agreed to be a sleuth, or informant, or whatever they wanted to call her. No matter what fancy term the police gave it, she would still be an office spy. But the thought of helping the detectives with a murder case gave her a thrill. Now here was a role she could sink her teeth into. Ever since high school, people for some unknown reason had told her their secrets. Maybe she could help to find a cold-blooded murderer.

She could also be the victim of a cold-blooded murderer.

Lara wanted, no yearned for, a purpose in her life. She thought back to when she worked for Exxon. She had time then to volunteer at the Houston Women's Center helping abused women, and their children, find a safe house. Looking back on that time, she realized her life had more balance. Now, real estate filled her days. She could never find the time to do volunteer work. She currently lived on her commissions, and a small trust fund left to her when her parents died. She envied the married agents. They had a partner to share expenses. Her livelihood hinged on a transaction making it to the closing table. That's when she got paid. The constant stress to close a sale coupled with the persistent office drama was emotionally, and physically draining on her. Maybe helping the police could bring some purpose back into her life.

This is not volunteering. This is putting your life in danger.

Passion. That word TV gurus used. Find your passion. Lara wasn't sure snooping was her passion, but she felt more alive thinking about the possibility. Then the fear came. Fear of the unknown, of danger. And yes, that old bugaboo, fear of failure. Lara felt her stomach tighten, and her hands moisten just thinking about it. She could still hear her dad's admonition when she brought home a poor grade. "Failure is not an option."

The ringing phone jolted Lara out of her reverie.

"Hey Lara, it's Sonya. Are you okay?"

"I'm tired, and need to rest. Other than that, I'm good."

"I was worried about you after I read Jackie's kooky office memo."

"What did she write this time?" Lara asked.

"I'll read it to you. Lara is home today, and possibly tomorrow to ease implications from a migraine."

Lara burst out laughing. "Thanks, Sonya, I needed that."

"Are you coming to my house tonight? You're welcome to stay."

"Thank you, but I've got my favorite robe on. I'm ready to crash. It is comforting to know I can stay with you if need be."

"I think you are just plain exhausted. Not surprising after what you've been through," Sonya said. "You know I'm here for you. How was your interview today with the detective?"

"Nerve wracking," Lara said.

"I'm dying to hear what went on, but I won't keep you. Take care of your implications!"

Lara grinned. "I will. Let's catch up tomorrow."

She turned her phone off, stuffed it in her purse, and continued sipping her tea. Sonya was a dear friend, and confidant. She hated keeping another secret from her. She hated secrets because keeping one meant lying.

Lying was painful. She was rotten at it. Even the thought of lying brought a faint soapy taste to her mouth. Where did her mother ever get the idea that a mouthful of soap would prevent her from lying? Or did her mother wash her mouth out when she cussed? She forgot. The one thing she remembered was the mouth washing didn't work.

Lara took another sip of tea, wishing her parents were here. If only they hadn't driven home from Austin on that stormy night two years ago. If only that drunk had stayed in his own lane. She'd always felt she and her brother were hapless characters in a Disney film.

Lara and Randy. Bambi and Tarzan.

Randy! Taking her phone from its hiding place she called her brother.

"How's it going, Rainey?" said Randy.

He was the only one who called Lara by her given name, Larraine. She had shortened her name when she went into real estate. Lara Maxwell fit better on signs, flyers, and business cards.

"I've been worried about you. Are you alright?"

Lara held back tears, and asked, "Do you have time to talk?"

"Of course, I do," Randy replied.

"My life has been turned upside down," Lara said. "I thought I was a major suspect in Todd's murder until today. Now I've been asked by the police to be an informant."

"What the hell! I thought you were just dealing with grief, and shock. You should have called me sooner," Randy said. "Are you sure you want to get more involved?"

"No, I'm not sure. I'm not sure about anything right now."

"I probably need to come to Houston," Randy sighed. "After all, you've seen the aftermath of a murder. That must have been a gruesome sight."

"It was. I wake up at night seeing that gaping hole in Todd's head. I manage to work, which helps a lot. It's good to know you're only three hours away," Lara said. "I need your level head to help me decide what to do. You know me better than anyone. Do you think I can be an informant? The detective seems to think I can do it."

Lara sat wrapping the end of her robe around a finger, waiting for Randy to respond.

Don't blow me off as your baby sister. I need you.

"I'm thinking," Randy finally said. "You've been through hell. I'd advise you to be careful, and not get in too deep."

"I'm in deep now," Lara replied. "I'll just listen to the people in the office, and report to the police if I hear anything suspicious. To be honest, I think I'm a small cog in the wheel."

"You're smart, a little flaky, but smart as hell. I know you can do anything you set your mind to. I think you can pull it off," he said.

"Thanks for the back-handed compliment. But, if you really think I can do this, I do too. I feel, and don't laugh, a little excited just thinking about it."

"Don't get too excited," Randy said. "Keep your head about you. Remember who you are, and who you aren't. You're not a detective."

"Okay, I'll only admit this to you. I tend to get into situations without thinking. This time is different. I've given it a great deal of thought."

"There's one thing you've absolutely got to promise me," Randy said.

"What's that?"

"You've got to really watch your step, and make sure the police are protecting you. I hate to think of you involved in a murder investigation. For God's sake, be careful. Do you promise me you'll do that?"

"Yes sir, I promise," Lara answered. "I wish you were here."

"Unless you need me now, I'm making plans to come to Houston in about a month. Meanwhile, I want you to continue calling to give me updates. I'll jump on a plane, and be there in a flash if you need me."

"Thank you," Lara sighed. "How are Cheryl, and the kids? Do y'all still like Austin?"

"They're doing great. They miss you. We love Austin, and want you to come see us."

"I have this urge to get in my car and go, but I can't run away from this," Lara said. "As soon as this mess clears up, I'll be there."

After saying their goodbyes Lara gave in to exhaustion, and went to bed. On her way to the bedroom she stopped, and looked at the mirror on the living room wall.

"Well, look at you. Fuckin' Sherlock Holmes in drag."

•   •   •

Outside Lara's condo, in the dark, Detective Ron Yates sat in a Ford sedan sending a text.

Edie. Lights out. All's well.

CHAPTER 15

No sooner had a rested Lara settled in her office than Jackie rushed in, and closed the door.

"So, tell me what happened with that detective," Jackie said.

"The interview went well," Lara replied, trying to look busy.

Jackie twisted a long silver necklace that hung against her white silk blouse. Lara was sure she'd seen the gray suit Jackie was wearing along with the silk blouse at Neiman Marcus. Jackie always wore beautiful clothes, shoes, and jewelry. A real fashion plate. Lara silently contemplated how if given a chance this strange woman could be better looking. Maybe trim those thick dark eyebrows enabling others to see the gray-blue eyes that matched her suit. And ditch those awful eyeglasses.

Jackie seemed unfazed by Lara's attempt to ignore her. Instead, she sat down across the desk, leaned forward, and said, "When will we be finished with these police interviews? I just want this to be over, and soon. Why do we have to be under such scrutiny?"

"Because Todd was murdered, and this is what police do when they don't have any obvious suspects," Lara said, trying not to show her irritation.

"I know all that," Jackie snapped back. "I thought you might have some insight into what's going on."

"I'm guessing as much as you are," Lara said, taken aback by Jackie's curt reply.

Hmm, maybe there is fire in her engine.

Jackie rose abruptly from her chair. "I'll leave you to your work. Hope that migraine is gone. You need to take better care of yourself," she said, giving Lara a crooked smile before leaving.

Now what was that all about?

Lara shook her head. She turned to the red blinking light on the desk phone, and began listening to her voicemails. A loud rap on the door announced Megan's presence.

"Lara, if you have a minute, I want you to come to my office." Without waiting for an answer, she left. Typical Megan, demanding that Lara drop everything with no explanation.

"Yes ma'am, I'll be right there," Lara said to the empty room.

Remembering her new role as office snoop, she took a notepad and pen from the desk, and followed Megan. She took a seat across from Megan, and opened her notebook. With pen at the ready she asked, "What's up?"

"I hope your migraine is better," Megan said. Without waiting for a reply, she continued. "I'm concerned about Drake Properties' survival. I know you had an interview yesterday with that woman detective. I had mine on Monday, and it was brutal. Anyway, I want to know if you think the police suspect someone in the office."

Here we go again with the police interview.

She didn't know how tight Megan and Jackie were, but it seemed fishy they both were so anxious about her time with the detective. She shook her head to rid the laughable image of Megan and Jackie conspiring together. Too ridiculous to be true.

"I think they suspect everybody," Lara said, trying to sound dismissive.

Megan stood, and walked to the window where she watched the traffic flow along the tree-lined street below.

"That's what worries me, Lara," she said, still looking out the window. "Maybe someone in real estate, or connected with our firm is the murderer. I'm also worried that our phones aren't ringing as much as they were five days ago. Drake Properties could lose clients, not to mention our standing in the community."

Megan walked away from the window, and moved to her desk.

"I'm afraid we won't survive the publicity, and stain of Todd's murder," she continued. "Imagine if someone in this office killed him! Goodbye business. I want Todd's murder solved soon. Do the police suspect you? After all you were the last one to see him alive."

Without thinking, Lara let out a short, contemptuous laugh. "Are you saying that because I was at the open house working my ass off, I've become the main suspect? Megan, you of all people should know better than that. To be honest, I think I'm at the bottom of the suspect list."

"You're right. I know better. Todd's murder, and the aftermath have screwed with my common sense," Megan said. She returned to her desk, leaned back in her chair, and swept her hand around the room.

"All this could be gone. All my hard work destroyed by some crazy ass with a gun. The longer the police drag their feet, the longer this firm is in the news. That's where you come in, Lara."

Watch your step!

"What? How in the world can I stop the press?"

"I'm not saying you can do anything about the press," Megan said giving a short low laugh. "The other agents talk to you, confide in you. I'm asking you to talk with them, and then tell me if you think someone here is involved with Todd's murder."

First the police ask me to snitch, and now Megan. Why me? Do I have a sneaky, back-stabbing personality?

"I'm not comfortable doing that, Megan. I've got clients who occupy my time. As you know I have three listings, one active contract, and several demanding buyers. You need to find someone else," Lara said.

I'm not the office gossip.

"I'm not asking you to take time away from your business. If you would let me know what you hear I'd be forever grateful." Megan rubbed the back of her neck. "Besides, you owe me. I've pulled your ass from the fire a few times."

Megan had helped Lara with difficult transactions, but in reality, that was her job as the broker. Lara acquiesced to the queen's demands in order to stop being pressured. Now was the perfect time to ask Megan about Todd's parties.

Careful!

"I'll do the best I can, Megan. I'll let you know if I hear something."

Megan rose from her chair, walked over to Lara, and smiled.

"Thank you."

Lara looked up at Megan. Her almond-shaped brown eyes actually had gold flecks, reminiscent of Lara's childhood cat. A sleek, beautiful cat. She never did like that cat. It killed baby rabbits, and brought them to the back door.

"Speaking of hearing things around the office, I've heard rumors concerning parties hosted by Todd. Apparently, he got a lot of business from the party goers."

Megan's smile vanished. She stared coldly at Lara, her body rigid. "I heard persistent rumors, but discounted them because I, oh I don't know, because I didn't want to believe it. It's nonsense."

"I think it's true, Megan."

"Damn! That may have something to do with Todd's murder. But from what I gathered not everyone in the office was invited."

"I'm among the fortunate who were left out," Lara said.

"Maybe not everyone felt the same as you. Those who were left out may have been angry. What about Jackie? She's never raised her voice, never showed anger even though she has the most stressful job in the office. Isn't that odd?"

"Odd, yes. Odd enough to commit murder? I don't think so," Lara replied.

"Just stay cool, and listen to those around you," Megan snapped. "Report back to me. Forget about the police. They seem incapable of solving anything quickly."

"I believe the police are doing everything they can," Lara said. "I'll let you know if I hear anything."

"By the way Todd's funeral is tomorrow," Megan said. "I've emailed all the agents. It's at St. Martin's at four o'clock."

"It will be tough, but I'll be there," Lara replied.

Megan's phone buzzed. She picked it up then mouthed goodbye to Lara who gladly left.

Returning to her office, Lara began going through the long list of unread emails. She immediately clicked on one from Jane Layton, listing agent for the house the Clark's made an offer on. The subject line read, "Offer Acceptance." She called Vanessa.

"Hi Vanessa, this is Lara. I just got an email from the listing agent saying the owners have accepted your offer as written. This doesn't happen often. Normally people take days negotiating a contract. I'm happy for you. Congratulations!"

Vanessa let out an excited shriek. "Wonderful. Now what do we do?"

"Set up an inspection with one of the companies I sent you. I'll take care of the paperwork, and getting your earnest money check, and executed contract to the title company."

"I'm so excited I could cry," Vanessa said. "I know Dick will be too. Thank you so much."

"This couldn't happen to a nicer family," Lara said.

After saying goodbye, she sat back in her chair, enjoying the moment.

Chaya Getz walked by her office. "What are you smiling about?"

"I just got an accepted offer for my buyers, the Clarks. The best thing yet, we aren't spending time with nit-picking negotiations."

"Congrats!" Chaya said. "Do you have time for a cup of coffee?"

"I'd love one!"

They sat together in the break room enjoying freshly brewed coffee. Lara kicked off her shoes. Chaya followed suit, kicking off her black strappy three-inch heels.

"These damn shoes are killing me," Chaya said. "I left my slippers at my desk. But enough about my aching feet. Congrats on the contract! Todd would have approved. God, I miss him."

"You two seemed to be friends, as much as anyone here could be Todd's friend."

"I liked Todd," Chaya said as tears welled up in her eyes. "I considered him a friend even though he could be a taskmaster. Do you know the funeral is tomorrow?"

"Yes. That's going to be hard to get through," Lara said. She watched Chaya sip on her coffee, and decided that now was a good time find out what she knew.

"Chaya, maybe you can shine some light on a rumor I heard that's really bothering me."

Chaya moved her chair closer to Lara.

"Go ahead. Ask me."

"Do you know anything about parties hosted by Todd?" Lara began. "From what I've heard these were not just mixers, but orgies fueled by drugs."

Chaya's mouth flew open, and her eyes popped out in horror while Lara continued. "Apparently, Todd was heavily involved. That may be why he was killed."

"Where in the hell did you hear that? I'll bet that little prick Billy is flapping his mouth," Chaya said. "Crap! I'll tell you what I know. This is just between the two of us. Promise me," she pleaded.

Lara sipped her coffee trying to decide how to proceed without lying to her friend. Why did she ever agree to being put in this untenable situation?

"I can't promise when I don't know what the hell you're talking about," Lara hedged.

"Okay. I'm taking a deep breath here," Chaya said putting her hand over her chest. "My husband doesn't know. I went to a party. Just one. Nothing happened, but still I went."

"We realtors go to business socials all the time alone. What made this different?" Lara asked.

Chaya got up from her seat to close the door. "The difference was, the type of party, Lara! I don't know why I went. Damn. Yes, I do. Money."

Chaya paced the small room, wringing her hands. "I was thinking I could just enjoy the party without the sex, maybe meet some wealthy guy who wanted to buy a house. Ha! Little did I know. No sex, no deal. Period, end of story."

"Actually, I understand," Lara said. "This is a tough business. We're always looking for clients. Isn't that why we go to cocktail parties given by builders, bankers, chambers of commerce? That's how we make contacts. It's part of the business. You were unprepared for what happened. I'm sorry you got lured in."

Chaya sat next to Lara and wept. "Thank you. I felt stupid for believing the bullshit about how the party could bring me business. Not the kind of business I wanted."

Lara reached over, patted Chaya's hand, and said, "My curiosity is getting the best of me. I'm dying to know who else was there. Anyone in this office?"

"No one the night I went, but that agent you're working with, Jane something? She was there."

"You're kidding! Jane Layton? I'll be damned."

"She was all decked out in a low-cut, short black dress, and fuck me stilettos," Chaya said. "You never completely know about people, or what they're capable of."

Chaya got up from her chair, and poured herself another cup of coffee. She offered the pot to Lara who shook her head.

"The one thing that bothered me was, I'm convinced some of the women were prostitutes. I know little about the world's oldest profession, so I don't know who invited them," Chaya sighed. "Todd? Could he have been involved in prostitution?"

"Are you sure they were prostitutes?"

"Several months before I went to Todd's party my husband and I went to the bar at *The Hilton* with a friend who is a police reporter for *The Houston Chronicle*," Chaya said. "There were several women at the bar talking with some men, you know, normal activity at a bar. Our reporter friend, who trusts us to be discreet, pointed out a couple of women he said were call girls. I guess he had inside information, or he may have wanted to impress us with his knowledge. Anyway, I'll be damned if I didn't see those same women at Todd's party."

"No! Todd the pimp! That's so sleazy," Lara said

Chaya looked around the room, sipped from her cup then suddenly grabbed Lara's hand.

"I saw someone else that night," Chaya said as tears welled in her eyes. "I'm so sorry."

"What? Who?" Lara said feeling her stomach flip flop.

"Your boyfriend, David."

Lara pulled her hand from Chaya's, then laughed loudly. "That's impossible. David doesn't fit the type. He doesn't have money, and he's not new to Houston. Are you sure?"

"I wouldn't bet my life on it," Chaya said. "But if it wasn't him, he has a twin."

Lara's voice cracked. "I'm afraid to ask this, Chaya." Taking a deep breath, she continued. "What was he doing?"

"He was talking to the bartender. That's all, honey. I left shortly after seeing him so I don't know what else he did, or didn't do."

Jackie's voice came out over the office intercom. "Chaya, you have a call on line two."

"I'm waiting for a call from a buyer," Chaya said. "I hate to leave you like this. We'll talk later. Don't be upset. I'm sure there's an explanation."

Lara watched Chaya leave, and remained at the table staring dumbfoundedly at her coffee cup. The only sound was the ticking clock on the wall. A silent scream came from her entire being. She took the plastic spoon from her cup.

David!

Twirling the spoon between her fingers, she wondered if it really had been him. Maybe someone who looked like him? But David wouldn't go to that type of party. The spoon fell from her fingers. He didn't do drugs, but if he did drugs that would explain his recent volatile behavior. She picked the spoon up and threw it across the room.

Damn him!

That meant he knew Todd. He never told her. The sin of omission. Everything she knew, or thought she knew was disintegrating around her. Why had she ever agreed to be an informant? Her conversation with Chaya could put David in the detective's cross hairs. David would become a suspect. Could she tell Edie about David? She picked up her phone, and called the detective.

"Edie, it's Lara. We need to meet."

"I have time later today," Edie said. "I'll meet you in the bar at the *Ramada Inn* on Dairy Ashford at four o'clock. It's out of the way, and quiet that time of day."

The line went dead.

Lara looked at her phone. "I'll be damned. She hung up on me again!"

CHAPTER 16

Ron and Edie

Ron Yates was eager to interview Alex Ricci. He paced the interview room where he and Edie waited.

"If Ricci doesn't show in two minutes, I'm going to go get him," Ron said. "I think he's going to be a tough nut to crack. If he wasn't cowed by those two narcs, Cline and Carter, he won't be by us."

"We'll see about that," Edie said. Her phone rang. "It's Lara Maxwell. Hold on to that thought, Ron."

Captain Henry burst into the room, looked at Edie with a frown then turned to Ron. "Ricci is here for his interview. I'll be in the other room watching. And get Edie off the damn phone!"

"Hey, Edie you heard the boss," Ron growled.

He looked up in time to see Alex brazenly enter the room with an eat-shit grin on his sensuous mouth. He wore jeans, and a red shirt unbuttoned just enough to show his smooth chest punctuated by a few dark curly hairs. He had a classic Roman nose, and a mop of coifed dark hair.

"Come in Mr. Ricci," Ron said. "Have a seat. Can I get you anything?"

Alex noisily pulled a chair out before easing into the cold steel seat. He looked up at Ron. "Yeah, you can get me out of here."

"This won't take long," Ron said. He sat across the table from Alex, and next to Edie. "This is my partner, Edie Ross. May we call you Alex?"

Alex slouched in the chair, tapping his foot. His grin faded. He glared at Ron, and shrugged.

"Call me whatever the fuck you want," Alex growled. "Why are you two harassing me? First the narcs bring me in on a phony drug investigation. Now you bring me in for what? How many times do I have to sit in this shit hole answering idiotic questions?"

What a total asshole, Ron thought as he pulled his chair closer to Alex, who threw his hands up in front of his face.

"Whoa! Can you back the fuck off detective? Next thing I know you'll be in my lap."

"Not likely. We don't want to harass you, Alex. Why would we want to do something like that? We just think you're an interesting guy on several levels. Today we want to talk to you about Todd Drake's murder."

"I don't have the vaguest idea who murdered Todd. End of story. I'm leaving now."

"Sit down wise ass," Ron said as he forcefully put his hand on Alex's shoulder. "Calm down. This is only an informational interview. We want to ask you some questions that will help fill in some gaps in our investigation."

"Alright then, fire away," Alex said, running his hands through his hair.

"Let's start with question number one. Where were you from noon to four last Sunday afternoon?" Ron asked.

Alex smirked. "I was with a lady friend. That makes it none of your business."

"See, that's where you're wrong," Edie interjected. "Everything you did last Sunday including who you did it with, is our business. Unless you want to spend the rest of the day sitting here you need to stop the bullshit, and be straight with us."

Alex rolled his dark eyes toward the ceiling. "Alright already. I get the drill. Let's get this over with. I was with a woman named Jackie Long."

"Jackie Long, the office manager at Drake Properties?" Ron asked.

"That's right," Alex replied.

"What is a woman like Ms. Long doing with a drug dealer like you?"

Alex sat up, clenched his fists, and slammed them on the table. "I'm not a drug dealer. Get off that shit."

"I'll give you the benefit of a doubt, Alex," Ron said. "Let's talk about your relationship with Todd Drake, and his office manager."

Alex squirmed in his chair, looking warily at the two detectives while blowing air noisily out of his mouth.

Ron leaned back. He'd known men like Alex. Men whose looks, and gift of gab got them perks, jobs, and women lesser men only dreamed of.

Alex glared at the detectives. "Todd was a regular at the bar I tend at *Ceres*," he began. "We became friends. One night after the bar closed, we were just sitting around, shooting the breeze. That's when the two of us came up with this great idea for executive mixers. He included me in his plan. That's how I got in with Drake Properties, as an idea man."

"C'mon, Alex cut the crap. We know all about the parties Drake gave. I wouldn't define them as mixers. I'd say they were more like meet hot women, suck up free booze and drugs, and then have sex," Ron said.

"You're a real comic," Alex said, laying both his hands on the table. "Listen, all I did was tend bar. I needed the job. I met Jackie at Todd's office. She was easy to be around. She asked me out. She was bold, and somewhat alluring. We started dating. That's all there is."

Edie sat quietly, then asked, "Are you still seeing Jackie?"

"Yes, we see each other often," Alex replied. "She's a great listener. She sends me gifts. She takes me out to dinner. Man, that doesn't happen often."

"What gifts?" Edie asked.

"There was a time, maybe six months ago, she sent me a gift certificate to Neiman Marcus. Thanks to her I have the finest bathrobe I've ever owned," Alex replied. "Another time she sent me a box of fine cigars. That's one generous, sweet-ass woman."

Ron briefly made eye contact with Edie, knowing she was probably thinking the same thing.

Jackie bought Alex's heart, if he had one.

He then turned his attention back to Alex. "Did Todd know about you and Jackie?"

"Nobody knew, and that's how we wanted it. Actually, Jackie's the one who kept our affair quiet. She didn't need the agents gossiping about her," Alex said. "I like Jackie. She knows how to keep her mouth shut. She spoils me."

Alex looked directly at Ron, and winked. "Just between us the quiet, shy ones are tigers where it counts."

"I think we've heard enough, Alex," Ron said. "This interview is finished. You're free to go, for now."

Alex stretched his long legs, got up from his seat, and stopped beside Edie. He bent down by her ear, and said in a stage whisper, "I'll bet you're a tiger too."

Edie jumped from her seat, reached for Alex's arm, and slammed him against the wall.

"Did you forget where you are, and who you're talking to?"

Alex's eyes opened wide as he put his arms up. "Slow down mama. I didn't mean any disrespect."

Edie gave him one last shove before taking her seat. "Just get outta' here."

Ron took Alex firmly by the arm escorting him to the elevator. As they stood waiting for the doors to open, Ron said, "Don't leave town. Watch your step. I'm just itching for you to screw up."

•　•　•

Edie returned to her office, sat at her desk, and clasped her shaking hands together. What was it that made her lose control with Alex? She took a long, deep breath. Could it be she felt protective of Jackie, and women like her? Jackie was just another in a long line of sad, lonely women Edie encountered in her job, only this time the woman in question paid for her man's affection. She'd actually bought Alex gifts!

Ron passed by her open door. "Remember, Mr. and Mrs. Bard will be here in five minutes."

"I lost track of the time," Edie said. "Come in."

Ron sat across from Edie, stretched out in the chair, and crossed his ankles. "That Alex is a piece of shit. You certainly put him in his place."

"He belongs in a sty with the rest of the pigs. But is he a killer?"

"He's being watched by narcotics, and homicide," Ron said. "Whatever he is, he won't get away."

"I agree," Edie said with a satisfied smile. "Before I forget, Lara wants to meet this evening. Seems she has already heard something that pertains to the case. I want you to come along."

Edie glanced at the wall clock. "As for now, I think we need to separate the Bards. You take Jack, and we'll compare notes when they leave."

Edie remembered Melanie as a buxom blond whose hair, clothing, and makeup were beautifully done. Today she was disheveled. Her appearance had radically changed since the day of Todd's murder. She wore jeans, a tee shirt, and no makeup except for a splash of red lipstick. Her light blue eyes were red, and swollen. Her hair hung limply.

Melanie entered the interrogation room and burst out in tears. She fidgeted in her purse for a tissue. Finding one she loudly blew her nose before taking a chair. Edie offered her a Styrofoam cup of water.

"My mouth is so dry," Melanie said after taking a large gulp. "I've never been in a police station before."

"I know it can be intimidating," Edie smiled. "Don't let it bother you. We'll just talk for a while. Why are you crying, Mrs. Bard?"

Melanie nodded her head. "Please call me Melanie. I can't stop crying when I think of Todd's death. My life has been ruined by all this," she said waving the tissue around. "Is there a reason my husband isn't in here with me? Are we under suspicion?"

"It's a matter of efficiency. It takes up more time when we interview people together."

"Makes sense," Melanie said. "I'm a wreck. I still can't believe what happened in my home, in our bedroom. I can't live in that house. We've moved into an apartment."

"I realize how tough it has been. This won't take long, Melanie. I just have a few questions. Think back to Sunday. Did you notice or sense anything different before the open house? Did you see any strangers in the neighborhood?"

Melanie shook her head, and took another sip of water. "I remember nothing. We left about an hour before the open house started."

"Where did you go?"

"We went to Galveston for lunch. Nothing out of the ordinary happened."

"Where did you eat lunch?"

"The *Shark Shack*. They have terrific seafood," Melanie said. "After lunch we walked along the beach, and boardwalk. We were biding our time until the open house was over."

"I have to ask if you know anyone who would want to kill Todd."

Melanie sniffed, brushed her hair back out of her eyes, and said, "I can't think of anyone who would want to hurt Todd let alone kill him. In case you're not aware of it, Todd was a highly respected realtor," she sighed. "Now he's gone."

Melanie rubbed the back of her head while looking sideways at Edie. "Before we go on, I have a terrible headache. Could I please have a cup of coffee?"

"Do you take cream, sugar or both?"

"Black, like my mood," Melanie replied.

Edie got up, and before leaving the room, gave Melanie a pat on her shoulder. She heard shouting as she passed the room where Ron was interviewing Melanie's husband, Jack. Slipping in the small area behind the one-way mirror Edie saw Jack pacing while Ron sat listening intently.

"When I got the transfer to Cincinnati, I was pleased when Melanie said she'd get a realtor. I believed she was finally taking control of something, taking the load off me. I thought she was handling the sale of the house. All along she was handling Todd," Jack fumed. "That wife of mine was in love with him."

Edie's shoulders slumped.

Now we have an angry, maybe jealous husband in the mix.

She leaned against the two-way window, and continued to watch the interview.

"Sit down sir, and let's talk about this," Ron said.

Jack walked to the empty chair at the table, and pulled it out, slamming the legs on the floor. He then sat with his arms crossed over his chest staring coldly at Ron.

As much as Edie wanted to hear more of Jack's rant, she had to finish her own interview. She stopped for the promised coffee, then returned to the room where Melanie was sitting stiffly, drying her eyes with a tissue. Edie placed the hot coffee by Melanie before sitting next to her.

She smiled, lowered her voice, and softened her tone. "You seem to have been quite fond of Todd. Was there something other than a business relationship between the two of you?"

"You're quite perceptive, detective. Oh, what the hell. My life, and marriage are falling apart," Melanie replied. "To be honest, detective, I had a thing for Todd. That was all. There was no relationship other than business."

"Did Todd know how you felt?"

"I don't think he did. We got along so well. We laughed together, lunched together, and flirted. I think that was Todd's way of doing business with women. I fell for him hard. I adored him. I guess you could say I was a bored, neglected housewife," Melanie said. "How cliché is that?"

"When was the last time you saw Todd?"

"Last Friday," Melanie said, softly crying while twisting, and turning a sodden tissue. "Todd came by to go over the details of the open house. He stayed for around an hour. Then he was gone."

"Were the two of you on good terms?"

"We were always on good terms," Melanie murmured.

"Did Todd ever do or say anything you or Mr. Bard disagreed with?"

Melanie lifted her reddened eyes toward the ceiling, sighing deeply. "Jack seemed irritated with Todd over a comment about smoking."

"Jack is a smoker?"

"He is. He tried to smoke outside most of the time, but it is so damned hot. One day he smoked in the house. Todd accompanied a showing the next day. The buyers smelled the smoke and apparently said something about the odor. Long story short, Todd told Jack and Jack hit the ceiling," Melanie said. "He yelled at Todd saying, 'This is my house, and I'll do what I want!' He was unreasonable."

"Is your husband a volatile person?" Edie asked.

"Not volatile. More like controlling. My way or the highway, is the best description of Jack's attitude toward everyone in his life."

"Was Jack angry enough to hurt Todd?"

"I think Jack had a right to be angry with Todd," Melanie said. "Todd could be demanding. I think the two of them were so much alike that they clashed. I don't think Jack was angry enough to hurt Todd."

"How does Jack treat you?"

"If you're asking me if Jack physically abuses me, the answer is no. He is more emotionally abusive. He treats me like I'm a dumb ass."

Melanie straightened her shoulders, and looked directly at Edie. "That's changing. My whole life is changing. I told Jack about my feelings toward Todd. The kids are grown. I'm ready to let Jack go to Cincinnati. I'm staying here."

"I'm sorry to hear that," Edie said.

"I'm not. It's time, detective," Melanie said with a slight smile. "Todd's murder was the catalyst for my decision to end the marital bliss façade, and part ways."

"I think we're finished here unless you can think of anything that will help with this investigation," Edie said. "Here's my card with my cell phone on the back in case you remember anything relevant to this case, or need to talk."

Melanie shook Edie's hand, and left the room to join Jack who was impatiently pacing the hallway clicking his cigarette lighter open, and shut. As they walked away Melanie looked back at Edie with a rueful grin, and a small wave.

Edie joined Ron in the interview room. "Let's go over our notes in your office, Ron."

Ron's office was sparsely furnished with a metal desk, and two matching wooden swivel chairs. Several framed citations decorated the wall behind his cluttered desk.

Ron sat, and opened up his notebook. "Jack, is one pissed off jerk. He's angry about everything, especially his wife lusting after Todd."

Edie sat across from Ron, looking at her notes. "I heard some of his rant when I got coffee for Melanie," she said. "I'm wondering if Jack knew how much time his wife spent with Todd before the murder. According to Melanie her feelings for Todd were unrequited. What did you get from Jack?"

"Jack's anger and resentment spilled over. He believes his wife had an affair with Todd. I think he needs to be watched," Ron said.

"I agree. Check for any criminal record. He's leaving for Cincinnati in a couple of weeks," Edie said. "Also, check with the *Shark Shack* in Galveston to see if there is a record of them eating lunch there on Sunday. That's their alibi."

Ron put his pen down, looked across at Edie, and sighed. "Did you get anything else from your interview with Mrs. Bard?"

Edie looked at her notes. "Melanie told me Todd chastised Jack for smoking in the house. Apparently, when a house is up for sale, smoking inside is taboo. It seems that Todd's non-smoking policy enraged Jack. In my opinion, that's not a strong enough motive to kill."

Ron gave out a hearty laugh. "I know many people who get pissed about not being able to smoke, but not angry enough to commit murder. I do think the wife's imagined infidelity is a possible motive."

"Jealousy is an evil monster," Edie said shaking her head. "This damn case is keeping me up at night. Nothing is breaking."

"Something will," Ron said. "I can feel it in my bones."

Edie shook her head. "I need some air. Let's get out of here."

"Where to boss?" Ron said, grabbing his jacket from the back of his chair.

"I say we nose around *The Hotel Zoie*, where Todd's parties were held."

"I'm right behind you. I'll even drive," Ron said, smiling broadly as he opened the door, bowing to Edie as she passed by.

CHAPTER 17

From the *Hotel Zoie* parking garage Edie and Ron walked half a block before seeing the unassuming facade of what Edie thought was the hotel. She studied the dark brown portico with a scarlet "Z" emblazoned across the front. She looked again at the address she'd written before leaving the squad room, then at the numbers on the building. They matched.

Ron opened the leaded glass door for Edie, who stopped mid-stride to stare at the shimmering Baccarat crystal chandelier hanging in the spacious entry. Turning left, they went directly to the mahogany front desk.

"Good afternoon," Edie said. "I'm HPD Detective Edie Ross. This is my partner, Detective Ron Yates. We'd like to speak with the manager."

The clerk's welcoming smile dropped. He left without a word, returning with a thin well-dressed man in his thirties, "Detectives, I'm Arthur Jordan, the hotel manager. Is there a problem?"

"We're here to look at your surveillance video, Mr. Jordan," Ron said. "Detective Ross called this morning."

"Of course!" he said with an oh-so-slight roll of his eyes. "I momentarily forgot you were coming. I'll show you to the security office. We have the tapes ready for you." He looked over at Ron. "By the way, you can call me Art."

"Art, before we watch the tapes, we'd like to see the venue where Mr. Drake held his parties," Ron said while looking around the sumptuous lobby.

"Certainly," Art replied with a wave of his hand. "Follow me, detectives. There are lots of interesting tidbits about this unique hotel. If you're interested, I'll point them out along the way."

"Sure, why not?" Ron answered. "I didn't even know this place existed."

Art looked Ron up and down, then slightly shook his head. "You might need to keep current, detective. This is the newest boutique hotel in Houston. We take pride in the carefully curated mix of antiques with contemporary furnishings. When we get up to the third-floor party area, you'll be surprised by the artsy, edgy look. Very innovative, and hip."

As they entered the elevator Edie glanced over at Ron, raising her eyebrows. Ron grinned, and slightly shrugged his shoulders. When the elevator reached the third floor Art stepped out first to switch the lights on. He smiled gleefully when the multi-colored globes lit up the entry.

Edie turned to face Ron, mouthing, "Wow!"

"Isn't the lighting wonderful? Our creative director went all out when he designed all the different shaped globes. Quite edgy."

Edie's gaze went from the myriad of vividly colored hanging globes to the rounded floor-to-ceiling glass walls, which gave a panoramic view of downtown Houston. She imagined how intoxicating it must have been to be a guest at one of Todd's parties.

"I can see why Todd chose this venue," Edie said.

"The lighting at night makes this area highly sensual," Art said. "Next time we have an event here I'll send you an invitation," he added, smiling at Ron.

"That's unnecessary," Edie snapped. "We're here to investigate a brutal murder, not book a party."

Art's smile turned to a frown. His freckled nose twitched. He turned his head, and sneezed three times. "Excuse me. My allergies are over the top today."

"I have the same problem," Edie said. "How many times did Mr. Drake rent this venue?"

Art leaned against the wall, holding his chin. "I believe it was six times over the past year. I'll check when I get back to my office."

"Was Mr. Drake easy to work with?"

"I didn't work with Mr. Drake. I worked with Billy, uh, Billy Parsons. He was so easy," Art replied. "I just made sure this area was available when he wanted it. I didn't know what went on at the parties, or who attended. I was shocked to see the news that his boss was murdered."

"Can you give me a list of hotel personnel who worked the parties?" Ron asked.

"I can," Art quickly replied. "There are a few waiters and a maid who are working today. If I'm not mistaken, they worked every party. If you want to talk with them, I can arrange it."

"Is there a place away from the lobby we could use to talk with them?"

Art looked at his watch. "The bar is closed. I don't think any of our guests would see you."

"Good. Ask them to meet us there, please," Edie interjected. "We will be here for about ten more minutes to look around. And don't forget, we want the entire list of employees who worked the Drake parties."

"I'll get that to you before you leave," Art said. He quickly went to the elevator giving the detectives a slight wave.

"I hope ten minutes is enough time to look this room over," Ron said. "It's so over-the-top."

"Doesn't this just fit everything we've learned about Todd? Glitzy to the max. No wonder he was one of Houston's top brokers," Edie said. "Imagine being invited to a party here. Glamor all the way. No wonder Todd was all the attendees go-to realtor."

"On the surface it's a perfect setup," Ron said. "I'm thinking if Todd had kept drugs out of the mix, he would still be throwing parties today. Supplying drugs almost never leads to longevity."

The detectives walked through the reception area, past the glass walls, and into a large room.

"This must be where the main party took place. I'm thinking the band was by the windows, the dance floor here, and the bar over in the other corner," Ron said, pacing and pointing as he talked.

Edie saw three doors off the main room. She walked over, opened a door, then switched on the light. A long, wide, deep red couch cluttered with large pillows, filled the small room. A side table held a lamp at one end of the couch.

"Well, I'll be damned. This must be where the party animals sowed their wild oats."

Edie turned to look at Ron who stood beside her.

"There are two more rooms like this. The only difference is the color of the couches," he said before letting out a long, slow whistle. "A perfect arrangement."

"It definitely matches up with what we've been told by those who were here," Edie said. She looked at her watch. "I think we've seen enough. Let's go talk with the help."

When they got into the elevator, Edie took one last look.

I can't wait to tell Ted about this place. Maybe we could save up for a weekend here.

Edie yearned for time alone with Ted. They both needed to unwind from demanding jobs, and the children. One weekend would be ideal. She made a mental note to talk to her mother-in-law about watching the kids.

The elevator doors opened, bringing Edie from her daydream to her reality. They exited the elevator and walked straight toward the bar where they saw Art, and three others sitting on a couch.

Art rose from the couch. "Detectives, I'd like you to meet Juan Moreno, Frank Manus and Lupe Badillo," he said pointing his hand to each person. "Juan, and Frank worked as waiters at the Drake parties, Lupe helped clean up. I'll let you talk to them. Call me if you need me."

Edie and Ron introduced themselves before sitting in chairs at either side of the couch. "We want to talk with you about the parties

Todd Drake gave. Do you remember the parties?" Edie asked smiling at all three who sat stiffly, nodding in assent.

"I want you all to know we are investigating Mr. Drake's murder. None of you is a suspect. We just need your impressions of the parties, and the people who were there," Edie continued before taking out her notepad. "Can you begin, Mr. Moreno? What do you remember about the parties?"

"Just the usual Roman Bacchanal," he said. "Lupe mixed with the crowd more than we did."

"Is that true, Lupe?" Edie asked.

"Si senora. Mr. Drake, and his beautiful women!" she said. The others laughed while Lupe smiled shyly. "I cleaned the side rooms. I saw pills left around the couches and on tables. I found uh, things, uh, condones," Lupe said as her cheeks turned crimson.

"I assume condones means condoms?"

Lupe nodded shyly while looking at her lap.

Edie smiled, and leaned forward. "Did you see anything unusual besides what you just described?"

"One time I did. The three side rooms have couches where many people went to be alone," Lupe said. "One time I went into the room nearest the bar to clean, and saw the bartender with a dark-haired woman."

"Did you interrupt them?" Edie asked.

"Yes, they stopped yelling when they saw me," Lupe said. "The woman was crying. I thought everyone was gone. I was frightened."

"Frightened? Why?"

"The woman turned, and screamed at me, 'Get out of here, bitch or I'll get your ass fired.' She was a very mean woman."

"Was anyone else there?"

"I think a man was in the main room picking glasses up."

"Can you describe the man?" Edie asked.

"I think he's the one who worked for Mr. Drake." Lupe said.

"Can you describe the woman who yelled at you?"

"She wore a short black dress. Her hair was long to her shoulders, I didn't see her eyes but I remember she had black running down her cheeks. Maybe mascara from crying? She was not as pretty as the others," Lupe said. "I'm sorry. That's all I remember."

Edie looked at Ron who was going over his notes.

"Lupe, did you witness any other, uh, disagreements between the party goers?" she asked.

"Yes. One night the man with yellow hair who worked for Mr. Drake, I think his name is Bill or Billy. He got angry, yelling about watered down drinks. The bartender told him to, uh, excuse me, fuck off."

Edie looked over at Ron who shrugged slightly.

"Is there anything else any of you can think of?" Ron asked.

Lupe, who continued to stare at her lap, shook her head and quietly said, "I can't think of anything more to say."

"Frank and I worked the main room," Juan Moreno said. "We served drinks, and tidied up. We saw nothing more than a bunch of drunks partying. Nothing unusual."

"If you think of something please call us anytime. This is a murder investigation. Anything you remember is important."

The detectives handed their cards to the three staff members, who mumbled goodbyes, and hurried away.

"I don't think we learned anything we didn't know," Ron said. "Maybe the fight between the bartender, and some random woman is important."

Art came striding toward them. "The security tapes are ready for you to view." He showed them to the hotel security office. "As you can imagine we have security cameras on every floor including the lobby, and bar. We keep security film for thirty to ninety days. Our security tech found, and isolated the party room tapes so you will only see the Drake events. This video only shows the elevator door, and short hallway into the main room."

"Why aren't cameras in the main party room?" Ron asked.

"Guests aren't comfortable with cameras rolling while they have meetings, or parties. We don't want to make our guests uncomfortable. Have a seat at the table with the computer screen. Just click the mouse to stop the video, zoom in, and re-start."

Edie sat on one side of the computer, and Ron sat on the other side with the mouse. He clicked *play*.

"This is state-of-the art quality," Edie said. "Look at the clarity. Not only can I see faces, but facial expressions."

She and Ron sat watching people come out of the elevator, gather briefly, and then walk over to Todd.

"This is great! It's like a receiving line," Ron exclaimed as Edie intently watched the parade of people waiting to greet their host. Women dressed in short, mostly black, form-fitting dresses with plunging necklines, streamed out of the elevator while men stood around gawking at the sexy array before them. Ron laughed, and pointed to a couple of men who stood open-mouthed.

"Stop it there," Edie said. "Right here. See Todd turn his head toward the camera? Can you zoom in on his face?"

Ron did what Edie asked, closing in on Todd's nose and mouth, then started the video. "There it is," Edie cried. "What is he mouthing?"

Ron looked closer, rewound the tape, played it again. "It looks like he's saying 'Ka-ching'. What the hell is that?"

"Ka-ching, like a cash register! That's it. All these people meant nothing but money to him," Edie said.

"That's no surprise," Ron replied.

They continued watching the first tape, then the second. By the third tape Edie was rubbing her eyes, and squirming in her seat as she watched a stream of overly exuberant women with large boobs, drunken men throwing their arms around every woman within reach, Todd shaking hands, patting backs of men, and the backsides of women.

"Oh my God," Edie said. "I think I saw Melanie Bard!"

Edie leaned in to the screen, and motioned Ron to back up the tape to where the elevator door was opening. Five women stepped out. Ron stopped the tape, then zoomed in on the group of women. It was Melanie, her blonde hair in an up-do, tight sky-blue cocktail dress, eyes aglow. Ron started the tape. They watched Melanie glide over to Todd, who pulled her to him before giving her a long passionate kiss. Melanie laughed, put her finger in front of his nose waving it back and forth, and then moved out of camera range.

"Well, I'll be damned," Edie said. "So much for the bored housewife crush. Let's copy this to a thumb drive."

The detectives took the thumb drive, said their goodbyes to the obliging Art.

Ron quickly followed Edie out the gold leaf doors, and into the humid air.

"Isn't it about time to meet Lara at *The Ramada Inn*?" he asked.

"Yes. Don't forget you're coming with me, right?"

Ron looked over at Edie with a wide grin, and said, "I wouldn't miss it for the world."

CHAPTER 18

Lara chose a small table in a back corner of the sparsely populated *Ramada Inn* bar, then told the waitress she was waiting for friends. She ordered a glass of ice water. She needed to think.

What the hell was David doing at Todd's parties? Who had invited him? None of the answers she came up with made sense. She played with the notion that David knew the bartender, Alex something or other, who invited him to the party. That had to be the reason. No other logical answer would suffice until she heard differently. Would David tell her the truth? Could it be that he knew Todd? If so, why hadn't he told her?

She knew very little about David. Of course, they'd only been to-gether for a few months, but still who was he? All she knew was that he was employed by Shell Oil as project manager for an off-shore drill-ing site, and that he had graduated from Rice University with an engineering degree. That was it. He had never mentioned his family, where he grew up, or if he had siblings.

All I know is he's good in bed. Dammit! Another shallow relationship.

Lara took a deep sip of cold water. She had decided for now, not to tell Edie about David. David was her problem, not a police matter. He may be possessive, and have a trigger temper, but he wasn't a killer. But what if David had found out about the affair, and confronted Todd? That would make him a suspect.

Stop thinking like that. Don't say a thing!

Edie and Ron appeared suddenly. Lara jumped. "Shit, you scared me," she said, trying to laugh off her self-absorbed stupor.

"Nice greeting," Edie said pulling a chair out from the small table. "You didn't see us coming?"

"No. I guess I was deep in my own thoughts. Please sit down," Lara said. "Detective Yates, what a pleasant surprise."

Lara quickly glanced at Ron. *What a hunk*, she mused before blurting out, "I could use a stiff drink."

She motioned the waitress over and ordered a dry Martini. Edie and Ron ordered club sodas.

"You sounded a little upset when you called," Edie said. "What's going on?"

"A little upset? I was about to explode," Lara said. "Not only that, but on my way over here I saw the same dark sedan I saw the other night. The car followed me for about ten minutes. This time I got a glimpse of a woman driver, but I didn't recognize her. It could have been a man with long hair. I'm so confused. Who's following me?"

"Be careful, and call one of us immediately if you see the car again, or feel threatened," Edie said. "Please, whatever you do, don't stop and confront whoever it is."

The waitress returned with their order. She gave Ron his club soda, and said, "Haven't I seen your picture in the newspaper? Do you play for the Astros?"

Ron smiled broadly. "If only I did, but I don't."

Not to be deterred the waitress studied Ron's lean face.

"I recognize those baby blue eyes from the picture. It was a big color photo. I've got it!" she exclaimed. "About a month ago you were on the front page of *The Chronicle*. It was about the arrest of our esteemed state legislator for distributing porn. I knew I recognized you!"

Ron's smile disappeared. "I think you've got the wrong guy."

"Then you have a double out there with the same beautiful eyes. Sorry if I embarrassed you," she said, smiling at Edie and Lara before leaving.

"That was weird," Lara said. She watched the waitress leave, then looked over at Ron. "Was it you in the paper?"

"Yes. Lower your voice. No need to draw attention."

"It's amazing that the waitress recognized you," Lara said in hushed tones.

Ron leaned in. "Let's concentrate on why we're here. Whatever you hear or see that could help us unravel this tangled web is vital." He looked around the bar. "This isn't a game. Your identity needs to be protected. This is the last time we meet publicly."

"Aren't you overreacting just a little?" asked Lara. "There's no more than six people in this bar."

"I don't think I am, Lara. That waitress recognizing me shows how any of us can be compromised. I see your photo in the real estate section of every Sunday paper. We need to keep our meetings discreet, preferably in a park somewhere."

Lara took a sip from her drink, then glanced over her shoulder. People were drifting in. Probably the happy hour group.

What have I gotten myself into?

Her entire body tensed. What she previously thought would be a great chance to work with, and befriend the police, had turned deadly serious. Ron and Edie were not amicable confidants. They were stone-faced police officers hunting a killer. Lara tried to steady her pounding heart.

"I understand, detective. The last thing I want is to screw up the investigation."

Edie took out a small notepad. "So, what do you have for us?"

The martini soured in Lara's stomach. She pushed the drink aside. "I've already told you that Billy Parsons gave me a luridly entertaining description of Todd's parties. Today I learned from an agent who went to one of Todd's parties, that the guest list was more far-reaching than I ever imagined."

"Who is the agent?"

Lara squirmed in her seat, pulled the martini glass over, and fiddled with the olive.

"This is confidential, right?" she asked.

"For now," Edie said. "Yes but, if need be, we will interview whoever you tell us about. That's how you help us with this investigation. Do you understand?"

Lara nodded in agreement. "Chaya Getz. She told me she only went to one party. Her husband doesn't know about any of this. She wants to keep it that way. Chaya went to the party to get business. Apparently, she wasn't successful in getting a client. Like she said, 'no sex, no deal.' Do you want to know the names of the other realtors Chaya saw, or is that hearsay?"

"We aren't taking testimony here," Ron said. "For our investigative purpose it would be good to know who your friend saw."

"Chaya told me she saw Jane Layton there. Jane is with another broker. The interesting thing, at least to me, is I'm working with Jane on a contract. She's a smart, professional realtor. I have a hard time imagining her at these parties. The other interesting part is that Chaya also saw a woman she recognized as a hooker."

"She recognized a hooker?" Edie asked.

Lara let out a short laugh. "I know, who would have thought? Chaya was at a bar in a well-known hotel with her husband, and a friend who is a reporter for *The Houston Chronicle*. He pointed this woman out, and said she was a high-end call girl. Imagine Chaya's surprise when she saw the same woman at Todd's party."

"Call girls hang out at all the big hotels in Houston," Ron said.

"That's true, but Chaya got the impression that several women were working the party," Lara said. She leaned forward. "Someone got them there. Maybe Todd?"

"Interesting," Edie said. "Thanks, Lara. We'll look into this. Do you have anything else?"

"Chaya said Megan probably knew about the parties, but ignored what was going on. I got the same impression when we talked."

"When did you talk to her?" Edie asked.

"This morning Megan called me into her office," Lara said. "I was surprised because she rarely speaks to me. She told me she wants this nightmare murder investigation over soon. She asked me to be find out who in the office could be involved in Todd's murder. Isn't that ironic?"

"Did you go along with her?"

"Rather than argue, I agreed. Until the case is solved, I'll do my best to avoid her," Lara said.

Ron shook his head. "I don't think that's a good idea. I'd like you to stay in close contact with Megan. You might learn something vital."

"I'll do my best, but she is one cold woman who pretty much keeps her distance," Lara said. She brushed a strand of hair out of her eye before continuing. "Toward the end of our conversation, I mentioned Todd's parties. Megan said she'd heard rumors. She told me to forget about the parties, concentrate on my business, and keep my mouth shut. Talk about a contradiction. The woman wants me to shut up, and then she flips, and wants me to blab." Lara shook her head. "I'm of the opinion that she knows Todd's partying brought business to the firm, so she looked the other way. Isn't that called the sin of omission?"

"Yes, but it's not illegal," Edie said.

"How would you describe the overall mood in the office?" Ron asked.

"Before Todd's murder the synergy in the office was geared toward success. Now there is a shroud of dread that permeates everyone, and everything," Lara replied. "Of course, we are all grieving, but this is a different feeling. Perhaps Megan isn't doing a good job of hiding her fear that Drake Properties is going down the drain."

Lara took a small sip of her drink. "That's all I've been able to find out. Todd's funeral is tomorrow at four, at St. Martin's. The entire office will be there."

"We'll be at the burial. You won't see us, but we'll be around," Ron said.

Edie stretched and looked at her watch, "If you see us, act like we're not there. I have one more thing. We've interviewed the bartender at *Ceres*. Have you met Alex Ricci?"

"I met him once. If I remember correctly, he's a dark, handsome Italian. He came to the office to see Todd."

Edie put down her note pad. "Was Todd the only one he came to see?"

"As far as I can remember, yes. I think Megan was in the office. I got the feeling they knew each other. Of course, Megan knows everyone from the mayor on down. That's why it wouldn't surprise me if she knew Mr. Ricci. From what I've heard he's a popular bartender in a popular restaurant, and Megan loves Italian food, and booze."

"Do you know why Melanie Bard would be at the *Hotel Zoie* on the night of the last party Todd threw?" Ron asked.

Lara's head snapped around. "What the hell? Sweet, sedate Melanie went to a wild party?"

"Did you ever see any signs of an affair between Melanie and Todd?"

Lara sat back. "I can't help you here. I met Mr. and Mrs. Bard for the first time the day Todd was killed. I know Todd's clients thought he was great, but this goes beyond appreciation."

Poor Melanie under Todd's spell. Was Melanie sleeping with Todd too?

How embarrassing to realize these detectives were probably thinking the same thing. Her face flushed as she looked down at her lap trying to recall her first impression of Melanie.

"I remember Mrs. Bard was distraught when we met," Lara said. "I also remember her saying how much they loved Todd. My God, how many women did Todd lure into his parties?"

"Apparently quite a few, but if it makes you feel any better, I think we're narrowing down our suspects," Ron said.

Lara reached for her drink, spilling it on the way to her mouth. She quickly grabbed a napkin wiping the liquid off her blouse.

Damn! Calm down!

"It seems to me you're adding more suspects," said Lara. "I'll continue keeping my eyes and ears open."

Edie put her notes in her purse, and motioned the waitress for the check.

"Y'all don't have to go do you?" Lara said. "At least stay while I finish my drink."

"We aren't off the clock yet," Edie said while paying the check. "Stay alert, Lara."

She walked away followed by Ron, who stopped beside Lara. "Don't worry. You'll be okay. I have a feeling this will be over soon."

Lara sighed as she watched Ron walk away. She reached over for the martini glass, then left it untouched. Looking around at the people filling the bar she rose to leave. It was then she felt a firm hand on her shoulder. Turning around she was surprised to see David's familiar grin.

"David! Where'd you come from?" she said looking furtively around the bar. "How long have you been here?"

"I just walked in. I'm surprised to see you," David said. "This place is far from your usual hangouts, isn't it?"

"My clients just left. We were looking at houses in this area. We stopped here to go over the showings," she said, pleased at how quickly she thought on her feet.

"Is this your drink?" David asked, picking up the martini glass. "Aren't you going to finish it?"

"Well, now that you're here I will," Lara said before she saw the cocktail waitress with the super face recognition ability coming toward them. "On second thought, do you have dinner plans?"

"I'm with a group from work. I'd rather have dinner with you," David said pulling Lara's chair out for her. "Let's get out of here."

Lara stood and forced a smile. "I'm ready if you are."

Lara watched David say goodbye to his co-workers, slapping the men on their backs and shaking the women's hands. They all waved to her. She waved back.

Her body felt limp with relief as she and David walked to the parking lot. What if David had shown up ten minutes earlier? How could she be sure he didn't see her with the detectives? Ron was right. From now on, discretion was of the highest order.

Lara's entire body shook even though the night air was hot and humid. She put her arm around David to steady herself.

"You aren't cold, are you?" David said.

Lara forced a smile. "No, I just wanted to give you a hug. This is a great way to end my day."

She got into her car, and gripped the wheel to steady her shaking hands. Dread filled her entire body ending in the pit of her stomach. David honked as he passed her. She moved in behind his car following him to the restaurant of his choice.

Lara spent the rest of the evening pretending to be attentive while her mind raced. What if David had been lurking in the crowded bar watching her? She ate little, drank even less. By the time the waiter had cleared their table Lara had a splitting headache.

"This was a better night than I expected," David said squeezing her hand. "I'll follow you home where we can continue doing the unexpected."

"Not tonight, honey. I've had a bitch of a day. My head is pounding."

"Okay, but tomorrow night I'm counting on you," David said with a wink.

Lara sighed heavily as she entered her condo. She shed her clothes before falling into bed. Sleep escaped her. She laid, eyes wide open, unable to quiet her thoughts. Why was she feeling so anxious? This evening's bizarre turn of events was unsettling, but something else was nagging at her.

Tomorrow is Todd's funeral.

She'd never see Todd again. Never hear him tell one of his obnoxious jokes. But David would go to the funeral with her. Having him by her side might help.

As she drifted off to sleep, she dreamed she was in a rocking chair with her mother. No words were said. Just mother rocking, holding her close.

CHAPTER 19

Lara anxiously looked at the clock in her office, the time ticking slowly toward Todd's funeral. Sitting in her chair made her antsy. Pacing the room helped.

She loathed funerals. The sickly aroma from the flowers, the weeping, the liturgy. Most of all she hated the loss of life. She hadn't attended many funerals, but after sitting through her parent's double service the thought of attending today's funeral made her physically ill.

If there was such a thing as funeral phobia, Lara was certain she had it. A year ago, her therapist prescribed tranquilizers for times like this. She'd put the bottle in the back of her desk drawer for emergencies. Opening the drawer, she reached to the back, pulled out the bottle, then popped a small pink pill on her tongue.

Down the hatch!

Lara sat back, and closed her eyes waiting for the pill to take effect. Todd's image burst into her head. She still had a hard time thinking of Todd as dead, let alone murdered. Megan's comment about a crazy ass with a gun ruining her business rang true. That same insane gunman had upended Lara's life. Her business was slower; her phone rang less, her listings sat without being shown. On a positive note, working on the Clark contract kept her mind occupied.

This morning Lara dropped the Clark's option check at Jane Layton's office. Jane was her usual friendly, charming self.

"I'm going to the funeral this afternoon," Jane said. "I think my entire office is going. We all thought Todd was one of the best brokers in town."

Lara was tempted to tell Jane to cut the feigned innocence. She wanted to sit Jane down, tell her Chaya saw her at one of Todd's parties, and ask her why she went. Did she get business? Was it all worth it?

Until now, Lara considered herself an open-minded, accepting woman, but the idea of intelligent women prostituting themselves for any reason bewildered her. She didn't want to slut-shame women she worked with, but how desperate could a woman be?

A knock on her office door snapped her back to the present.

"David!" she said with a smile. "Thanks for being here."

"You're welcome," he murmured. "Let's get this over with."

Lara had been in St. Martin's Episcopal Church sanctuary, known in Houston as, *The Church,* but had forgotten how beautiful it was. The exquisitely designed nave boasted seventy-foot arched ceilings over an Appalachian white oak altar. The afternoon sun shone through stained glass windows, the light reflecting on mourner's faces.

Lara and David sat in the second row reserved for Drake Properties behind Todd's family and Megan. Sonya sat across the aisle with her mother. She winked at Lara, and blew her a kiss.

Lara turned to watch people filling the pews. She saw Houston's mayor, and several members of the city council who had sat with Todd on city planning committees. The others who were seated came from every business section of Houston. Realtors, clients, friends, title company personnel, contractors and of course, the men, and women who had partied with Todd. Lara's gaze passed by Melanie Bard who sat alone, to Jane Layton who was dabbing her eyes with a tissue.

They both look heartbroken.

How many broken hearts had Todd left behind? It was becoming quite obvious to Lara that she was one of many Todd had seduced. Jane looked up, saw Lara, smiled, and gave a small wave. Lara discreetly waved back.

Megan gave a eulogy chronicling the years of her partnership, and friendship with Todd.

"If I hadn't met Todd my life would be totally different, and incomplete. Todd stood by me while I proved that a woman of any race can be successful in Houston." Megan wiped a tear. "He leaves a big hole in his office, in the city, and a huge hole in my heart."

A hush fell over the mourners. A few sniffles were heard as Megan, holding her head high, walked to the pew, and sat beside Todd's father.

The burial ceremony was brief. David stood behind Lara with his hands on her shoulders. Todd's father, Kevin, stood with his hand on Megan's waist as she leaned into him.

Todd's twenty-three-year-old brother, Stephen, rigidly stood beside his father and cried. *Poor guy*, Lara thought, *losing his mother five years ago, and now his big brother.*

Lara wept for Todd, and his family.

The Reverend Father offered a closing prayer. Everyone at Drake Properties walked by the family before placing a single rose on the casket. Lara's knees shook as she placed her rose with the others. She looked around the cemetery, and saw Edie and Ron standing under a sprawling live oak.

"Are you okay?" David asked.

"I'm a little shaky," she replied. "Let's leave now."

Suddenly, Billy sidled up to Lara. "Well, that was some send off."

"Yes, Billy it was," she said taking David's arm.

"Lara, introduce me to your fella," Billy chirped.

Lara turned slightly, and introduced Billy to David.

"My, he's a looker, Lara. Better not fool around and lose this one," Billy slurred.

Oh no! He's high!

Lara grabbed David's hand pulling him away from Billy, and his big mouth. Undeterred, Billy lurched forward following them through the pine trees.

"Lara, don't be so damned rude," David said.

"He's stoned," Lara whispered looking back over her shoulder, not noticing a tree stump in her path.

"Shit!" she said as she stumbled, falling to the ground.

"Oh, poor Lara," Billy shrieked as he rushed over to help her up. "Your knee's bleeding!"

"It's okay, I'll be alright. Just leave me alone, and go sober up," Lara said through clenched teeth.

"Well, 'scuse me princess," Billy slurred. "You forget, missy, that I'm as broken up about Todd's death as you are, and I didn't sleep with him."

Without warning, David turned toward Billy, grabbing him by the arm, "What did you just say?"

Billy twisted out of David's grip. Standing unsteadily Billy looked at Lara as she brushed dirt from her suit. He then turned to David with an oily smile.

"Oh, sorry, I thought you knew. Really, Lara you should be open, and honest with all your lovers."

With a toss of his head, Billy staggered toward a group of people hanging around the gravesite.

Lara looked at David whose color had drained from his face, and started to speak.

"Don't say a word," David said lowering his voice. "Just get in the fucking car."

Lara opened the passenger side door, and slid into the seat. David sat in the driver's seat. He looked over at Lara with a dark glare before slamming his door.

As soon as David turned the ignition, the radio came on. He flipped the switch off. "Damn crappy music."

Silence filled the car as David recklessly drove the short distance to Lara's condo.

She glanced over at him, his mottled skin, and set jaw giving him a monstrous, frightening appearance. She'd never seen him this angry. Billy, and his loose tongue may have just destroyed their tenuous relationship.

Light traffic, and David's speeding provided scant time for Lara to process what had happened. All she knew was to keep quiet, and hope David's anger would pass.

When the car stopped Lara opened the door, and started to get out.

"Don't you want me to come up?" asked David staring straight ahead.

"No. It's been an awful day, and I want to be alone," she said as she got out of the car.

Before Lara could react, David had exited the car, and was by her side grabbing her arm. "We need to talk."

"Ouch, you're hurting me," she said pulling away. "David, I'm exhausted. Let go. We'll talk later."

Her heart raced. The tranquilizer had worn off, and her mind was clearing. Clear enough to recall a realtor's safety mantra. *If you feel things aren't right, they aren't.*

David gave her a violent shove, making her stumble across the walkway.

This definitely isn't right.

Lara looked around. No one! She looked over to her left, and saw a car turn into the parking lot. Should she scream? Before she knew it, David had shoved her through the front door of her condo.

"David, stop pushing me. You're hurting me, and I don't appreciate it."

"You don't appreciate it? You don't appreciate it?" David stormed, jabbing his finger in her face. "Well guess what?" he said grabbing her shoulders. "I don't fucking appreciate being told by that little prick that the woman I love screwed Todd Drake."

Lara fought back nausea while trying to appear calm. Spittle gathered around the edges of David's lips as he furiously paced the room opening, and closing his fists.

Calm him down!

"David, honey you're getting worked up over nothing. It's not what you think."

"Oh really, what should I think? Did you, or did you not, screw Todd?"

Lara's mind scrambled for the right words, but would they be lying words or the truth?

There has to be a way out!

"David, please settle down, and listen with an open mind. Yes, I…"

She didn't see it coming. The fist flying at her face, the ugly animal growl from the man she thought she could love. David grabbed her blouse scrunching it up around her neck before slapping her again. Her blouse ripped as he threw her to the kitchen floor.

"You cheating bitch!" David roared.

Lara laid still on the cold tile, and put her hands over her face. From above her, she heard David curse, then slam the door as he stormed out.

Silence. The only sound Lara could make out was the faint ticking of a clock, and her own shallow breathing. She tried to lift her head. Hot pain shot through her eyes. Her breath slowed. Darkness surrounded the room.

"Ms. Maxwell, Lara?"

A male voice! Oh no, he's back!

Lara opened her eyes, and saw a sandy-haired man leaning over her. Gripped with fear she threw her arms over her face trying to scream, but nothing came out.

"It's going to be okay, Lara. It's Ron. You're safe now."

"What?" she croaked. "How did you get in?"

"The man who did this to you forgot to lock the door," Ron said. "Edie told me to watch you after the funeral. She had a feeling something was wrong."

Lara tried to smile through swollen lips, "Edie, the clairvoyant."

"Stay still. I've called an ambulance."

Lara turned her head slightly. "How'd I get on the couch?"

"I put you here. When I came in you were on the floor," Ron answered.

"Where were you?"

"I was in my car in the parking lot. I saw a man come out of your place, slam the door, and run to his car. That's when I came in," Ron replied. "I wish I'd come in sooner."

Lara grimaced. "I wish you had too."

Ron sat by her side, putting his arm around her shoulders. "Quiet now. Help is on the way," he said.

Lara eased into him, closed her eyes, and wept.

CHAPTER 20

She heard voices coming through a misty fog, male voices drifting in and out behind soft female voices. She willed her eyes open enough to see a slit of long bright lights against a white ceiling.

Is this heaven? Angel voices?

She quickly rejected the idea when she saw Sonya enter her limited vision.

"Sonya, where am I?" Lara whispered.

"You're in the emergency room," Sonya said as she gently patted Lara's hand.

"It hurts," Lara moaned, as she desperately tried to take in her surroundings. She heard a free-floating male voice.

"The doctor will be right in to talk to you, and will order some pain meds."

Lara focused on a man's ebony face. "Who are you?"

"I'm James, the ER nurse at Methodist Hospital," he said soothingly. "Don't worry. We'll take good care of you."

A woman dressed in a white coat entered the small room, and nodded at James. "How's our patient?"

"Lara, this is Dr. Linda Bailey," said James.

Lara saw a thin, blonde woman who didn't look a day over twenty-five, peering down at her. "Are you in a lot of pain?"

"Yes," Lara answered while blinking away the flow of tears stinging her eyes. "My head."

"How bad is your pain on a scale of one to ten, with ten being the worst?" Dr. Bailey said while gently wiping tears from Lara's cheeks.

Lara thought for a moment. "Six."

"Okay. I'm going to give you some mild pain medication. Then I'm sending you to X-ray for a CT scan of your head, and neck. After I see the results of the scan we'll talk," Dr. Bailey said. She squeezed Lara's hand, smiled and added, "Hang in there."

Edie, Ron and Sonya stood outside the examining room. As soon as Dr. Bailey left, they went to Lara's side.

"Lara," Edie said. "Who did this to you?"

Looking around the room, Lara tried to clear the fog. She wiggled her right hand out from under the sheet, touched her face, winced, and turned to Edie.

"David King did this to me. My David," Lara said, and began to cry.

"Are you willing to press charges against him?"

"Yes, I will."

Edie walked over to Ron who stood rigidly. "Did you hear that?"

Ron nodded.

"Arrest that son-of-a-bitch," Edie said in a low growl.

"Gladly," Ron said turning to leave. "I'll be in touch."

Sonya sat in a chair beside Lara's bed. When Ron left, she stood by the bed gently holding her friend's hand.

"You're going to be fine," she said. "I'm here until they let you go, and then you're coming home with me."

Lara smiled weakly. "Thank you. My face hurts."

As if on cue, James came into the room with one small pill, and a cup of water. "Take this pill, sweetie. It will take some of the edge off the pain. We'll give you a stronger med later. We need you to be awake for the CT scan."

Lara closed her eyes, waiting for the pain to lessen. She heard Edie's voice in the distance.

I need to tell her everything!

"Edie, I want to tell you something important."

Edie moved over to the side of the bed. "What is it?"

"David was at Todd's party. Chaya saw him."

Edie's eyes widened. "Really? You should have told me. We can talk about that later. Right now, we need to take photos of your injuries."

"I'm too tired. Is that really necessary?"

"You've been assaulted. We need photos for evidence," Edie replied.

"If you insist. Wake me when it's over," Lara said. At least the pain was not as bad, and she could relax some.

Edie quickly took the head shots before the nurse wheeled Lara to X-ray.

Twenty minutes later Lara was brought back to the room followed by Dr. Bailey, who nodded at Edie and Sonya before moving to Lara's bedside.

Lara saw a young woman in scrubs holding a clipboard. "Hi. Dr. Bailey, right?"

"You remembered my name. I'm impressed. Most people forget names after the pain pill. I've ordered a stronger pain med. Here it is now."

James entered the room. He rolled Lara to her side, injecting the medicine in her hip. "There you go, sweetie," he soothed. "This will help."

"You're a lucky woman," Dr. Bailey began. "You only have facial contusions, and a bruised jaw. You have a mild concussion probably caused by hitting your head on the floor."

"So, that's what makes me lucky?" Lara asked.

"I've seen worse. Be glad the damage done to your face will heal without scarring or disfigurement. "

Tears welled up in Lara's eyes, and she whispered, "Thank God."

"When can she go home?" asked Sonya.

"She can go home as soon as we finish the paperwork." Dr. Bailey said turning to her patient. "Do you have family, or someone who can take care of you for a few days?"

"I'm her family," Sonya said. "My mother and I will take care of her."

"In that case you need to apply ice on her jaw every two hours for about 20 minutes. She also needs ice on her eyes for at least two days."

Dr. Bailey looked at Lara. "Even though your jaw is not broken you can only eat soft food. After a week, if you're up to it, you can resume normal food."

"A week?" Lara exclaimed sending hot pain along her jawline. "I work. I have clients who need me."

"Try not to talk much. I know how tough it will be, but you can do it," Dr. Bailey said. "The bruising and swelling will take one to two weeks to go away. Whenever you feel strong enough you can return to work, but remember to be gentle, and kind to yourself. Don't run any marathons for a while. In fact, no strenuous exercise until the pain lessens, and you are stronger."

Doctor Bailey shook Edie and Sonya's hands and patted Lara on her arm, "You're free to go. I'll see you in my office in a couple of weeks. Stay strong, Lara."

Lara gave the doctor a feeble thumbs up. She looked at Edie and Sonya who remained by her bed. "What a mess!"

Edie took a notebook out of her bag. "If you're up to it, Lara I need to take your statement. I know it's hard to talk, but just a few words will be good for now."

Lara told Edie all she could remember in a minimal of words. "Stoned Billy, told David about Todd, he slugged me." She looked over at Edie. "That's all."

"That's enough," Edie said as she turned the tape recorder off. "I will get a written statement for you to sign. Then I'll go to the Harris County DA who will pursue criminal charges."

Lara lay quietly trying to imagine David in a jail cell. The scene made her smile.

"The prosecutor will take the photos, and your statement to a judge in a probable cause hearing," Edie continued. "What happened to you is a third-degree felony assault that can carry a prison sentence."

"What about a protective order?" Sonya asked. "She needs to have her safety guaranteed."

"I will ask the prosecutor to request an emergency protective order, but only if Lara agrees."

Lara sat up slowly, and felt her entire face throb. Lowering her eyes to avoid looking at either woman, she thought about David, the man who had turned into a monster. She moved her right hand to her jaw.

"Mirror?" she muttered.

Sonya took a compact mirror from her purse, and handed it to Lara who hesitantly raised it to her face. Her heart raced as she stared at the image of both eyes not only black, but green mixed with patches of blue. One eye was swollen shut, her bottom lip gashed, and her jaw was flaming red. Her entire face, made swollen by David's fists. Lara felt an uncontrollable rage fill her body.

Her mind quickly went back to her first day volunteering at the Houston Area Women's Center. She was working at the reception desk. The woman's name was Gwen. She came to the Center for protection. She had been beaten bloody.

So bruised, so broken.

"I'm Gwen," Lara said through the swelling.

If only I had caught the signs. David was arrogant, demeaning, and controlling. All the red flags waving in my face!

"I'll do it," Lara said. "That piece of shit."

"Keep that anger. It will help you push through this," Edie said. "I'll go now and do my job. Your job Lara, is to heal." Edie looked at the large wall clock. "It's two a.m. I'll get your statement typed up, and sent to your email. We have DocuSign at HPD. Just follow the directions, and email back to me."

"Thank you, detective," Sonya said. "I'll have her well in no time." She shook Edie's hand before returning to help Lara dress.

James came in with a prescription for pain meds, and more advice.

"When you get your prescription filled remember to grab a bag of frozen peas," he said. "You might also want to pick up a baseball bat for the next time some asshole tries to take a swing at you."

Lara started to chuckle, then stopped when the pain returned. "Don't make me laugh. Great advice."

"No laughing for a while," James said as he helped Lara into the wheelchair.

Sonya walked alongside Lara, squeezing her hand. "You'll be alright. I have confidence in you. That S.O.B. will rue the day he thought he could take you down."

CHAPTER 21

Ron and Edie

Ron pounded on David's townhouse door. No answer. He looked over at the backup policeman, Dan Morales, shrugged, and banged at the door again shouting, "Police! King, we know you're in there. Open up!"

David opened the door just enough to look out. Ron only saw the chain, and left side of David's face.

"What the fuck?" David barked.

"Open the door now or we'll break it open!" Ron yelled. When the door failed to open Ron shoved it hard enough to break the chain. He burst into the room followed by Officer Morales. The first thing he saw was an open suitcase on the couch.

"Going somewhere, King?" Ron asked.

"What the hell business is it of yours?" David said, looking over at the uniformed policeman stationed between him, and the door.

"I'm HPD Detective Ron Yates, and this is officer Dan Morales. We're here to take you downtown for questioning concerning the assault of Lara Maxwell."

"Lara's been hurt?" David asked in a slurred voice. Ron smelled stale booze.

"Come on, King. Let's get you downtown."

David rubbed his face then ran a hand through his hair. He furtively glanced around the room. He took a wind breaker from his suitcase, and slid into a pair of sandals before following Ron out the door.

Officer Morales escorted David to the patrol car, and opened the back door. He placed his hand on top of David's head, pressing down as he guided him into the back seat.

"Make yourself comfortable," Morales said.

Ron followed the patrol car where his suspect sat slumped in the back seat. When they reached the downtown station house, Morales escorted David to an interrogation room, sat him down, and closed the door.

"He's all yours, detective. Looks like he was packing for a trip," Morales said. "I hope you nail his ass."

"I've got this one dead to rights," Ron replied. "Thanks for the backup."

Ron made a pot of coffee. He poured two cups, one for him, the other for David. He slowly opened the door to the interrogation room, setting both cups of coffee on the table, and watched David pace the room like a caged animal.

"What the hell took you so long?" David growled. "I have to be on a rig in the Gulf in four hours."

"I'm sure you do," Ron said. "You may have to postpone that trip."

David yanked a chair away from the steel table. He sat down and reached for a cup. "Make this quick."

"Before we begin, Mr. King I want you to know you have the right to remain silent. Anything you say can, and will be used against you in a court of law. You have the right to an attorney. If you cannot afford an attorney, one will be appointed for you. Do you understand?"

"Of course, I do. I'm not stupid. Am I being arrested?" David asked.

"Not yet, King. Right now, we just need answers to some questions," Ron said placing his pen, notebook, and a small tape recorder on the table. "May I call you David?"

"That's fine. Call me, or ask me anything," David said opening his arms wide.

"Drink that coffee before it gets cold," Ron said. "Looks like you need some sobering up."

"You can cut the shit, detective. I'm wide awake, and sober. You've read me my rights. Let's get started. I have the right to know why I'm here."

"I'll tell you why. I found your girlfriend, Lara Maxwell out cold on her tile floor. I just left the hospital where she is being treated for two black eyes, a split lip, and badly bruised jaw," Ron said while tightly gripping his pen.

"I didn't hurt Lara. I love her," David said, squinting his eyes to make tears.

Ron's fury rose as he watched David's performance. He'd lost count of the times he'd seen women beaten by men who later shed tears of remorse.

He rubbed his forehead in an effort to calm his anger.

I'd love to bash his head in.

Ron tapped his pen vigorously on the notebook page. "This is what we're going to do. I'm turning this tape recorder on, and you're going to tell me what happened yesterday, beginning with Todd Drake's funeral."

David took a gulp of coffee. "That funeral meant nothing to me. I only went because Lara wanted me to be by her side. For support, she said." He shrugged then gave a short laugh. "Little did I know she had fucked the deceased."

"Just tell me what happened," Ron said.

"After the funeral Lara and I were leaving when that asshole, Billy something, stopped us. He told me my girlfriend had screwed the *King of Real Estate*. I was angry. I'll admit to that. What man wouldn't be?"

"Most men would," Ron muttered.

"Damn straight!" David exclaimed thrusting his chest out. "When we got to Lara's place, I confronted her. The little bitch confessed. She acted like it was okay."

"Then you slapped her around?"

"I didn't. Okay, I slapped her. That's it, detective, a little slap."

"Enough for her to wind up in the hospital all bloodied, and bruised? Do you really want to stick with a little slap?" Ron asked.

"I guess she injured herself when she took her drama queen fall."

"What type of fall is that?"

"You know what I mean," David said. "She threw herself against a chair screaming, and then she did a face plant on the floor. It was a totally unnecessary, Lara-type drama over a small slap."

Ron's stomach turned. "You're saying she injured herself on purpose?"

"She must have. I didn't."

Ron could feel his temperature rise as he fought to slow his breathing. He watched as David's eyes moved upward, and to the right corner of the ceiling. The body language of a liar.

"Yep, that's what I'm saying," David continued. "That woman is a piece of work. You don't know how emotionally over-the-top she can be."

"Let me get this right," Ron said. "Your emotions were controlled, calm, in check, and hers were out of control? Is that what you're saying?"

"Well, no one's perfect, detective," David said with a slight grin. "She's, uh, how can I say, uh, a hot-blooded redhead."

Ron shook his head. "Few of us are perfect," he said drilling down on David. "Every relationship has flaws. Lara was trusting. You're a liar."

"A liar? What the hell makes you come to that conclusion, detective?"

"You know you're lying."

Ron waited to hit David with his next question. Edie had called him when she left the hospital about David supposedly being at Todd's party. Ron wondered how David would try to weasel out of this one.

"Did you tell Lara about the party you attended at *Hotel Zoie*, hosted by her broker, Todd Drake?" Ron asked.

"Did I tell her about a random party? I don't understand what you're saying."

"C'mon, David, cut the crap. You kept it from Lara. Why were you at Drake's party? Who invited you?"

David glanced at the exit door, then shifted in his chair. "I was invited by a realtor I know," he said sighing deeply. "I didn't know Todd was the host. For the record, I didn't lie to Lara about that party. I just didn't tell her."

"Who's the realtor?"

"Her name is Jane Layton. She isn't with Drake Properties. She's just a friend."

"A friend with benefits?"

David smirked. "Clever, detective. Yes, but no commitments. She wanted me at the party so she could talk business with the party goers. I was the pretend boyfriend."

"So let me get this straight," Ron said, narrowing his eyes. "It's okay for you to screw around, but it's not okay for Lara?"

Suddenly David swung his leg out kicking over the empty chair beside him. His face reddened. Clenching his fists, he started to stand, then sat back down. "I refuse to qualify that fucking question with an answer."

"Where were you the day Drake was murdered?" Ron asked.

"What are you insinuating? That I killed Todd? That does it," David exclaimed, glaring at Ron. "I'm exercising my right to an attorney."

"You can talk to your attorney from a holding cell," Ron said before jerking David out of his chair.

"I want to call my attorney," David demanded. "You can't keep me here. I have an important job."

"Oh yes we can, David," Ron said while pushing him toward the cell. "We can detain you for up to forty-eight hours on suspicion of a felony. Meanwhile I suggest you call your supervisor, and chill out."

"Asshole," David yelled as Ron locked the cell. "I'll have your job for this!"

"Now, David, I'd be careful if I were you about threatening an officer of the law. That mouth of yours could keep you here longer than you want," Ron grinned. "By the way, your cell phone works in here. Knock yourself out making all the calls you want."

•   •   •

The next morning Edie stopped by the police station on her way to the DA's office. Throwing her purse on the desk she went to Ron's office, knocked sharply, and entered.

"I'm beat. I slept all of four hours. How much rest have you had?" Edie asked.

"Less than you've had. King is in a cell. What a worm."

"What did the worm have to say? Did he confess?" Edie said pulling a chair up to the desk before sitting.

Ron eased back in his chair, brushing his sandy blonde hair off his forehead.

"No. He said she beat herself up."

"Now that's a new one," Edie said.

"Laughable if it weren't so pathetic. According to King, he gave Lara a little slap, and she threw herself against a chair before falling face first on the floor. He called her a drama queen. Of course, he shed tears over the woman he loves," Ron said. "It was all I could do to not jump across the table, and strangle him."

"What did he have to say about Drake's party?"

"He went with a friend, Jane Layton. I'm thinking it's more than a friendly relationship. When I asked him where he was the day Drake was murdered, he asked for a lawyer."

"Of course, he did. What a dick. We know Layton was at the parties, but didn't know about her connection to David. I'm adding her to our list of people to interview."

"How's Lara doing?" Ron asked.

"She went home with her friend, Sonya."

Edie watched her partner fidget in his seat.

What's going on with him?

"How are you doing, Ron? You're angrier than I think I've ever seen you."

"I admit seeing Lara all bruised, and swollen has set me off. What is it with these bastards who beat women up?" Ron said.

Edie watched Ron rub his eyes, then his neck. She thought back over the three years she'd known him. Ron was the happy-go-lucky guy who took his job as just that, a job. Today was different. This case was different.

I think he's got a thing for Lara. How sweet is that?

"I remember when I first became a detective, my older, wiser sergeant told me to be careful of getting emotionally involved with victims," Edie said. "When you do, this job will get you down."

Ron nodded, sighing deeply. "Good advice. I'll try to remember it." He sat back smiling slightly. "Now what else have you got?"

"I have photos of Lara's injuries that I'm going to take to the DA along with Lara's signed statement," Edie said.

"We need to get this done quickly," Ron said. "King has an attorney already working on getting him out. By the way, he was packing a suitcase when I picked him up this morning."

Edie's eyebrows shot up. "So, on top of everything he's a flight risk?"

"Maybe he isn't. He's an offshore manager with a major oil company. He said he was packing to go to work on a rig in the Gulf. I'm thinking he won't skip town. He doesn't want to jeopardize his job. He's arrogant enough to think he can beat this. He'll stick around to play the innocent man wronged by a cheating woman."

"After interrogating him do you think he's a suspect in the Drake case?" Edie asked.

"Let's not take him off the list, but my gut tells me he didn't do it," Ron replied. "He's a chicken shit who beats women. I don't think he would take on a man."

A knock on the door gave Edie a start. "Come in."

The station administrative assistant entered handing a paper to Edie. "Here's Ms. Maxwell's statement, detective. By the way you both need to know King's attorney was quick, and efficient. Your perp is about five minutes from walking."

"I'd better get this over to the DA's office now," Edie said. "I'm confident we have enough to bring felony charges. Do you know who's on intake duty this morning?"

"I think Rita Chandler," Ron replied.

"Good. Rita, and I have worked together on several cases. She's a sharp prosecutor," Edie said. "By the way, I really want to say something to that son-of-a-bitch David before he leaves."

"Great minds think alike," Ron said. "I've been thinking about what I'd like to tell him before he's sent out into the world."

Ron pushed his chair away from the desk, got up, and pulled his jacket off the back of his chair before opening the door for Edie.

"Let's both meet him outside, and give him a little pep talk."

The detectives stood outside of the tall, gray edifice that had formerly been known as the Entex Building, and was now Houston Police Department headquarters. The early morning wind blew down Travis Street in small gusts. Edie turned toward the entrance watching for David. In no time at all he burst out of the main entrance, taking the concrete stairs at a clip.

Ron sprang after David, and grabbed his coat sleeve. Edie ran to catch up, positioning herself in front of both men.

"Before you go, David I need to talk with you," Edie said. "I'm detective Ross, and you know detective Yates."

"What do you want? I've already given my statement," David said trying to walk around Edie. "You'd best back off, detective! I'm close to filing a harassment suit against the entire police department."

Edie stood close enough to feel David's breath on her cheek.

"Mr. King, shut up and listen. There will be no lawsuits. You need to know the damage you did to Lara," Edie said. "She has a concussion, black eyes, and a swollen jaw. She can't go to work for at least a week."

"I told Detective Yates I didn't cause those injuries. Leave me the fuck alone."

"I don't think we'll do that," Edie said. "In fact, we will never leave you alone. If you touch one hair on Lara's head, I promise one of us will find you."

"If you find me, what will you do? Scratch my eyes out? Get out of my way."

David gave a contemptuous little laugh, and pushed Edie aside. Suddenly, Ron grabbed his jacket lapels.

"Listen you piece of shit. This woman detective can take you down. Pay attention, and do everything we tell you."

Fear flashed momentarily across David's face. "Get your hands off me, or I'll file a complaint. That's my promise to you. Obviously, you don't know who you're threatening."

"You're just another low-class, scum assailant," Edie interjected. "Maybe you didn't understand us. You will not touch or see Lara again. You will not file any complaints."

"If you do, we will find you," Ron said in a low bone-chilling voice. "You can count on that."

It was then that Ron released his grip, brushed David's lapels off, and patted his cheek.

"See you in court," Edie said as she and Ron walked away, leaving David standing alone, the wind whipping the hood of his crumpled jacket across his ashen face.

CHAPTER 22

Edie purposefully strode into the District Attorney's office where Assistant DA, Rita Chandler sat at the intake duty desk. She was pleased Rita was on duty this morning as she was one of the most professional, trustworthy ADAs Edie had ever worked with.

"Good morning, prosecutor," Edie said while trying to juggle her file, and two paper cups. "I grabbed some caffeine for you on the way."

"Great to see you," Rita said. "I've got a couple more hours left on my shift, so the coffee is most welcome. What've you got?"

Edie opened her folder taking out the photos detailing Lara's facial wounds. "A woman, Lara Maxwell was beaten by her boyfriend, David King around six p.m. yesterday. Here are the photos taken in the hospital."

Rita reached for her glasses, "Ouch! Is she okay?"

"As okay as someone who looks like that can be. The doctor released her from the hospital around two this morning," Edie said. "I also have the victim's statement. By the way, when detective Yates picked up the boyfriend for questioning, he noticed an open suitcase on the living room couch. He may be a flight risk."

Rita read over Lara's statement, and sighed. "It looks like we have enough here to get an affidavit for an arrest warrant. Is the victim the same Lara Maxwell who was with Todd Drake when he was murdered?"

"You're good, Rita. But of course, you'd pick up on that with all the press this case has gotten," Edie said. "Lara had a sexual tryst with

Drake. Her boyfriend found out yesterday, and took his rage out on her. This is turning out to be one hell of a tough case to get our heads around."

"What makes it so difficult?" Rita asked.

"To begin with Drake had these sex and drug parties where he invited realtor, and others, mostly women, whose businesses could benefit from being with moneyed men," Edie said, taking a deep breath before continuing. "Lots of women in Houston attended including the woman who owns the house Drake was killed in. My problem is sifting out what is true, and what is just pure Houston society gossip," Edie said. She slowly shook her head as she tried to make sense of this complex case, and its complex characters.

"Then we have the drug aspect. Was Drake involved in drug trafficking? Which brings in Alex Ricci, who according to a reliable witness, supplied the party drugs. He was the bartender at all the parties, and was tight with Drake. It's all a combination of little details that in the end, may not be so little."

"Knowing you, Edie, you'll figure it out. Meanwhile I'd better get this affidavit ready for you to take over to the court. I'll call you when it's done."

"My partner, Ron Yates, is getting a protective order. We'll both breathe easier when King is arrested," Edie said. "By the way, he already has an attorney."

"Don't they all?" Rita laughed. "Good job, Edie. I'll be in touch."

•   •   •

Ron saw Edie enter the squad room, and followed her into her office.

"Did everything go well with Rita?" he asked.

"She's working on the affidavit for the arrest warrant as we speak. It looks like Mr. King will once again be calling his attorney," Edie said with a smile.

"Good news," Ron said as he slumped down in a chair. "For all it's worth, I got the protective order filed. I called Lara's cell phone. Her friend Sonya answered. I brought her up to date. She said she'll pass it along to Lara."

"It looks like we've done all we can," Edie said, tapping her fingers on the desk. "Rita asked me how we're doing with the Drake case. Now that Lara can't be our eyes and ears at her office until she heals, it may slow this investigation down a little. Maybe we need to pull some surprise interviews. We're not through with the partygoers yet."

Ron sat up straight, and leaned forward. "That's a good idea. The funeral's over. People are relaxed now, and possibly open to speaking out."

Edie looked closely at Ron, who stared with glazed eyes. "You look exhausted," she said. "Go home and get some sleep. I'll handle the interviews."

"I promise to go home after I interview Jane Layton. I will call her office when we're done here to make sure she is in. Her office is close to my house."

"That's a great idea. I'll interview Megan James and Chaya Getz. We'll compare notes after you've gotten some rest."

Edie immediately picked up the receiver on her desk phone. "Jackie, this is detective Ross. Will Ms. James be in the office in the next twenty minutes? Great. Tell her I have a few more questions. I'm leaving now. I'll be at your office soon."

•　　•　　•

Ron entered the spacious reception area of Wykoff Properties. He'd barely sat down when a tall, thin woman with unnaturally dark hair burst into the room.

"You must be Detective Yates. I'm Jane Layton," she said slipping her hand into his. "Come to my office where we can talk."

Ron followed her into a small cubicle where he sat in front of a cluttered desk. Behind all the clutter sat Jane. Ron's eyes lingered on a framed quote on the wall that read:

CRITIC – A person who enters the battlefield after the war is over and shoots the wounded.-Murray Kempton

"That's very good," Ron said pointing at the wall.

Jane looked back over her shoulder. "Oh, that. Obviously, it has nothing to do with real estate. In my spare time I'm writing a novel. I've run into many critics so that definition helps take the sting out."

"Is it a mystery novel?"

"No, it's a bodice-ripper, you know, a romance novel, or if you will a woman's erotic fantasy novel," Jane said moistening her lips. "I wish you were here to talk about me, but I'll bet you're here to talk about Todd Drake's murder."

"Yes, I'm investigating the Drake murder," Ron smiled. "I've always thought writers were skilled observers. Is that true, Ms. Layton?"

"First, please call me Jane, and I'll call you Ron," she said leaning forward exposing her ample cleavage. "I think you're right. I take pride in my ability to figure people out. I think that skill results from being a realtor for fifteen years. I know it's a factor in my writing. Enough about me. How can I help you?"

Ron took a small spiral notepad and pen from his jacket pocket. "I just have a few questions," he said, wondering how he would keep this overtly flirtatious woman on topic.

"From what I understand from witnesses you attended Todd Drake's parties at *Hotel Zoie*."

"Whoa! I wasn't expecting to talk about those parties. What does that have to do with Todd's murder?"

"We're investigating all aspects of Todd's life," Ron replied. "Apparently you were with David King at one of those parties. Is that correct?"

A flush creeped across Jane's cheeks. She coughed several times then sat up straight wrapping her arms around her waist.

"It certainly is. David is my friend. I took him with me to take part in the fun," Jane said with a wink. "Is that a crime, Ron?"

"Not a crime but an interesting connection between Todd, David, Lara Maxwell and you, Miss Layton. Are you aware of David's relationship with Ms. Maxwell?"

Jane smiled broadly. "Ah, now I see where you're going, the jealousy angle. I know about Lara and David. She's not the first one he's been with since I've known him, and she won't be the last."

"Are the two of you more than friends?"

"Detective, detective," Jane said shaking her head. "David and I have a, shall we say, a unique relationship. We have sex, we're friends, yet we aren't in a sexual relationship."

It was Ron's turn to shake his head. "Does it bother you that his girlfriend, Ms. Maxwell, was in the dark about all this?"

"That's David's problem, not mine," Jane snapped. "All I know is that David is not a killer. Neither am I. I think you're off the mark here. Lighten up, handsome."

Ron's eyes narrowed. "Ms. Layton, this isn't fiction. This is a real, cold-blooded murder we're talking about."

Jane sighed deeply. "David and I are honest and open with each other. We're friends, not lovers. At least not now. Todd's parties aren't the only ones in town," she said with a wink. "I go to all the parties. When David isn't busy, he goes with me."

"Okay, so tell me about your relationship with Todd."

Jane sat back in her chair, playing with a strand of her hair. She studied her inquisitor. "I didn't know him in the biblical sense, if that's what you mean. I worked a few real estate transactions with him. He thought I would benefit from an invitation to his parties, and I did. I got business. I liked him because of the opportunity he gave me to get more clients."

"Do you know anyone who disliked him?"

Jane placed a manicured finger on top of her lip. "I always thought that blonde guy who was Todd's assistant, Billy Parsons, hated him. One time I saw blondie, I mean Billy, at a party standing and glaring at Todd," Jane said. "Gives me the chills just thinking about it. Makes my hair turn grayer," she said running her hands through her hair. "It takes a ton of money to keep up this facade."

Jane threw her head back laughing at her own self-deprecating humor. "That's all I know, honey. Hell, everyone loved Todd. Who wouldn't? He gave fab parties. He was a juicy hunk with a deep sensuous voice. To top it all off, he was devilishly witty."

"How well did David know Todd?"

"Not at all," Jane replied. "I don't think they ever spoke. Todd was too busy with the invited guests. David wasn't with me all the time, but I never saw him speak to Todd."

"Can you give me some insight into Todd's parties. Did you see drug use? Did you see people pair up sexually?"

"That's an interesting question. I'm not into drugs, but I saw pills in dishes. I'm a drinker, and dancer," she said smiling at Ron. "Todd always had the best band. Do you like to dance, detective?"

"Ms. Layton, please just answer my questions."

Does this woman ever give up?

"What other questions? Oh yeah," she said with a twinkle in her eye. "Sex pairing. I saw people pair off, and go to other rooms. Nobody I knew personally. In fact, to tell you the truth I didn't know many people there. But I wasn't there to make friends."

"One last question. Do you remember the people Drake interacted with?"

"Sure I do, and they were all women," Jane said with a laugh. "Now that I think of it all the women looked the same, plastic boobs, and blonde hair. I was an exception," she said gazing into Ron's eyes. "The answer to your question is no one person spent more time with Todd than anyone else. I'm sorry, detective, but I can't help you with much more."

Ron stretched, closed his notebook then handed his card to Jane. "Thank you for your time. If you can think of anything that would help this case, please call me."

"There's a party tonight in Sugar Land," Jane said as she showed Ron out of the office. She looked over at him, and gave his arm a squeeze. "Want to come?"

Ron stifled a yawn thinking how this woman was like a cat seeking prey. No wonder Todd had asked her to his parties. She fit the description. Beautiful, seductive, and aggressive.

"Sorry, I'm not a party guy. I'm just a worn-out cop who'd bore you to death."

CHAPTER 23

Megan's office was grander than Edie had imagined. She had to resist the urge to run her hand over the edge of the mahogany desk. A large painting of a black woman's face with almond shaped eyes commanded her attention. The artist had liberally splattered forest green paint on the woman's mouth, cheek, tip of nose, and part of the forehead.

"That's an interesting painting," Edie said. "I don't think I've seen anything like it before. It looks like you, Megan."

"It's by my favorite local artist," Megan said as she pulled a chair over next to Edie. "Kevin Drake, Todd's father, gave it to me."

Megan stared at the painting for a moment then looked back at Edie. "What's going on? I told you everything I know in our last interview."

"Lara's boyfriend slapped her around yesterday after the funeral. She was taken to the emergency room. She is recuperating at Sonya's house."

Megan's deep brown eyes widened, and her mouth dropped open. "Why would her boyfriend do that? It's like there's an evil spell over this office," she said. "Drake Properties doesn't need more negative publicity. We've been the major local news story, and now Lara's been beaten!"

Megan clasped her hands together before breathing deeply. "Can you do anything to help keep this out of the papers?"

"That's a valid concern," Edie replied. "Reporters who have the police beat avoid domestic violence cases. Sometimes I think it would be a good thing to expose violent men. But for now, you don't need to worry about any extra publicity."

Megan's arms dropped to her side. "There's the good news. Poor Lara."

"Do you recall ever meeting her boyfriend, David King?"

"Yes, I met him about two weeks ago here in the office. In fact, I've met several of Lara's boyfriends," Megan replied.

"What was your impression of King?"

"He seemed amiable. I will say that Lara chooses the best-looking men," Megan said with a slight smile.

"Did you get the impression David knew Todd?"

"No. Why do you ask?"

"You're aware that Todd gave several uh, parties for uh, prospective clients. Apparently, David was seen there," Edie said.

"Crap! Those parties again. I told you before that I was aware Todd hosted many social events. I will admit I heard talk around the office, but I wasn't aware of the extent of Todd's party giving," Megan said. "Lara's boyfriend went? You don't think he had anything to do with Todd's murder, do you?"

"We're still investigating. That's why I'm asking what you know."

"Apparently, I've been in the dark about several goings on in this office," Megan said with a slight shrug. "I wish I could tell you more, detective. I'm really at a loss."

"Tell me what you heard."

Megan looked around the room before resting her gaze on Edie. "I heard so many unsubstantiated rumors, ranging from Todd having social meetings, to hosting sex parties, to Todd taking drugs. I ignored the wild rumors because I thought I knew him better. What I'm trying to say is, Todd was a solid, strong business partner."

"Where did you hear these rumors?"

"I picked up conversations in the office," Megan said. "I also overheard conversations about Todd when I attended luncheons, and went to board meetings. I'm on several real estate, and civic boards. No one said anything to my face. I probably should have paid attention. Do you think someone who attended the parties murdered Todd?"

"We're working on several theories. I can't say we've narrowed them down." Edie glanced at her watch. "I appreciate your time, Ms. James. I won't keep you any longer. Can you show me to Chaya Getz's office?"

"Why are you talking to my most reliable, stable agent? Chaya isn't a suspect, is she?"

"Apparently, she's known Todd since high school. I'm just getting some background information while I'm here," Edie replied.

Megan went to the door, and pointed down a hall to the left. Before shaking Edie's hand Megan said, "Please try to wrap this investigation up soon so we can return to some semblance of normalcy."

"We're doing the best we can. Thank you for your time."

Edie walked to Chaya's office, and knocked lightly on the open door. Chaya, who was on her phone, looked up, giving Edie a startled look before waving her in. Edie moved a chair in front of the desk. She sat, and waited until Chaya finished her conversation.

"I'm sorry, I don't think we've formally met. I recognize you as the detective who is working on Todd's case," Chaya said.

"Yes, I'm working on the Drake case. I'm Edie Ross with HPD. I'd like to ask you some questions, Chaya."

Chaya began wringing her hands. "Of course. I've got a client coming here in thirty minutes. Until then I'm okay to talk."

"This won't take long," Edie said with a soft smile she hoped would put Chaya at ease. "I only have a few questions. How well did you know Todd Drake?"

"I've known Todd for a long time. We grew up in the same neighborhood. He's the reason I went into real estate," Chaya said.

"What kind of relationship did you have with Todd?"

"We worked well together, and yes, we liked each other. Todd and I go way back. He was more or less my real estate mentor," Chaya replied while taking a tissue from the box beside her phone. "Excuse me, but I get emotional when I talk about Todd. I still have a hard time believing he's gone."

"When did you last see Todd?"

Chaya leaned back in her chair closing her eyes. "It was the Friday before his open house," Chaya said, opening her eyes, and looking straight at Edie. "Yes, I remember it so well. He was in a good mood, laughing, and joking with the few agents who were in the office. He was quite witty, you know."

"I've heard that," Edie said. "I also understand he threw great parties. Did you ever go?"

Chaya got up from her desk, and went to shut her office door. "I need to be assured that what I say will be confidential. I have a good marriage. I did nothing wrong, detective," Chaya said with tears welling up in her eyes.

"I never said you did wrong. You went to a party. What you know about the parties may, or may not, lead us to Todd's killer. I will promise to keep your name out of the investigation unless absolutely necessary," Edie said.

"I'm embarrassed, and frightened. Shit!" Chaya said while quickly sitting behind her desk. "What do you want to know?"

"How many parties did you attend?"

Chaya ran her hands through her blonde curls, licked her lips, and took a deep breath. "I only went to one party. I quickly realized that Todd's party was different. It became obvious if I didn't screw the men, I shouldn't be there. I know, detective, why did I even agree to go? I will tell you that realtors go to a ton of business-related parties without their spouses. I needed the business badly. I guess I hoped to meet people who really needed a realtor," she said patting her eyes with the tissue.

"Did you recognize anyone else?" Edie asked.

"I saw Billy Parsons. I heard he hosted parties for gay men. I will admit that I was surprised to see several people I knew. Several were in this office. I'm not sure at this point if I should give names."

"If you want to write who you saw, that would be helpful. No one will know where I got their names," Edie said. She waited for Chaya to scribble names on a scrap of paper. Chaya handed the list to Edie who glanced be at the paper, folded it, and put it in her jacket pocket.

"Did your relationship with Todd change when you didn't go to any additional parties?"

"It certainly did. He was cooler toward me. One day he took me aside, and in what I thought was a threatening way, told me to never mention the parties. He implied if I didn't keep my mouth shut, he'd tell my husband. That certainly put a chill on our friendship," Chaya said with a nervous laugh. "That's all I know. Now, I've got to get ready to meet my client."

Edie closed her notebook, and rose from her chair to shake Chaya's hand. "Thank you for your time. Here's my card. Call me if you re-member anything more."

"By the way, detective, I'll bet you've heard how tough Todd was on the agents. Just between you and me, sometimes they deserved it. I don't want you thinking the agents hated him enough to kill him. Most of the time they all got along with him."

Edie nodded and turned to leave, then snapped her fingers. "One more thing, Chaya, do you know David King?"

Chaya stiffened, and brought her hand up to her cheek. "Isn't that Lara's boyfriend? I never met him, but he was at the party I went to."

"You never met him, but you recognized him?"

"I never formally met him, but I saw him rummaging around in Lara's office a couple of weeks before I saw him at the party. She was out with clients, and he was like, snooping around. When he saw me, he waved as if he knew me, and then scurried out," Chaya said. "If you ask me, he was way too weird for someone as classy as Lara."

Edie smiled and thanked Chaya again. On her way out of the office she saw Jackie look at her, then jump up from her desk, and hurry over to a file cabinet.

"Goodbye, Ms. Long," she said to Jackie's back. "I'll let myself out."

Edie got into her car and looked at the small clock on the dash-board. Her day was coming to a close. From Drake Property's parking garage, she headed straight for her office to retrieve the raincoat she absent-mindedly left behind.

Every muscle in her body was crying out for rest. Stress and sleep deprivation sapped her energy. She quickly parked her car, walked into police headquarters, and dashed up the stairway to her office. Without looking or talking to anyone she grabbed her coat from the stand.

As she hurried out, she noticed a familiar shape in the booking room. Stopping outside the open door she saw a hefty officer taking David King's fingerprints. David casually looked around the room. He stopped cold when he saw Edie.

With a self-satisfied grin on her lips, she lifted her head high, and walked away.

I'm sleeping like a baby tonight!

CHAPTER 24

Five Days Later

Lara reclined in a deck chair on Sonya's spacious back patio with her eyes closed, enjoying the warm morning breeze gliding over her bruised face. Majestic oak, and magnolia trees, reminiscent of Southern grace and charm, provided much needed shade. This lovely setting had now become a haven for physical, and emotional healing.

Sonya appeared at Lara's side with a pot of coffee. She filled Lara's cup, and then her own before sitting on the red cushioned wicker couch across from her friend.

"So, how's my courageous friend today?"

Lara touched her face, and flinched as pain shot up her jaw. "The pain is still with me, but getting better. I'm sleeping better, but sometimes I wake in terror thinking David is in bed with me. Then I have a hard time getting back to sleep. My mind goes over the reasons I should have recognized David for the monster he is." Tears began to build and sting her eyes. "The times when he put me down, glared at me, or did his best to pick a fight. I chalked it all up to his nasty mood. Now I realize there's a big difference between being a grouch, and a thug."

Sonya sighed, and rested her head back on top of the cushion allowing the breeze to caress her face, and neck.

"Isn't it sad the way so many women fall for so many brutes?" Sonya asked. "In fact, I can't think of a woman I know who hasn't been involved with at least one violent man. Is it in our upbringing? Here's the big question. When we finally get rid of the slobs, why do we blame ourselves?"

"I don't know, Sonya. I think I've told you that my parents fought constantly. I was brought up in the middle of a marital war. No hitting, but lots of yelling that left wounds that never healed," Lara said, wincing as she recalled her tumultuous childhood. "You would think with that background my antenna would have been highly tuned to detect an angry, potentially dangerous man. I guess women in bad situations, blinded by love and lust, feel guilty when the veil drops, and reality strikes. I know I feel guilty for being so blind, and so damn dumb."

"Don't beat yourself up, honey," Sonya said. "You are definitely not dumb. Blind maybe."

Lara smiled. "Thanks for the backhanded compliment."

The back door slammed and Betty, Sonya's mother, appeared. Lara smiled warmly at the woman who had been her loving, and caring nurse for the past week.

"Good morning, girls. I brought you some sausage kolaches, and cantaloupe. Just sit there, and enjoy your breakfast."

Before Betty went inside Lara asked her to get a cup of coffee, and join them.

"No, you two enjoy this beautiful weather. I've got to run to town," she said as she waved goodbye.

"I love that your mother calls us girls," Lara said. "In fact, I love everything about your mother, Sonya. She's been my rock through this. By the way where is your beauty queen?"

"She and her friends are mall hopping as we speak."

As far as Lara was concerned, Sonya's fifteen-year-old daughter, Justine, was a model teenager. She was full of life, never frowning, always smiling.

"I enjoy being around that girl. I think I'll just stay in this lovely place forever. No more work, no more men, just this," Lara said as she swept her hand toward the yard. "Speaking of work, I forgot to thank you for going to the Clark's inspection, and successfully negotiating repairs."

"It was all good, and really didn't take up much of my time. Dick and Vanessa are so excited about their new home. They asked me about you. They are looking forward to seeing you at closing."

"You realize they rank among my favorite clients," Lara said. "I'll call them."

Lara put her empty coffee cup on the small table. "So, how is everyone at the office? I'm thinking I can go back as soon as Monday. I'm looking for thicker makeup to hide my black eyes."

"I told everyone that you were in a minor car accident, and that the air bag exploded bruising your face. So, when you return to the office no one will be surprised that you have a little black eye."

Lara smiled gratefully. "Any news of David?"

"When you were in the hospital, I asked Edie to keep me up to date on him. She called the next day to tell me David was arrested for assault and battery. Apparently, he was behind bars for four hours before he made bail. I'm sorry I didn't tell you sooner. I figured I'd wait until you were off the major pain killers."

"Thanks for waiting. Now I can savor the vision of him behind bars, even if it was only for a short time."

Lara sat back as her fear mounted.

Out on bail. Where was David now?

"Does he know I'm here? If he does, I'm afraid he will find me and finish the job!" Lara said feeling her throat tighten.

"Remember, I told you that Detective Yates filed a protection order."

"I don't remember you telling me that, Sonya. Those pain killers messed with my mind. Damn! I've heard those orders aren't worth the paper they're printed on," Lara exclaimed. "He can still find me, and hurt me."

Sonya reached over and took Lara's hand. "David is being watched by the police. He won't find you, or hurt you."

Lara breathed deeply trying to clear her head.

Calm down. Trust Edie and Ron.

When she wasn't dreaming of David and his brutality, she was dreaming about Todd, the parties he threw, and the bloody way he ended. Ever since she found out about the parties, she had wanted to talk to Sonya about what she knew, but the time never felt right.

"Lara, are you okay?" Sonya asked. "Why are you looking at me that way?"

"Oh, I'm sorry, I didn't know I was," Lara demurred. "I have a lot on my mind."

"Let's hear it. It's Saturday. Neither one of us are going anywhere. We have time to talk," Sonya said.

Lara took a deep breath, and looked at her dearest friend. It was time to ask the one question that had been bothering her ever since Todd's murder.

"Tell me the truth, Sonya. Do you know anything about the parties Todd hosted?"

Sonya sat straight up. "You asked me this the other night at *Carrabba's*. Does it really matter?"

"Yes, it does because apparently several people I know attended. You avoided my question before. The detectives are poking around finding out who went. I think it's time you leveled with me."

Sonya sighed heavily. "Okay, yes, I went. Along with several agents in our office, and grab your seat, Mrs. Melanie Bard."

"I know about Melanie, but not about you. Really, Sonya?" Lara gasped. "What the hell!"

Sonya nodded and sat quietly. A couple of Blue Jays screeched in the tree behind her.

"Oh my God, Sonya you've got to be joking," Lara exclaimed, scattering the noisy jays. "What kind of bubble have I been in?"

Lara sat back, and began laughing. "I'm picturing Mrs. Bard in an apron, partying hearty at Todd's bacchanal. I feel like I'm in the middle of a trashy reality show." No longer able to sit still, Lara jumped out of her chair, and started pacing as she talked.

"Why, Sonya? Why would you cheapen yourself when you have everything a woman could want? A terrific daughter, a loving mother to help raise her, and a thriving business."

Lara looked at Sonya who sat with her hands over her eyes. What was it mother always said when she couldn't explain someone's behavior? When in doubt, think money.

"Sonya, did you get clients at these parties? Is that why your business has boomed? That's it, isn't it? It's all about money!" Lara threw her arms up. "Is there anyone in our office who wasn't tainted by Todd?"

Sonya leaped off the couch. Her eyes flashed as she furiously stomped over to where Lara stood.

"Tainted? Who do you think you are Miss Priss?" Sonya said. "Of course, I got clients at the parties. By the way, you're tainted too. Look at the way you pounded signs in the ground for Todd's open houses hoping to get a moneyed client. Look at the way you bite your tongue instead of firing a client who is a vulgar, wretched excuse for a human being. You just put up, and shut up! Every one of us who pushes the ethics envelope in order to get a commission is tainted."

"Todd was always nicest to agents who made him more money."

"I think you can include the one who slept with him," Sonya said.

Lara stepped back, clenching her fists. "You'd better stay in your own lane, girl. That's hitting below the belt."

Sonya stood rigidly looking Lara straight in the eyes. "Yes, it was below the belt, wasn't it, Lara?"

Lara did a double-take, unclenched her fists, and began laughing. She pointed at Sonya. "Now that's funny!"

Sonya gave in with her own whoop of a laugh.

"Oh, Sonya your mascara is running, you look like a possum. A sharp-witted possum," Lara gasped. "Below the belt! Very good!"

Lara's laughter suddenly turned to sobs. Her life was a mess. She was close to screwing it up even more with her temper.

"I just can't be angry with you, Sonya. Can we just sit down and talk this over?"

Sonya put her arm around Lara's shoulder, "Of course we can. We'll talk slut to slut. I could use a cool stiff drink. I think we can have mimosas this morning, don't you?"

Sonya disappeared into the house returning with a bottle of champagne, a carton of orange juice, and two glasses.

"I shouldn't have freaked out at you," Lara said as they sat back on the red cushioned couch, sipping their drinks. "I just have a hard time getting my mind around why you, of all people, went to sex parties."

"I really want you to understand why I ended up at Todd's parties," Sonya said. "You don't have any idea what it is like to be a single mother, and the sole support of a family. I'm in real estate to make money, period. That means I need every client I can get, and the wealthier the better."

"I may not be able to put myself in your shoes, but I can somewhat relate," Lara said. "It's difficult being alone without a salary to rely on. In fact, it's damn scary. I tend to be judgmental. The truth is I envy your ability to handle what life has thrown you."

Lara leaned forward taking another sip of her Mimosa. "That said, I'm about to burst with curiosity. How many men did you have sex with?"

"You stay in your lane! You don't need to know every detail," Sonya said. "Alright, I'll tell you, but no names, no lurid details. I had sex with one man, and the others I met really needed a realtor. Now don't give me that deer-in-the-headlights look, Lara. I liked him, and I still do."

Lara closed her mouth, and willed her eyes to normalcy. "You haven't mentioned the one person I'm just dying to know about," she said. "I heard that the new agent in our office, Jason Morris went to the parties. It may just be gossip. I think Jason is a stand-up guy. He's an ex-Marine for crying out loud! Did you see him there? Or maybe he was at Billy's gay parties? Is he gay? Please don't tell me he's gay."

"No, no, no," Sonya laughed. "Jason was there. He went because, believe it or not, there were wealthy women there, and he wanted to meet people. That's all, really quite innocent."

Innocent my ass.

All these people she thought she knew well were involved in what she considered sleazy activities. Was she jealous? Maybe that was why she had such an angry reaction to finding out about these parties. She never did like being left out.

"Are you okay?" Sonya asked.

"Oh, I'm just having a hard time wrapping my brain around all this," Lara said. "Chaya went to a party, and saw David there."

"You forget. I was in the hospital room when you told Edie. You don't think he killed Todd, do you?"

Lara looked deeply into her glass of bubbly orange juice. "No. I've thought long and hard, and concluded he's a mean son-of-a-bitch, but not a crazed killer," she said. She took a gulp of her mimosa, and looked over at Sonya realizing she hadn't asked her friend about the drugs.

"There's something that frightens me about the parties that I'm thinking could be the reason Todd was killed. Apparently, drugs were available for the guests."

"I took nothing," Sonya said lifting both hands in front of her shoulders. "I may have had too much to drink, but no drugs."

"I know that, Sonya," Lara said. "Drinking and dancing are enough for a good party. When you add drugs, you're bringing in a dark underbelly of suppliers."

"Was Todd a dealer?" Sonya said. "That's brutal, scary shit. From what I see on TV, you don't want to mess with drug dealers."

Lara felt a sudden chill go through her. She wrapped her arms around her chest before continuing. "Sonya, I need to confess that I agreed to tell Edie everything I hear at the office."

"You've been telling the police everything?"

"No, Sonya, not everything. Just what seems odd or out of place," Lara replied. "I didn't tell them what I heard about David until he slapped me around. My agreement with the police lasted less than forty-eight hours before I was taken out of commission. I think Edie needs to talk to you about what you saw, and heard at the parties. Would you agree to meet with her?"

"You're putting me on the spot," Sonya said. "If I say no, does that mean you're telling Edie I went to the parties?"

Lara sat still, silently wishing she could walk away from this bizarre turn her life had taken.

Do I really want to involve Sonya?

"I would have to tell Edie," Lara sighed. "But I think it's better coming from you. Who knows? You might help the detective put a murderer behind bars."

"Dammit, Lara! Okay. But only if you'll be with me."

Lara smiled broadly while she poured the last of the mimosas into their empty glasses. She passed a glass to Sonya, then raised her own. "I'm with you!"

CHAPTER 25

Edie

Edie opened her car door to a blast of suffocating heat. She eased out of the car seat, grabbed a tissue from her purse, and wiped the sweat from her neck before walking the short distance to Sonya's lemon-yellow cottage. Taking the wide steps two at a time, Edie rang the doorbell. She looked down the street and saw sycamore, post oak, and a smattering of palm trees shading the sidewalks. Once again, she removed the wilted tissue from her pocket, wiped her brow, and glanced at the weather app on her phone.

Ninety-seven degrees with ninety percent humidity! What a perfect environment for plants, trees, and cockroaches.

Even though Edie had grown up in Houston, she had never become accustomed to the mid-summer heat. Her summers were spent traveling in an air-conditioned car, to an air-conditioned police station, then back to her air-conditioned car taking her to her air-conditioned home.

The door squeaked open causing Edie to jump. "Good afternoon," she said to a tall, silver-haired woman in black tights, and tee shirt with the familiar Nike swoosh across the front.

"I'm detective Edie Ross, and I'm here to see Sonya and Lara."

"Oh, of course," the woman said jutting her hand out. "I'm Sonya's mother, Betty. Come on in."

Betty led Edie to a large sunroom at the back of the house where Lara, and Sonya were standing silently looking out the window. They both turned to greet her.

"Hi, Edie," said Sonya. "We've been waiting for you. There's iced tea on the table next to you. Help yourself."

"Thanks, Sonya. That's exactly what I need."

"I'm off to exercise class," Betty announced, giving a small wave goodbye. "Nice meeting you, detective."

Edie smiled before sitting on a cushioned glider. She took a long draw of tea before removing a tape recorder from her purse.

"With your permission, Sonya, I'm going to tape our conservation."

"Recorders make me nervous. But I guess you need this for your investigation. Sure, tape away," Sonya said before sitting next to Lara, and across from Edie.

Turning to Lara, Edie said, "Before we start, I want to say you look one-hundred percent better than when I last saw you. The swelling in your face is less noticeable. How are you feeling?"

"Great!" Lara said. "Subject to immediate collapse."

Sonya gave a quick laugh at Lara's remark, looked at Edie, and said, "Thank you for coming to my home detective instead of insisting I go to your office."

"I actually prefer interviewing people outside the office," Edie said. "I understand you are more comfortable here. When you called this morning, I was ready to get away for a while. Besides, Saturday traffic is always lighter, and I enjoyed the ride here."

Sonya smiled, and sat back on the cushion. "Is it okay if Lara is here? She's the one who encouraged me to call you."

"Of course, it's okay. I know Lara is here to support you," Edie replied. "Before we start, I want you to understand it is important to provide complete, and accurate facts. Be open and candid. Your interview is being recorded for accuracy."

Edie pushed the recorder on, gave the time and date, Sonya's full name, and then Lara's full name.

"This interview is related to the Todd Drake murder investigation.," Edie began. "The interview is voluntary, and can be ended whenever you want. All comments will be kept confidential to the degree possible. You will be protected against any retaliation. Do you have questions, Ms. Brown?"

"No, I understand. Please call me Sonya."

Edie smiled briefly. "Sonya, you told me on the phone that you attended a few of Todd's parties. Is that correct?"

"Yes, it is. I probably went to five or six."

"How many people do you think were at the parties?" Edie asked.

"I'd estimate fifty, more men than women," Sonya answered. "Before we go on, I want you to know I have a good memory. It served me well in college, and now in real estate. I rarely forget a name or face."

"That means you make a good witness," Edie said. "Sit back, relax, and let your memory work its magic. My first question is, why did you go to these parties?"

Sonya looked directly at Edie. "Todd invited me. He told me he was giving a party at a hotel downtown for professional men, and women. He said I could get business. I wasn't making a lot of sales, so I thought, what the hell, and went."

Edie stopped the tape, took off her jacket, and fanned her face with one hand. "Sonya, keep that thought. I'm about to burn up. Would you mind turning the A/C down?"

"The controls are in the other room," Sonya said. "I'll be right back."

As soon as Sonya left the room, Lara turned to Edie. "Wow! This is a day full of surprises. First, I found out Sonya went to the parties, then I'm blown away by her great recall ability. What's next?"

Before Edie could answer, Sonya was back in the room. Cold air flowed from the A/C vents.

"That's better. Thank you," Edie said before pressing the record button. "To continue, you said you went to the parties to get business. Can you tell me what you observed?"

Sonya combed her fingers through her hair, looked at the tape recorder, and sat back.

"The men were drunk or high, and playing grab ass with the women. I had to slap a couple of hands. There were several rooms where people went to, uh, get to know each other better. Some couples didn't mess with a room. They screwed in front of everyone, for God's sake. In fact, Todd had sex on a couch for all to see."

"Besides the sexual activity, what was Todd's demeanor at these parties?" Edie asked.

"Todd was completely charming, laughing at other's jokes, and just being everyone's friend."

"Can you tell me about the arrangement in the main room? Did you see drugs?"

"A small stairway led down into the main room where a three-piece band was set up. Along the side wall facing the floor to ceiling windows was an impressively stocked bar. Beside the bar were two tables with the usual party food," Sonya said. "Another table had red, blue, and white pills in separate bowls. The handsome bartender not only made drinks, but I saw him give out lines of coke for people to snort."

She paused, then crossed her legs putting an elbow on one knee.

"It's a wonder I didn't run out, and never return. I'll admit that was my first inclination. But I stayed, and danced, probably drank too much, but didn't take drugs. I promise," Sonya said looking at Lara who smiled, and patted her friend's hand.

"It was like a scene out of a Roman bacchanal with people dancing, gulping pills, and booze, plus an intrepid few snorting coke," Sonya said. "The odd thing is once I got over the shock I relaxed, and tried to have a good time. I was determined to stay in the main room where the band was. I met some nice people who in retrospect were probably stoned," Sonya sighed.

"Did you see many people you knew?" Edie asked.

Sonya flashed her eyes at Lara, and turned to Edie.

"Are you going to interview the people I name? I don't want to put anyone in an embarrassing position."

"Remember, we are looking for a cold-blooded killer," Edie replied. "Your memories could give us a clue to this difficult puzzle. Can you tell me who the people were?"

"Okay, I'll focus," Sonya said. "The only people I know were a few agents from our office plus a few from other real estate offices in town. I recognized some women I've seen at social functions at the Chamber of Commerce. Some women were recognizable from their photos in the *Houston Chronicle's* society page. Most of the women were strangers to me, but not to Todd," she smiled wanly, and looked at Lara who was hanging on Sonya's every word.

"The more I think about it, the more I wonder why so many well-known people went to these parties. I've come to the conclusion that the men came to get business, and meet women. The women who were there had a good deal to lose if anyone found out what they were doing. That still confuses me. Why would these women who were big in Houston's business, and social scene risk a possible scandal just to meet dopey guys? I imagine they came like the rest of us. To make contacts and possibly, if you can imagine, find the man of their dreams."

"Can you give me names, Sonya?" Edie asked.

Sonya took a deep breath before continuing. " I saw Jane Layton with Wykoff Properties. Chaya Getz and Jason Morris are the only ones who came from Drake Properties. Todd's client, Melanie Bard partied until she literally dropped. She danced all night before passing out on the couch. Eerie that Todd was killed in her house. I don't understand why Melanie was there. Sex? I don't think so. I never saw her pair up. Jane, Chaya, Jason and Melanie laughed, danced, and had fun. I never saw one of them take drugs or go into the other rooms. Since this is confidential, I will tell you Jason and I hooked up later."

Lara smiled at Sonya, and said, "Why you hussy, you got to Jason before I could."

Sonya chuckled, and continued. "I almost forgot. Jackie Long, our office manager was there. Why she came is puzzling because she isn't a licensed agent, and doesn't need business. I didn't see her dance or leave with anyone. She just stood with a drink in her hand staring at every-one. It was kind of creepy."

"Was there anyone in particular she seemed to concentrate on?"

Sonya put her head against the cushion. Edie and Lara sat on the edge of their seats not wanting to interrupt Sonya's thought process. Suddenly Sonya sat up.

"I've got it!" she cried.

"What do you remember?" Edie asked.

"Jackie watched only one person. She followed him around, stand-ing in the background, spying on his every move. I thought it was strange, but then Jackie is an odd duck."

"Who the hell was it?" Lara said.

Eyes wide in disbelief, Sonya leaned forward, and whispered.

"Todd."

CHAPTER 26

Silence filled the sunroom. Lara sat back into the cushion wrapping her arms around her waist. In the quiet she heard the roar of skateboard wheels on the sidewalk outside accompanied by children's gleeful laughter. The laughter drifted away replaced by the sounds of traffic.

Lara stared at Sonya and Edie. "For heaven's sake someone, say something!" She got up from the couch, opened a nearby cooler, and reached for a beer. Thinking better of it, she reluctantly grabbed a ginger ale, popped the lid, and took a swig.

"I'm confused. What the hell? Why was Jackie at those parties in the first place?" Lara asked.

Edie sat looking at her notes. She glanced over at Sonya who sat with her head down biting her lower lip.

"Dammit to hell," Lara said. "Once again, I'm blown away by how out of touch I am. But that's not important now. The main thing here is what Sonya's memory brought out. How did mousey Jackie show up at, of all things, a sex party? It's laughable."

"I'm with you," Sonya said. "If memory serves me right, Jackie just showed up. I saw her sometimes at the bar, but most of the time she was in the shadows never talking to anyone. I suppose I was too caught up in all the goings on that I didn't give Jackie much thought."

"Why do you two think Jackie was out of place?" Edie asked.

"Have you met her?" Lara replied.

Edie smiled and nodded.

"She's so solemn," Lara continued. "She does wear expensive, tailored suits. For such a dreary woman she has great taste in clothes. Other than that, Jackie just melts into the background. She's quiet, efficient, and otherwise unimpressive. I don't have the vaguest idea how old she is, anywhere from thirty-five to fifty."

"I'd be betting on fifty," Sonya sighed. "She definitely is the best office manager. So much so, that instead of giving my clients a closing gift, I give Jackie one. I don't know what I, or the entire office, would do without her. I'm still left wondering why she came to Todd's parties."

"Do either of you know anything about her life outside of the office?" Edie asked.

"I don't know where she lives, or who she lives with," Lara said.

It was then Lara realized she had ignored Jackie. She thought Jackie wore lovely clothes, but didn't compliment her. When Jackie found errors in Lara's contracts, saving her from embarrassment or worse, Lara never thanked her. As far as Lara was concerned, Jackie was just doing her job.

"I think everyone in the office treated Jackie like a diligent machine spewing out paperwork, and cleaning up messes," Lara said. "I don't think Jackie likes me. Now I understand why. I didn't care enough to pay attention to her."

Sonya sat with her head resting on her hand, listening intently to Lara. "Someone paid attention to her. I think that someone was Todd. I always thought Jackie had a crush on him. What do you think?"

"I never thought about it, but you may be right. He treated Jackie with some regard by not yelling at, or berating her," Lara said, looking over at Edie. "Believe me. When Todd didn't treat someone in the office like shit, that meant he liked them. I wouldn't be surprised if Jackie had a thing for Todd."

Edie acknowledged Lara's statement with a nod and then continued asking Sonya if she knew anything about Jackie's personal life.

"I took her to lunch one time to thank her for helping me with a closing. We talked about work, and then she opened up about her past,"

Sonya said. "Apparently, she was married at the ripe old age of seventeen to a boy around the same age. They lived somewhere in Kansas. Her husband was killed in a tractor accident leaving her poor, and uneducated. She once told me she has a degree in accounting. I don't know where she went to school."

"She was married!" Lara exclaimed. "To be married at such a tender age. I wonder what seventeen-year-old Jackie was like."

"I imagine she was the same as she is now," Sonya smiled. "I can see her managing the farm, can't you? I can also imagine her as a young widow selling the farm to pay for school."

"We aren't in Kansas anymore," Lara said. "She's come a long way alone. I wonder if she ever remarried."

"Not that I know of," Sonya replied. "I do recall I was surprised at how alluring she looked at the party. She had her hair down. She wore a short black, low-cut dress showing cleavage! It was a stunning metamorphosis. Her makeup looked professionally done with soft eyeshadow, and dramatic black liner painted on her eyelids. Her hair was done in that messy, sexy style. Todd looked shocked when he saw her, you know, did a double take. After the initial shock wore off, he was on to better, and um, bigger things."

"Can you think of anyone else at the party Jackie may have been interested in, Sonya?" Edie asked.

Sonya thought for a moment, then shook her head. "Maybe the bartender? They talked while he mixed her a drink. Other than that, she just stood around, poor thing. Even with all that makeup on, and a great hairdo, no one paid attention to her. Jackie never smiled or displayed any social skills. She was like a fish out of water."

Edie looked at her watch, and checked the tape recorder. "We're almost finished. Is there anything else you remember? Anything you think would throw light on this investigation?"

"I think that's about all I can recall. I heard rumors of Billy Parsons being in on the fun, but in a different way. Apparently, he had boys only parties," Sonya said.

"Were Billy's parties held on the same day as Todd's?" Edie asked.

"Yes, I believe so."

"Of course, it was tied to Todd," Lara exclaimed. "Billy followed Todd around like a puppy dog. He also got paid for setting up the gay group. Billy's the one who told me about the parties. He's got a big mouth. The little shit."

"I don't know Billy as well as Lara does," Sonya said. "He was fun to be around, but other than that I don't have any insights into his psyche."

Edie turned to Lara. "I know you're angry with Billy for telling David about you and Todd, but can you tell me more about him? You said in our initial interview that you two were friends."

Lara rubbed her forehead. "Even though he was a shit, and betrayed me, I'll admit he was a charmer. I'm afraid he got caught up in Todd's web."

Lara looked over at Sonya who nodded in agreement.

"Todd seemed to pick on Billy," Lara continued. "He could be downright cruel to him."

"How was he cruel?"

Lara leaned forward, hands on her knees. "Here is an example. There was this time I held an open house, and asked Billy to help me. The house was too big for me to work alone. We had a large crowd, and I was glad to have someone as witty, and professional as Billy there with me. We had such a good time laughing, and getting to know each other."

She sighed, and continued. "Then suddenly Todd showed up at the house all red faced, and furious. Apparently, Billy didn't get the boss' permission to help me. Todd was such a control freak. I was shocked, then angry. I tried to defend Billy but Todd wouldn't listen, told me to 'shut the fuck up,' and stormed out of the house."

"What a jerk," Sonya said. "He was definitely a good candidate for anger management classes."

Edie closed her notebook, and stopped the tape recorder. "I think we're done here. Sonya, your recall has helped me a great deal."

Lara got up from the couch, and walked over to the sunroom windows. Edie packed the recorder in her purse, and joined Lara who was watching the Blue Jays fight over apple pieces left on the lawn.

"So, Lara, when will you return to work?" Edie asked. "I still need you to be my eyes and ears." She turned toward Sonya who was getting a club soda out of the cooler. "By the way, Sonya, if you hear or see anything unusual while you're in the office would you let me know? Your power of recall is invaluable."

Sonya joined the other two women. "Lara told me she is helping the police," she replied. "I'm reluctant to spy on my colleagues."

"I'm not asking you to be a spy, Sonya," Edie said. "I'm asking you to let me know if you hear anything that may help us find a murderer."

Sonya looked from Lara to Edie and said, "I'll do whatever I can, detective."

"I'm hoping I can go back to work soon," Lara said. "I'm going to the doctor Monday. I've got my fingers crossed she'll give me the green light."

"I want you both to be careful when you're in the office," Edie said. "Don't, I repeat *don't,* go around thinking you're Veronica Mars. That means you just look, and listen. You do not go into someone's office desk or files. No snooping. Call me when you see or hear something suspicious. The person who murdered Todd is still free. I don't want to scare you. Just watch what you do, and be smart."

"Shit, Edie, now I'm scared," Sonya said with a slightly nervous laugh.

"No need to be frightened. Do as I say. Don't snoop, don't pry. Watch quietly, and you'll be okay," Edie said. "I'm leaving now. Thank you both for your time. You've been a big help. I'll let myself out."

When Lara heard the front door close, she turned to Sonya. "Welcome to my snitch world. See how hard it is to tell Edie no?"

"It sure is," Sonya sighed. "By the time she was finished I felt like it would be un-American to say no."

"I agree. I struggled with my decision," Lara said, putting her arm around Sonya's shoulder as they walked into the house. "After Edie's pep talk, I felt like crying out, 'Give me the job so I can die with a purpose!'

Sonya chuckled, and patted her friend's back. "We're in some deep shit now."

•   •   •

The traffic was light, making Edie's trip to headquarters short. She trudged up the four flights of stairs to her office. She grabbed the tape recorder and notebook out from her purse, and scurried out of her office.

Slow down girl!

Halting her pace, Edie pulled her shoulders back, and smoothed her skirt before calmly walking the few feet to Captain Henry's open door.

"Captain, I need to talk with you," Edie said.

Captain Henry put his paperwork aside, and leaned back. "So, what's going on?"

"I've just interviewed Sonya Brown and Lara Maxwell, the two realtors at Drake Properties. I think I may have a breakthrough," Edie said.

"Okay, Edie. I'm all ears."

Edie leafed through her notes before beginning. "Sonya Brown is an interviewer's dream. I now have an eyewitness to Drake's parties whose recall power is impressive."

"That's wonderful Edie, but so what?"

Edie tapped her pen on her notebook. "We now have a clearer picture of the parties. I've interviewed agents who were there, and the people they remember seeing match with what others say. I originally thought Drake's murder was committed by a jealous husband, or lover. I thought the parties were simply realtor events. Not so!"

Edie felt her heart beat faster with each sentence she uttered. She stopped, took a deep breath, and then continued. "Come to find out the party goers were the upper echelon of Houston's best, and brightest with a few realtors thrown in. Todd was the overlord if you will.

Imagine the scandal that would erupt if the overlord's bacchanals were exposed. There were gay parties too. Think of the scandal if any of the parties were exposed. And we can't forget the drug angle. Maybe someone tried to shut Drake down. When that didn't work, maybe that someone shut him up."

"Damn, Edie," Captain Henry said. "This case has tentacles that could invade corporate Houston, and open up a whole new bag of worms."

Edie nodded, pulled her chair closer to Henry's desk. "So, Captain, where the hell do we go from here?"

CHAPTER 27

Lara sat on the examining table watching Dr. Bailey look over her notes.

"Your contusions have healed, Lara. I'm going to let you go back to work," Dr. Bailey said, "but only if you promise not to overdo it."

"Obviously Doctor, you've never been in real estate."

"I get it, but try to rest during the day."

"Okay, I promise to be good," Lara replied. "I've sworn off open houses for obvious reasons. No more hammering, and yanking signs out of the ground. I'll slow down physically for a while, but it's hard to keep a good woman down."

Dr. Bailey smiled before asking, "Are you still having nightmares?"

"No, the nightmares are gone, but when I leave the house, I watch everyone, and every car expecting to see David," Lara replied. "I'm angry as hell. I'd love to see that son-of-a-bitch in jail. But no, he's out on bail awaiting trial. Out on bail! Oh, and he's been charged with a Class A misdemeanor. Can you believe that? A misdemeanor!"

Lara tried to fight back the tears that began stinging her eyes. "Damn. I always seem to cry when I'm angry. I'm angry at the legal system. I'm angry at David, and I'm angry with myself for not being aware of David's cruel streak. The blinders are off now."

"Don't be so hard on yourself. Many of us have a blind spot for someone we love, or think we love." Dr. Bailey said. "Your fear, and anger are understandable."

Dr. Bailey closed Lara's file and continued, "Domestic violence is the leading cause of injury to women, more than car accidents, muggings, and rapes combined."

Lara sighed deeply. "You're a fountain of knowledge, doc. Now I'm a statistic, and I'm furious about it."

Dr. Bailey patted Lara's knee. "Good. Your anger is understandable, and will lessen as time passes. Do you have a restraining order against David?"

"Yes, for whatever that's worth. The police assure me they are watching him, and that makes me feel safer. I've put my condo on the market. I'm looking for a place in the same neighborhood my friend Sonya lives."

"Sounds like you're moving on in a positive manner," said Dr. Bailey. "I want to see you back here in two weeks, but if your pain increases call me. I'm here for you. As far as I'm concerned, you're good to go."

Lara got off the examining table, and before the doctor could leave the room, Lara gave her a grateful hug.

CHAPTER 28

Jackie

Jackie sat rigidly in a chair outside Detective Ross's closed door thinking how irritating it had been to hear that detective's voice on the phone this morning, demanding she come to police headquarters for a second interview. She had tried to resist by saying her workload made it impossible to leave the office, but to no avail. That bull dog of a woman had insisted.

The longer she waited the worse Jackie's agitation became. She watched the detectives in the squad room talking in groups of two or three. No one seemed to notice her.

Looking at her watch she saw ten minutes had gone by. The hard chair made her butt hurt. The air was stifling.

She stood up, smoothed her skirt, and looked around. Fighting the urge to run she took a few faltering steps toward the exit when she heard Edie's voice.

"Good morning, Ms. Long. Sorry to make you wait. Come with me, please."

Edie placed her hand on Jackie's elbow, and without another word escorted her down the hall to the interrogation room.

"May I continue to call you Jackie?"

Jackie pulled out a chair near the door, and sat down. Folding her hands neatly in her lap she looked blankly at Edie. "Of course. You don't need to be formal with me."

"Thank you for coming in on such short notice," Edie said. "Our first interview was for your initial statement, and observations. Today I called you in because some new evidence about Todd has come to my attention. I felt you could help me fill in some blanks."

Edie leaned slightly back in her chair, and looked directly at Jackie. She remembered Jackie having straight shoulder length hair that turned up slightly at the ends. Today her hair was loosely pulled back into a bun. Wisps of hair haphazardly fell around her neck, causing her to appear somewhat disheveled. Her deep-set gray eyes darted back and forth from Edie to the walls, to the floor, and back to Edie.

"What blanks? What evidence?" Jackie asked in a soft, almost inaudible voice.

"From what I've been told, you attended Todd's parties," Edie said stopping to look at her notes. "When I initially asked if you met Alex at one of those parties you said you had never been to Todd's parties. Why did you lie?"

"I've been to parties, and events where Todd was present."

Edie remembered that during her first interview Jackie's soft, child-like voice had made her wonder if it was an act to keep the hard questions at bay.

"Could you please speak louder when answering my questions?"

"Yes, of course," Jackie said clearing her throat.

"That's better. I'm talking about the parties Todd hosted at *Hotel Zoie*. Where people needed an invitation. Where sex and drug use were prevalent."

"I don't understand, detective. I think you have wrong information. The parties were more like a local Chamber of Commerce social. You know, a gathering where new people in town have a chance to mix, and mingle, exchange business cards, and make connections."

Edie stifled a derisive laugh.

"That's an interesting concept you have, Jackie. The people I talked to who attended the parties were not new to town, and they exchanged much more than business cards."

Edie sat silently watching as Jackie fidgeted with one earring while furtively glancing at the door.

"Okay, alright! Todd invited me," Jackie replied. "I don't get asked to many parties. I was flattered. So, I went."

"Why did you lie before?"

Jackie flashed Edie a wanting-to-please-the-boss smile. "I was confused and frightened. I'm sorry I wasn't up front with you."

"No more lies, Jackie," Edie said. "How many times did you go?"

"Once."

"Then you must know that most of the people who went took drugs, and paired up," Edie said. "Did you join in?"

Jackie raised her head slightly. "I didn't hook-up with anyone if that's what you mean. I bought a cocktail dress because Todd said it was a cocktail party. I even went to a big deal hair salon for a makeover. It was fun up to a point. I just didn't fit in."

"What about drugs, Jackie?"

"I'm afraid of drugs," Jackie whispered. "I'm afraid I'll go crazy wild if I take drugs. I saw pills on a few tables at the party, and I saw people take the pills, but not me."

Edie crossed her arms over her chest, leaned back, and waited.

"Detective, I just want you to know I was shocked. I didn't know what kind of party it was. I originally thought I was going to a social get-together," Jackie whined.

Edie leaned over slamming her hand down on the steel table enough to make Jackie jump.

"Okay, you and I both know these parties weren't Chamber of Commerce meet, and greet socials. So, you can cut the goody-two-shoes crap. We can continue talking in circles with you putting on the poor little me act. Or, better yet, you can answer my questions directly, and truthfully. If not, you and I will be in this room for a long time."

Jackie flinched, then cast her eyes down at her lap. "Okay, detective. I'll answer your questions to the best of my ability."

"Good," Edie said thinking Jackie's demeanor hadn't changed a bit. "Let's start over. "

"Oh, before we start, detective can I have a glass of water?"

"Sure," Edie said. "Anything else?"

"Some crackers would be nice to get my blood sugar up. I didn't know this would take so long. And some tissues?"

Edie left the room without speaking. She walked down the hall to the water cooler, filled a cup, banged around in the condiment cupboard, found a packet of saltines, and pulled some tissues from a box on top of a desk. She turned, and saw Ron standing by the two-way mirror motioning her over.

"Now that's one cool cucumber," he said. "Look at her now. No tears, no worries."

Edie looked in the room, and saw Jackie leisurely get up, walk to the bulletin board, put her hands behind her neck, and stretch before slowly returning to her seat. Edie looked at Ron, rolled her eyes, turned with a wave of tissue, and walked back to the interrogation room.

"Here's water, tissues and one packet of crackers," Edie said before pulling her chair closer to Jackie.

"Thanks," Jackie said dismally.

"Let's continue. Why did you go to Todd's parties?"

"I already told you. I was flattered. Okay, I was also curious. I honestly didn't know why Todd had invited me. I still don't know. Unless he wanted to…" Jackie gazed up at the ceiling then placed her head in her hand. "I think he wanted to be cruel."

She began to softly cry. "The more I go over the reason why, the more I believe Todd probably knew about my affair with Alex. He may have wanted me to see how the women fawned over Alex, you know, to hurt me. I went, I saw, and I was repulsed. End of story."

"What repulsed you?"

"Pretty much everything," Jackie replied. "The women were out of control. Alex was in his element."

"How did Todd act toward you?"

"I liked Todd. He was always a gentleman around me," Jackie replied.

"Did he act like a gentleman at the party?"

"Not really. I saw another side of Todd, you know, the party side. He let the women fawn over him like horny bitches, same as they did with Alex. I wanted to leave as soon as I got there, but that would have been rude."

"Were you attracted to Todd?" Edie asked.

Jackie rose from her chair then sank back down. "Maybe. A little. He was quite handsome. He was also kind to me. At least at the office. At the party he ignored me."

She looked pitifully at Edie. "I read somewhere that if you want different results, try different approaches. I tried to change my appearance. I even bought a padded bra, but nothing seemed to work."

Edie didn't know whether to laugh or cry. She chose neither.

"Let's change the subject here. How long have you worked at Drake Properties?"

"Five years," she replied.

"Is it true that you were fired from your previous job in Corpus Christi?"

"I wasn't fired, I quit." Jackie snapped.

"It just seems odd to me you worked for a financial firm in Corpus, came to Houston, and ended up with a job as office manager in a real estate firm. You have a degree in finance, don't you?"

"Yes."

"It just seems you'd get another job matching your education," Edie said looking at her notes.

"My background is needed at Drake because I take care of the business end of the company," Jackie said, smiling tightly as she rose from her chair. "I'm now wondering why I'm here, and where these inane questions are going," she said as tears welled in her eyes. "I have a feeling I need an attorney with me."

"Sit down, Jackie," Edie commanded.

"No, I don't think I will. I'm confused, and honestly, you frighten me. The next time we talk I'll be accompanied by an attorney. If I'm not under arrest I'll be going." Jackie grabbed her purse, opened the door, and turned to Edie.

"Please don't call me again, detective. I'll email you the name of my attorney."

The interrogation room door softly closed, leaving Edie in a deep folding silence. She looked across the room at the long mirror, shook her head, and said, "Well I'll be damned. She almost had me feeling sorry for her."

. . .

Jackie controlled her urge to run by taking a long, deep breath. She walked slowly down the row of detective's desks, steadying her shaking hands before pushing the down arrow on the elevator. She fought back tears as she rode the elevator to the main floor. After getting out of the elevator she wiped her eyes, adjusted her purse on her shoulder, and walked a little more briskly out of police headquarters, and into the sunny Houston morning.

CHAPTER 29

Lara felt her heart beat quickly in anticipation as she burst into Drake Properties' warmly lit entry. She made her way down the hall to the office she had missed for two weeks. It was then Megan emerged from the copy room.

"How great to see you, Lara! You look terrific. I've heard those air bags can break a face up," she said giving Lara a sly wink. "I can tell you're a little swollen, but other than that you look healed."

"Thanks," Lara said. "I found this great makeup to hide my bruises. It's nice to know it works!"

Megan called the other agents over. Sonya joined them, hiding a vase of mixed flowers behind her back. She danced a little jig before handing the bouquet to Lara who bowed in front of her small audience.

"Thank you. I'm so glad to be here!" she said smiling broadly.

"We all missed you. Now get to work!" Megan said with a laugh.

Lara gave a short wave, opened her office door, and surveyed the room. She placed her purse on a chair, and the flowers on her desk before sitting.

Finally!

The desk phone's red blinking light demanded Lara's attention. She turned on her computer, then listened to her voicemails. Most of the messages were junk except three who were possible clients wanting to sell their homes.

"Alright, I'm back!" she exclaimed to the empty office, then picked up the phone to call the prospective sellers. One had already found an agent, but two were eager to meet with her.

She began building listing presentations, and was deep into comparable sales sheets when she heard a slight knock on the door.

"Can I see you for a minute?" Sonya asked.

"Of course, come on in."

"How does it feel to be back?"

"It feels great. I'm happy to be in my cozy office again," Lara said. "By the way, thanks for the flowers, and entertaining dance."

"You're welcome on both counts. I had a feeling you missed this crazy business. Speaking of crazy, have you noticed Jackie isn't in the office?"

"I was so excited to be here that I didn't notice her absence," Lara replied. "She's always here. Is she sick?"

"Well, scuttlebutt is she left the office this morning for an interview with Edie, and hasn't returned," Sonya said. "I also heard Billy has been summoned for an interview. Edie sure doesn't let any grass grow under her feet."

"I don't think she'd be an HPD detective if she did," Lara said. "I think you told her enough to warrant calling both of them back in. Wouldn't you love to be a fly on the wall in that interview room?"

"I would rather be on the other side of that one-way mirror," Sonya said. "This is the first time I've actually envied a detective."

She looked distractedly around the room before continuing. "I need to ask you a favor."

"Sure, go ahead."

"I just got a call from a woman who drove by my listing on Shady Glen, and wants to meet me there at quarter to four to show her the house. I've got an appointment I can't get out of. I doubt I can make it in time. If you could be there instead, I'd be so grateful."

"Isn't that house vacant?" Lara asked. "Maybe I should call that woman, and ask her to come by the office first."

"I asked her to come by, but apparently, she has a demanding job at Halliburton with little time to look at homes. Today she only has an hour off. She sounded really excited about the house. She isn't working with an agent. I'm giving you a chance to represent her. Even if she doesn't want to buy this house, she could be a good client."

"I don't know, Sonya," Lara said thinking of how many times agents were warned about meeting strangers at a vacant house. Didn't Megan strongly suggest at the last sales meeting that we take a buddy when showing an empty house to a stranger?

"Let me check and see if someone can go with me."

Lara walked around the office. A few agents were at their desks. She saw Chaya.

"Hey, Chaya! Sonya wants me to show an empty house to a woman who called in. Can you go with me at three forty-five this afternoon?"

"Sorry, Lara. I've got an appointment. You know I would if I could," Chaya replied.

Lara continued walking around the office asking agents to go with her, but none were available. Lara walked back into her office where Sonya waited patiently.

"No luck, Sonya. So much for the buddy routine. I guess if you have a good feeling about this woman, I'll go."

"Thanks. I'll make it up to you."

Lara looked at the wall clock. "That gives me a little over two hours to finish up here. What's this woman's name?"

CHAPTER 30

Billy

"Billy, thank you for coming in," Edie said as she ushered him into the nearest interrogation room.

Before taking a seat at the table he looked directly at the mirror across the room waving exuberantly, "Hi y'all."

Edie groaned. "Been in many police interrogation rooms?" she asked, before pulling her chair over next to Billy.

"Heavens no," he replied. "I watch a lot of crime shows though, so I know there are other detectives watching, and listening to us."

Smiling mischievously, Billy winked at Edie before looking directly at the mirror. "Hope you're enjoying the show, fellas," Billy said, with an exaggerated lilt in his voice. "At least I hope they're all fellas."

"Billy," Edie sighed, "It's time to focus on why you are here, and not on who you think is here."

"You don't need to be so peevish, detective," Billy said tossing his head to the side just enough for his blonde curls to bounce. "To be honest I'm not sure why I'm here."

"I think you're aware there is an ongoing investigation into Todd Drake's murder. You are here because as we interview people who knew Todd, your name keeps popping up," Edie said.

"It's that bitch, Lara, isn't it? She hates me for telling her cute boyfriend about Todd."

"I just have a few questions, and then you can go," Edie continued, ignoring the anger she felt toward this man who fueled Lara's beating.

Billy sat back with his hands behind his neck. "Okay, go ahead. My life's an open book. Do you want to start with chapter one?"

"I'm sure your childhood is fascinating, but let's cut to the chase," Edie snapped. "Were you involved in the decision to throw the *Hotel Zoie* parties?"

Billy sat up, dropped both his hands to his chest, and said, "What? You think I came up with the idea? Ridiculous. Todd came up with that brilliant concept. He only needed me to, once again, be his lackey. My duty apart from my day job was organizing the parties. I even organized an alternative lifestyle party that was held the same night as Todd's parties. I had my day job, and then my party job. It was exhausting."

"What exactly is your job at Drake?"

"I was Todd and Megan's assistant, and now after Todd was, uh, murdered I'm Megan's assistant."

"Why did you say you were Todd's lackey?" Edie asked.

"Because I was. I ran all his errands," Billy replied. "Todd treated me like a lackey. Megan didn't. She would thank me for my hard work. I never got a thank you from Todd. I guess he thought my paltry salary was thanks enough."

Billy looked up at the ceiling then turned his face toward the mirror. "An assistant at a large firm like Drake Properties is a big job. I took care of all Todd and Megan's client's paperwork, phone calls, and inspections. Pretty much everything they needed to facilitate a closed sale. This freed them up so they could attend to marketing, and running the business."

"Billy, do you mind looking at me when you talk, and not that damn mirror?" Edie said.

"You're in a touchy mood today, detective," Billy replied before turning his entire body directly at Edie. "Is this better? Anyway, we were a great team if I say so myself. If Todd were alive, he might disagree. He often seemed to find fault with my work. Todd and Megan spent most of their time out in Houston pressing the flesh. They were busy serving on committees, speaking at area luncheons, and schmoozing Houston's power players while I stayed in the background."

"Since you worked closely with both of them, do you think Megan knew about the parties?"

"Probably. She must have questioned Todd about the sudden surge of new business. Maybe she just thought Todd was working doubly hard. Honestly, I really don't know the answer."

"Okay, back to the parties. Did you get paid extra for helping?"

Billy leaned forward, smiled at Edie, and said, "Great question, detective. That's where I made good money. I got paid well for organizing, and hosting the boy parties," he said turning ever so slightly toward the mirror. "To be truthful, the boy gatherings were poorly attended. The venue I chose in West University wasn't as splashy, and popular as the gay clubs. One time, no one showed at the boy party so I went to Todd's party."

Billy sighed, folded his hands on the table, and continued. "Even taking into consideration the collapse of the gay festivities, the whole party thing was a bonus not only for Todd, but me too. Just think of it. Anytime you offer free sex, drugs, and booze to a bunch of lonely guys, and girls, you are guaranteed to become their favorite realtor. What's not to love? You have big time salaried people who want to spend their new found wealth on luxury homes. Luxury homes bring in substantial commissions."

Billy gave a self-satisfied smile. "High-end synergy."

"Did you bring drugs to the parties?" Edie asked.

Billy's blue eyes popped wide open along with his mouth. His entertaining demeanor disintegrated. He sat up straight wringing his hands.

"Are you kidding me? Drugs almost killed me," he exclaimed. "I didn't bring the drugs in, I used them." It was then Billy began to sob. "I did nothing illegal. Just ask anyone who knows me. I'm not a brave person. I don't hang out with thugs, or drug lords. Oh God, I can't go to jail."

Edie watched Billy wail, then handed him a box of tissues.

"Let's not go off the deep end here, Billy. No one said anything about jail. All you have to do is tell me truthfully everything you know. If you didn't supply the drugs, who did?"

Billy looked straight at Edie, and with a tightly wound voice said, "You know it's the bartender."

"Does the bartender have a name?"

"Alex Ricci. I know you've interrogated, and threatened him," Billy said between sobs.

"Did Ricci tell you he was threatened?"

"Yes. I went to his bar for a drink, and he told me. He's an acquaintance, not a friend. I met him through Todd," Billy replied.

"How did Todd and Alex meet?"

"Alex is the bartender at *Ceres*, Todd's favorite watering hole. They became friends, like everyone did with Todd. I believe it was Todd and Alex who generated the party idea. I think during the initial planning phase Alex told Todd he had drug connections. When you think about it, it was a genius concept," Billy said no longer facing the mirror but looking intently at Edie. "I thought it was genius, especially when they brought me in. I was so fucking flattered. I felt honored, and bulletproof. So much so I began taking the pills everyone around me was taking. Actually, not everyone. Todd and Alex just drank."

Billy slumped forward. "Then my world took a spin. I couldn't get through a day without popping a pill or snorting a line. Expensive habits take money. Even though I was paid exceedingly well, I was drowning in a tsunami of financial debt. I was actually scared shitless."

"What were you afraid of?" Edie asked.

"I was afraid of losing it all. Afraid Todd would have one of his rages, and let me go."

"Were you in love with Todd?"

Billy's mood got darker; his body stiffened.

"No. I mean yes. I don't know," Billy stammered. "It's not like I haven't asked myself the same question. I think when I first met him, I had a silly crush. I will tell you that after the funeral I started seeing a therapist. I've been clean since, but I'll probably have to go into rehab. Anyway, the therapist tells me there is a fine line between love, and hate. If I were absolutely honest with myself, and with you, the answer would be no. I detested him."

Billy shed a stream of tears. Edie left the room to grab a cup of water. When she returned Billy drained the cup in one large gulp.

"Thanks," Billy said as he waved his hand above his head. "It's all these memories flooding back. Todd was a brutal, sadistic man who delighted in demeaning, and taunting people around him. He knew I had become dependent on drugs. He laughed and called me a weak Nancy. I was so proud of being at Drake. I loved my job. But working for Todd destroyed my pride. I can say I truly hated him. I wasn't at all surprised someone killed the son-of-a-bitch."

"Was there anyone Todd wasn't cruel to?"

Billy wiped his eyes. "Yes, Megan, Lara, and our super top producer Ginger. He was screwing Lara, and no one messes with a top producer. As far as Megan goes, I think he was in awe of her and her position of power in the community. She is a cunning woman, and I sensed he loved that quality in her."

Billy fidgeted with his curls, and waited for Edie to say something. He lowered his head looking at the tiles on the dirty floor. Suddenly he stopped counting tiles, and looked over at Edie.

"Now that I think of it there is one other person Todd never hassled, at least that I knew about. Weird Jackie. Do you know who I'm talking about, the office manager?"

Edie nodded.

"She held Todd at bay, and if I remember correctly, she had a thing with Alex. Yes! I don't know how I could have forgotten. I saw Alex hugging, and kissing her after everyone had left a party. It was that night I told you about when no one showed up at my party. That's when I saw the two of them. Can you imagine Alex the stud muffin with dull Jackie? Maybe Todd left Jackie alone because she was with Alex. Who knows?"

"Other witnesses said they were fighting? Were they?"

Billy shook his head, and stretched his arms wide over his head. "Yeah, then they made up. Who gives a fuck?"

"I give a fuck, Billy," Edie snapped. "Who do you think murdered Todd?"

"I wish I knew. I'd give him a medal."

CHAPTER 31

Billy

Edie closed her notebook, and stood up. "Wait here, Billy. I'll be right back."

"What? Why? Where the hell are you going, detective? Can't we just put an end to this?"

Without saying a word Edie left. She found Captain Henry and Ron in the small observation room watching Billy.

"What do you think?" Edie asked. "Should I let him go?"

"I see no reason to keep him here," Captain Henry said. "Do you, Yates?"

Ron looked at Edie, and shrugged his shoulders. "I think you've squeezed this one tight enough."

"Let him go," Captain Henry said. "Yates, tail him. He's hiding something."

Billy paced back and forth, glancing nervously at the clock on the wall. Edie re-entered the room.

"You're free to go now," she said. "Don't leave town. I'll be in touch."

Without looking back Billy scurried out of the building. He speed walked to his car, opened the door, and slamming down on the gas pedal, squealed out of the parking lot.

Fear, and anxiety gripped him as he fought to bring his breathing under control. The thought of going to prison for anything sent him into a panic.

Stop thinking like that! Breathe deeply. Be calm.

Looking up at the road he realized he'd gone past the office toward the Galleria. Turning left on Voss, Billy ended up in front of *Ceres*, his favorite bar. This was where he had met Alex, who made him smile. He felt comfortable with Alex, who always treated him like just another man to talk and laugh with. This bar had always been his comfort zone, where he could relax without fear of ridicule or scorn.

He had only seen Alex twice since Todd's death, the first time when he went to the bar for a drink, and the next time at Todd's funeral. At the funeral, Alex had acted like he didn't know him. Billy chalked Alex's rudeness up to grief. Of course, he was high at the funeral, which could have been another reason. Alex's rejection hurt. Surely by now Alex was over his initial grief.

After his frightening, depressing interview with the detective, he felt a need to talk to Alex. Billy had a gut feeling the police detectives were zeroing in on Alex, and possibly him, for Todd's murder. It wouldn't surprise him if Edie arrested Alex on drug charges. The shit was getting ready to hit the fan. He needed to warn his friend.

Normally he would get an intense rush of excitement when entering *Ceres* with its rich, dark wood bar, red plush chairs around low tables. But not today. This time he entered in a state of anxiety with sweat dripping down his cheeks. Fanning himself with his shaking hands he walked directly to the bar, and past Alex who was chatting with a few customers. He waved briefly at Alex, who ignored him.

Taking a stool at the far end of the bar, Billy could hear his heart pounding in his ears. He rubbed the back of his neck, and looked over at Alex.

He's ignoring me again!

He waved. "Can I talk to you?"

Alex's dark eyes narrowed as he looked down the bar. Smiling at his customers he excused himself, exhaled loudly, and slowly made his way to where Billy sat.

"What can I get you?"

"Scotch neat. We need to talk."

Alex rolled his eyes. "Can't we talk some other time? I'm busy."

"You're not busy, Alex, so don't give me that shit. We need to talk now because I just got out of an interview with the police. They're trying to nail my ass."

Alex sighed, poured a jigger of scotch, then passed it over to Billy. He wiped the bar top with a towel, turned his back, and flipped the towel in the air. "I don't have time for this. We'll talk later."

Billy's face reddened and his voice shook. "I'd think you'd want to talk, seeing that you were one of the main topics of the interview. You, my friend, are in deep shit too."

Alex's back went rigid. Suddenly he turned and grabbed Billy by the arm.

"Ouch. Take your hands off me," Billy squealed.

"Listen to me," Alex whispered through perfectly straight white teeth. "Keep your voice down. Take your glass and quietly go to a table as far from the bar as possible. Now!"

"Okay, but I won't sit there forever."

Billy pulled his chin up, hopped off the bar stool, and hurried to a nearby table, confused by his friend's display of contempt.

Alex followed him, scowling all the way.

"Is this far enough away?" Billy asked. "I've missed talking to you, Alex. You're much more handsome when you're angry."

Alex sat beside Billy. His chiseled features hardened. With a tight smile he reached under the table, and with one hand latched on to Billy's crotch.

"Cut the crap. Tell me what happened, you little fuck or I'll tear them off."

CHAPTER 32

Billy shrieked in pain. The few men sitting at the bar stopped talking. Alex gave one last crotch twist, sat back, smiled, and patted Billy on the arm. Alex waved at his customers who smiled back, and continued their conversations.

Anger rose in Billy's chest, and grabbed his throat like a vice. "Okay, okay, but don't touch me again, Alex or I'll…"

"Or you'll what? Tell the scary policewoman on me?" Alex said laughing at his own joke. "What happened during the interview? Make it quick."

Billy flinched from the intense pain between his legs, and took a quick sip of scotch. "That detective, Edie, has it out for me. She zeroed in on the parties. She knows you supplied the drugs."

"How does she know? Did you tell her?"

"I told her what I know. I know you brought drugs to the party. How you got them, or who you got them from is something I don't know. That's pretty much all I said."

Alex grinned slightly, but his eyes remained cold as he stared at Billy. "What else did you tell her?"

"Well, uh, I uh…I told her I organized the parties, and that you and Todd originated the whole party concept. I also said it was a genius of an idea. She was interested…no, obsessed with the relationship you and I had with Todd. That's what makes me think we are suspects,"

Billy said. "Oh God, I'm so scared. I don't want to go to jail. I think I may disappear to Mexico."

"Stop your fucking whimpering," Alex said. "I think we're okay. I'll let you know if you need to leave town."

Billy smiled weakly, wiped his eyes, and sat back. He sipped on his scotch.

"Thanks. I was so worried, but you've made me feel slightly better. You know when the detective asked me about Todd, all the memories came flooding back. Like I told the detective, I really detested him. While I was talking to her, I remembered something else."

"I've got to get back to work." Alex said. "What did you remember?"

The scotch was making Billy feel looser, more at ease. "I remembered seeing you and Jackie getting it on after a party. Like I told the detective, I always wondered what the attraction was. I mean, you're a hunk, and she's a, well she's nothing. What were you thinking?"

Alex looked at Billy in disbelief. "Why would you tell the detective that?"

"I was telling her my memories of the parties. One of them was of you and Jackie," Billy whined, shrugging slightly before taking a last gulp of scotch. He closed his eyes as the warm liquor slid down his throat. Suddenly he felt hands clenched around his neck. Pain flashed through his head. His throat closed. He opened his eyes, and saw Alex's red face next to his.

"You little fucker!"

"I can't breathe! I'm dying," Billy croaked.

It was then he heard a loud male voice. "Police. Stand back." He felt fingers being pried from his throat. Gasping and coughing, Billy struggled to a standing position. His eyes focused on a man standing before him who was holding Alex's arms back. The man glanced over at the small group of patrons who were rushing over.

"I'm HPD detective Ron Yates. Will one of you call 911, and ask for backup?"

A tall blond with shoulder-length hair pulled out his cell phone.

Ron took hold of Alex's shirt collar, and pushed him toward the bar, then slammed him down on the bar stool.

"Now stay put!" he commanded.

All at once four uniformed policemen burst in. Ron yelled, "Over here," and pointed at Alex, who they immediately surrounded.

Ron looked toward the blond man. "Thanks."

Out of the corner of his eye he saw Billy limping toward the exit. "Where do you think you're going? Get over here."

Billy stopped mid stride, then limped over to the bar, rubbing his throat. Strangulation was not the way he wanted to end his life.

"Grab a stool, and tell me what's going on," Ron said.

Billy hung his head saying nothing.

Alex fidgeted with a torn button on his shirt. He took a deep, long breath, forced a smile, and said, "It's just a mild disagreement. No reason for the cops to be concerned."

"Except you fucking tried to kill me," Billy interjected. "I'm pressing charges."

"You do, and you'll rue the day. You keep talking, and blabbing nonsense. You're like some mindless, gossipy bitch. Why is it you can't keep your fucking little mouth closed?" Alex sputtered before lunging toward Billy.

Two policemen blocked Alex's lunge, and sat him back down.

"Boys, boys. Calm down," Ron said.

"Just give me a couple of minutes alone with this irritating little worm." Alex shouted. "I'll make sure he never opens his mouth again."

"Calm the fuck down. Just sit where you are, and shut up," Ron said before walking behind the bar.

"What are you doing back there?" Alex barked.

"Oh, just seeing if I can find a towel to wipe my hands. Is this your backpack, Ricci?"

"Yes," Alex answered. "Leave it there."

Ron looked again at the backpack resting on a shelf under the bar when something caught his eye. He reached in, felt a soft plastic bag, and pulled it from the backpack. The baggie was filled with white powder. Unable to hide his enthusiasm, he held the baggie up in the air for all to see.

"Well, gentlemen, look what we have here."

Alex doubled over in laughter as tears poured down his cheeks. "You fuck. That's sweetener for my tea. Taste it, and after you do, get the hell out of my bar."

CHAPTER 33

Lara's first day back at work was one of those days that made her glad to be a realtor. It was a relief to be back in the groove of talking with clients, and making appointments instead of talking to police detectives, and doctors. So far, the whole day had gone smoothly, and she left the office in plenty of time to prepare for Sonya's prospective buyer, Marie Campbell.

The leisurely drive along Memorial, lined with tall pine, magnolia, and oak trees, was pleasantly serene, in sharp contrast from her usual rush through dense traffic. As she turned on Piney Point Drive, she took time to appreciate the beauty of this neighborhood, the gracious homes of differing styles sitting on over-sized lots. Each house, without exception, had a manicured vibrant green lawn, and perfectly trimmed bushes. She turned on Shady Glen taking the wide circle drive lined with flowering lantana and black-eyed Susan. She saw Sonya's sign in the yard, and pulled in the driveway stopping under the porte-cochere. She glanced at her dashboard clock, and sighed with contentment.

Perfectly timed. No need to rush.

Lara unlocked the dark mahogany door and stepped into the open hallway, which was showcased by a winding staircase.

"Wow!" she said loud enough for her voice to echo through the empty rooms. She walked through the magnificent dining room, through the butler's pantry and into the kitchen, flicking lights on as she went. Bright sunlight filtered through the windows in the dinette and large den off the kitchen. Dropping her purse on the granite countertop she stood to admire the vast rooms.

Exquisite! Nice listing, Sonya.

As she continued through the house she glanced at her phone and noticed she had ten minutes before Sonya's client was scheduled to arrive. Thinking she had more than enough time she went up the stairs to turn on more lights.

The media room was her last stop. She flipped a switch, turning on the wall sconces to reveal dark brown walls, a large screen and two rows of plush theater seats. She sat in one, taking in the extravagant surroundings.

Thump!

The hair on the back of her neck stood up. *What was that?*

She jumped up. Her heart and mind raced.

Silence. Dead, dark silence.

Oh shit! The front door is unlocked.

"Get a grip," Lara muttered as she willed herself to move out of the media room. She stood on the landing, calling out, "Hello. Who's here?" No answer.

Get down the stairs. Run, dammit.

Commanding her legs to move, Lara turned and ran smack into a body. Her scream resonated throughout the empty house as she continued down the stairway. Her heart jumped, and her mind froze as she tried to make sense out of her terror.

"Lara it's me," said a familiar soft voice

Her head snapped as she looked back over her shoulder.

"Jackie! Where did you come from? You scared the crap out of me."

"Why are you here?" Jackie asked in a disquietingly calm voice. "I expected Sonya. I want to talk to Sonya."

Lara grasped the stair railing, and took a deep breath, trying desperately to calm her mind. She looked at Jackie in disbelief. "Why am I here? Why are you here acting like a, like a goddamn stalker?"

Lara's fear was suddenly replaced by a blind rage. She lunged at Jackie, grabbing her by the arm.

"I'm supposed to meet Sonya's client here in about five minutes so tell me why you're sneaking around, and make it quick."

"Okay, okay," Jackie said as she pulled her arm away. "I made the appointment. I wanted to meet Sonya, and talk to her outside the office."

"So, you sneak up the stairs and scare me to death? Why go through this stupid charade? Why not just talk to her at the office?"

"I didn't think Sonya would meet with me. She's always so busy. I figured I'd come here with this listing form Sonya forgot to sign, and tell her I was on my way home, and stopped by for her signature. That way Sonya would think the buyer stood her up, and crap, I guess it was a bad idea. I didn't mean to scare you."

"This makes no sense to me," Lara sputtered. "Last time I felt this fear, Todd was murdered. Are you crazy?"

Jackie slumped against the wall and wailed. "Nothing makes sense. My life is falling apart. I'm not going back to the office. I'm leaving town tomorrow. And yes, I feel crazy. I just need someone to talk to. I've known Sonya longer than anyone in the office except for Megan. I think Sonya knows me well enough to understand."

"Sonya will be here soon. I'll text her saying you're here."

"No, don't do that, Lara. I'm going now. Please forget this happened. I'm sorry I scared you," Jackie moaned as she started down the stairs.

Lara followed. At this point she didn't know whether to hug this pitiful woman, or push her crazy ass down the stairs, and out the door. When they reached the end of the stairway, Jackie scurried out. Lara immediately locked the door, and then ran to the kitchen to retrieve her purse. Without touching a single light, she rushed out to find Jackie standing between her and her car.

Lara froze. "What is it now, Jackie?"

"I can't leave thinking you're mad at me. I'd like to buy you a drink to make up for scaring you," Jackie said.

Lara's mind raced, trying to decide if she should give Jackie a break. What harm would it do to have a drink and listen? Besides, didn't she promise Edie she'd keep her eyes and ears open? Now would be the time to find out what was going on with Jackie.

"I definitely could use a drink. Okay, Jackie. It's four-thirty. Where do you want to go?"

"Thank you, Lara. I'm spending the night at *The Lux* in the Galleria. If it's okay with you, we can go to the hotel bar."

"Alright, I'll follow you."

Lara locked the house and followed Jackie the short distance to the hotel. Taking her phone out of her purse, she hit Sonya's number.

"Sonya, don't interrupt, just listen. Your so-called client, Marie Campbell, turned out to be Jackie. I was turning on lights upstairs, and I literally ran into her. I almost fainted with fright. She is distraught, says she's leaving town."

"You've got to be kidding me, Lara. Are you okay? Where are you now?"

"I'm in my car. You'll think I'm nuts, but I'm following Jackie to that new hotel in the Galleria called *The Lux*. I know it's crazy, but Jackie needs a friend right now. She really wanted to talk to you, and when you didn't show she pleaded with me to have a drink at the hotel bar. I don't have the vaguest idea what she wants to talk about. Do me a favor. Call Edie, let her know where I am, and who I'm with. Jackie is acting odder than usual. On top of everything she's planning on leaving town tomorrow."

"Lara, you're not making any sense. I'm having a hard time understanding what's going on."

"I'm pulling into the hotel now. Just do what I ask, call Edie," Lara said, and disconnected the call. The valet took her car, and Lara slowly walked into the bar where she saw Jackie frantically waving from a corner table.

"I ordered you a Manhattan, Lara. I hope that's okay with you."

"Fine, thank you. Now what is going on with you, Jackie?"

The waitress swept toward them with four Manhattans, and two glasses of water. Lara looked at her quizzically.

"It's Happy Hour," the waitress said dully. "That'll be twenty-four dollars, or do you want to run a tab?"

Jackie mumbled something sounding like, "Run a tab," turned to Lara, and raised her glass, saying, "Here's to Drake Properties." Before she could reply Jackie took a big gulp of her drink and began sobbing.

Lara's stomach tightened, and her heart beat faster. She willed herself to concentrate on the hysterical woman before her.

She heard a faint, familiar ding coming from her phone. Trying not to let Jackie notice, she read the text from Sonya:

Stuck in traffic. Per Edie. Record J.

Lara quickly clicked voice memos on her phone, pushed the red record button, then turned her attention to Jackie who was loudly blowing her nose.

"What is going on with you, Jackie? I want to help, but I can't unless you open up."

Looking up at Lara with dull red eyes, Jackie gulped down her first drink. "I've been miserable for a long time, Lara. I'm leaving soon, and it will all be over."

Jackie looked furtively around the crowded bar while shredding tissues in her lap.

"Why do you have to leave town? Are you sure running away is the best thing for you, or do you need someone to help you?" Lara said. "I have a great therapist who can get you through this unhappiness. I know because she helped me."

Jackie took a sip of her drink. "Not everything can be cured by a therapist. I once heard someone define psychiatry as, the care of the id by the odd," she said with a sardonic laugh. She sat back, looking intently at Lara, "You want to know why I'm leaving? Alright I'll tell you why, but you've got to promise me you won't tell anyone. Can I trust you, Lara?"

Lara dropped her eyes, stared at her lap where the iPhone sat, and considered turning the recorder off. Not wanting to lie, yet also not wanting to let Edie down tore at Lara's sense of duty. She honored Edie's request.

"You can tell me everything," Lara said, re-checking the phone to make sure the red light was still on record.

"I've taken money from Drake for two years, and haven't been able to pay it back."

Lara's back stiffened. "What? Why would you do that?"

Jackie took a sip from her second drink. She wiped her eyes before continuing.

"You're so naive you wouldn't understand."

"Try me," Lara said.

"My sister was in a bad marriage, and needed money to get away. I get paid enough to help her, but at the end of the month I was running short of cash. Since I handle all the bookkeeping at Drake it was easy for me to take a couple hundred. I really meant to pay it back. No one noticed the missing money so I thought, what the heck, I'll pay it back later. I felt a little guilty, but you wouldn't believe how much money comes into Drake. I promised myself I'd pay back what I took."

Jackie took a mouthful of water and swallowed hard. Fresh out of tissue she took a cocktail napkin, and began tearing at it.

Lara sat back in stunned silence.

"A month or two later I was short of money again, so I took more. It just snowballed on me. Whenever I wanted money, I took it, a little at a time. No pain," Jackie sighed. "Until now."

"Drake Properties became your private bank account," Lara said. "How much did you take?"

"I was always going to give the money back, Lara. It's just that something always came up. It was so easy," she said looking furtively around to be sure no one could hear. "Give or take a hundred-thousand dollars."

"Shit," Lara said before taking a large swig of her drink. "Does Megan know?"

"I have a sneaking suspicion she does. She started asking me questions last week about my bookkeeping. Then today that detective Edie Ross, asks me about my degree in finance, and my past work in Corpus Christi. I think she has a good idea I've done something illegal."

"Rather than leave town, why not tell Megan? She's averse to bad publicity. She may work with you."

"Come on, Lara. You know Megan. Do you really think she's going to pat me on the head, and put me on a monthly installment plan? She'll go straight to that bitch detective who would love to put me in jail. I have no choice but to leave. I have no friends, no one cares who I am, I'm nothing, I've never been anything, and I never will be anything. I'm invisible, so I won't be missed," Jackie cried.

"That's not true, Jackie. The entire office likes and respects you. I don't know what we'd do without you."

"Cut the bullshit," Jackie sniffed. "You know as well as I do what a bunch of snobs there are in the office. They all make fun of me behind my back. They don' realize what I do, and how hard I work to cover up their mistakes so they can get their commissions. What a bunch of over-rated, over-the-top narcissists."

"I can't argue with that. I will admit there are some prima donnas in that group."

"Thanks for listening, Lara. I'm tired. I think I'll go to my room now. I promise to think about what you've said."

"Don't leave, Jackie. There must be something we can do to make this right. Think about talking to Megan."

"I can't talk with Megan. That woman has a heart of stone."

Lara's mind raced trying to think of ways to keep Jackie talking until Sonya came.

"Megan knows you well. She may surprise you, and be human"

"No, no a thousand times no, Lara. That train left the station a long time ago. I'm in too deep to ask for forgiveness. I'm out of luck, out of excuses, and out of time."

Lara looked desperately toward the bar entrance. No Sonya. She looked at her phone. No texts.

Jackie rose from the table to leave.

"Don't leave. Stay, and have another drink with me," Lara said.

"I'm too tired. Thanks for listening. Goodbye."

Lara sat back in her chair watching Jackie's unsteady walk out of the bar, and then looked at the blinking red light on her phone.

"Oh my God," she said directly into the recorder. "There she goes, leaving me with a splitting headache, and the bill."

CHAPTER 34

Jackie

Jackie's hands shook as she tried to unlock the door to her premium suite. After three tries the key finally slid into the lock. She hurried through the spacious living area. As she did, she looked around the room. A sectional sofa sat across from a picture window, showcasing Houston's skyline in the soft, red glow of sunset. Her pace slowed as she entered the bedroom where she tossed her purse, and then her body on the king-size bed.

Her mind raced as she lay on the soft comforter. She stared into the gathering darkness. If only money, and the things it bought could last.

I know better! Nothing, least of all money, lasts.

Back to the reality of running from the past, of finding a new job in a new town. A place where she would always be looking over her shoulder. Jackie sighed deeply as her eyes became accustomed to the dark. She began to cry.

What am I supposed to do now?

Once again, those childhood memories flooded in. She closed her eyes, wrapping her arms around her stomach, willing herself to think of the good times. High school was a calmer, better time. No more playground plain Jane taunts. What a relief to not be constantly on edge, always aware that without warning the verbal assaults could fly. Now the girl's attention turned to boys, and parties, leaving Jackie alone, totally alone.

Jackie's hand snapped the band out of her tightly held bun. She shook her thick chestnut brown hair loose, turned on the bedside lamp, then walked over to the mirror above the dresser.

God, I look like shit! Like a plain piece of shit!

She reached for the bottle of her favorite gin, *Bombay Sapphire*, that she had left on the dresser. Twisting the lid off, she took a deep pull of the familiar elixir. "Aah, never leave home without it," she said to the mirror.

All she wanted was to forget. No such luck. Thoughts kept bubbling to the surface as she wiped hot tears from her cheeks. Looking at her mirrored image she gave a short laugh and said, "You never had a chance." She grabbed the gin, and drifted into the living room where she reclined on the sumptuous couch. She put the bottle to her lips, and stared at the setting sun's last glow, painting the clouds a pale tint of orange.

Taking another sip, her mind drifted back to her senior year when she met a gangly, rusty-haired, sweet farm boy, Chad Paxton. He told her she was pretty, and graceful. He kissed her, made love to her, made her feel sexy. Was it any wonder that she said yes to marriage? Chad's warmth surrounded her. They laughed, made love, planned to raise rosy-cheeked children on the farm. If only he'd had that decrepit tractor repaired. She wasn't surprised the damn thing flipped on him, pinning him to the ground, killing the love of her life.

My dreams went with him. Alone again.

Jackie rubbed her temples trying to stem the surge of long-held grief. After selling the farm she'd finally had the money to pay for her dream of enrolling at the University of Kansas. The quiet campus library became her haven.

She sat back, closed her eyes, and smiled at the thrill she felt when in three years, she received a degree in accounting, and a job offer from an accounting firm in Corpus Christi.

Goodbye Kansas. Texas, here I come!

She threw herself into her new job like she had her studies. Only this time she was determined to change her persona into the woman people knew today. She smiled as she recalled the nights spent in front of a mirror practicing placid facial expressions, small smiles and perfect posture. Satisfied, she completed the outward transformation by pulling her thick hair back from her face, and ditching any makeup except a light lipstick.

She couldn't help but sneer, thinking how perfectly she had changed to resemble a shy, plain, efficient woman, and model employee. No one dared make fun of her now. In her mind's eye she was perfect. But damn, the pay was a measly amount. After all, she was a degreed accountant. She deserved so much more.

It was just a little bit of money. No one noticed. Every two weeks she'd put a little more into her personal account.

That nosy secretary. Why didn't she just keep her mouth shut?

Jackie picked up the gin and returned to the bedroom. She had to pee. When she returned, she picked up her bottle, and sat in a chair by the bed.

Darkness settled in. Jackie reached over to turn the desk lamp on. She settled back, took another sip of gin, and then closed her eyes. She thought how she had pleaded with the owner of the accounting firm to give her a chance. He did, the chance to leave town or face prosecution.

Houston!

A beautiful city of bayous and lush greenery. Moving to Houston was the best decision she'd ever made. No one knew her, and no one really cared to. Her job at Drake Properties was tailor made for someone like her to melt into the background of handsome men, and beautiful women, driven by their egos, and quest for success.

Chaya had once told her, "I want it all, and I want it now!"

You wanted it, I got it.

Jackie sat back, thrust her chin out, and thought about how Todd, Megan, and the agents went about hungrily grabbing what they could, while she silently, and efficiently began taking what she was entitled to.

Jackie's edgy laughter echoed through the bedroom as she tipped the bottle to her mouth.

What a group of egotistical sharks! All scared to death they would stop moving in real estate waters, and die.

All the agents were too busy career building, and filling their own pocket books to pay much attention to Jackie, who worked behind the scenes to correct their mistakes, clean up their contracts, and make their success possible.

Jackie's fist slammed down on the desk. "What damn fools!" she slurred. "Fuck 'em all."

She tossed her hair back as she recalled the pleasure she got out of playing the efficient office manager while she borrowed money, (she really meant to pay it all back) and kept Alex, who made her feel wanted. A companion to go on trips with, to buy designer clothes for. No longer alone.

He confided in me. Told me he sold drugs. Promised me he didn't use. What a fool I was.

So what if she originally had hired Alex for the night? What would those self-absorbed agents think if they knew Alex the bartender was also Alex the male prostitute, and a drug dealer? No one would believe that after two paid nights of pleasure, sexy, handsome, Alex would find Jackie so desirable he refused payment. Well, that wasn't totally true. A lot of the money she took from Drake she used to give gifts to Alex. Expensive gifts like clothes, booze, trips. Sometimes money, but only because he needed extra cash. No one knew. That wasn't true either. Todd had known. Alex told him.

She was certain Todd suspected she was stealing from the firm, because several months ago he had taken a sudden interest in her accounting, checking and re-checking her work.

Why didn't Alex keep his mouth shut? He destroyed everything!

The one secret she kept from everyone was her love for Todd. She was proud of her ability to hide her emotions by not smiling, or laughing too much when she was with Todd. She also knew if she had been foolish enough to give the slightest hint of her love, Todd would have taunted, teased, and thrown her aside.

That cruel son-of-a-bitch.

Thinking about this didn't help! Her scream echoed through the suite. It didn't help! She took another belt from the bottle.

Stop drinking from a bottle. You're a lady. Act like one.

She found a glass next to an empty ice bucket. She slowly poured gin into the glass. Why did Lara show up at the house today? She needed Sonya, to talk to. Sonya appreciated her, listened to her, took her to lunch, acted like her friend.

Not like Lara who ignored her.

Jackie took a gulp of gin, thinking back to the day Todd took her to lunch to celebrate her birthday. She was so excited. Todd drank a little too much. So did Jackie. They were getting along so well. Todd complimented her on her looks, her hair, her eyes. He was flirting with her! Could it be possible? Could Todd love her the way she loved him? Then it happened. Todd confessed he screwed Lara.

The self-centered whore!

He began whining because Lara wasn't interested anymore. He pleaded with her to talk to Lara. Put in a good word for him. She assured Todd she'd talk to Lara, knowing all along she never would.

Another rejection!

Tears streamed down her cheeks. Her heart beat so fast she expected it to explode. Life after that was never the same. Jealousy is a hellish obsession.

Now I'm running, always running.

Time to get out of town before winding up in a small, unbearable, claustrophobic jail cell.

Didn't the detective say if I left town, they would come looking for me?

Jackie began rocking back and forth, hugging her trembling body.

How am I ever going to get out of this?

She glanced over to the open suitcase next to the bed. She stumbled slightly as she walked over, and pulled out her favorite nightgown, and her favorite weapon, a Ruger .22 magnum pistol.

She held the Ruger in her hand. The gun Chad had given her. The gun she always carried with her. She fondled the grip before putting it down next to her gin.

I need to get that bitch Lara back here.

Straightening her shoulders back, Jackie wiped the tears away, and took a deep breath before picking up her cell phone.

"Hi Lara, Jackie. I hope you haven't left the hotel yet," she said trying to not garble her words. "No? Well do you have time to come up to my suite, number two-fifty? The view from here is beautiful. I'd like you to see it."

Jackie bit on her thumb, and held her breath waiting for Lara's response. She smiled, and exhaled when she heard Lara say, "Okay. I can't stay long. I'll be there in a minute."

CHAPTER 35

Lara surveyed the crowded bar looking for the cocktail waitress. Tapping her nails on the table's edge she looked at her phone. Out of the corner of her eye she saw a man weaving through the crowd before taking the empty chair beside her.

"Excuse me? Did I ask you to sit here?"

What the hell happened to that waitress?

"No, honey you didn't," the man slurred. "I just want you to know my friends, and I think you're the most beautiful redhead we've ever seen," he said, sweeping his arm around his left side toward a group of men sitting four tables away. The men smiled, and raised their glasses.

Dumbfounded, Lara looked at the group, and back at their spokesman.

Why do some men think a woman alone is a woman up for grabs?

"I'll bet you think I'm flattered. I'm not. I'm insulted," she snapped at the intruder.

She looked directly at the man who had the bluest eyes she'd ever seen. He appeared to be in his thirties with dark hair that cascaded halfway down his forehead.

Had she spoken too soon? He was quite good looking, and maybe she could forgive his rudeness. But David had been oh-so-cute, and charming before he turned into a brutal monster. She rubbed her finger over her upper lip feeling the wound that was still healing. No more bar flirtations. No more chance sexual encounters. A bar full of frogs would never again be a place to find her prince.

"Don't go," the intruder slurred. "My buddies and I have a bet. Is your red hair real, or not? They chose me to find out."

Lara stood, and without comment smiled derisively, leaving the drunk, and her urge to slap the shit out of him, behind. She pushed through the crowd to the bar where she paid her tab.

The lobby hummed with activity making it difficult for Lara to find a place to sit. She found a chair along the wall, and texted Sonya:

Where are you?

She sat back and watched all the impeccably dressed, elegant men, and women drifting through the lobby.

Watching people was one of her favorite pastimes. Tonight, was no exception. Her phone softly rang. "Hi Jackie. I'm in the lobby. Why do you want me to come to your room?"

Why not see her room? Sonya will meet us. It will give her a chance to talk to Jackie.

"Okay, Jackie. I can't stay long. What's that room number again?"

Lara hung up, let out a long sigh, stood, and quickly scanned the lobby for any sight of Sonya. She texted Sonya:

I'm going to J's room #250. Come on up.

Sonya immediately texted back:

Traffic horrible, almost there. Wait for me? If not, record. Be careful.

As she stepped out of the elevator, Lara texted Sonya again:

No worries. Just hurry.

She turned the phone voice recorder on, and walked to the end of the dimly lit hall where she found Jackie's room. She started to knock before noticing a chair leg jammed in the door. Lara stuck her head into the opening, moved the chair back, and then called Jackie's name.

"I'm back here. Lara. Come on in." Jackie answered.

Lara walked briskly through the living room but saw no one there. "Jackie, where are you?"

"I'm back here, in the tub."

In the tub?

"I'll wait out here."

"No, come on in, Lara. I'm decent. I just decided to have a farewell party here."

Lara stopped cold. Her heart raced, and her hands shook so hard she put the phone in her jacket pocket. Her body stiffened with an intense feeling of dread. She heard Jackie crying, a heart-wrenching sob like a wounded bobcat. Leaving Jackie like this seemed cruel. Maybe she could at least get her out of the bathroom before Sonya arrived.

She went through the bedroom, and entered the dimly lit bath area. "Jackie?" she whispered.

"Over here," Jackie replied.

Lara let out a small gasp. Jackie lay in the spa tub still wearing her perfectly tailored suit. Behind the tub was a floor to ceiling window view of the Houston skyline. Lara crept closer. Jackie had a bottle of *Bombay Sapphire* in one hand, and in the other…*Is that a gun?*

"Don't look so shocked, Lara. I'm just having a pity party while drinking in the nicest room in this suite. Didn't I tell you the skyline is fabulous? Join me," Jackie said as she swung the bottle toward the windows.

Lara put her hands to her cheeks. "What's with the gun?" she gasped.

Jackie laughed in a tight, squeaky way that Lara had never heard from her, or anyone.

"Get out of that tub, and come into the living room so we can talk," Lara said, trying to make her hands stop shaking. She reached out to take the bottle from Jackie who pulled it closer to her chest.

Jackie raised the Ruger, pointed it at Lara, and said, "No, let's talk here."

Lara screamed and jumped back. She tripped on the rug by the tub, and fell against the sink. "Holy shit, Jackie, put that gun down. You're scaring me."

Jackie's voice lowered, and her eyes narrowed. "Oh, so you're scared? Sit down. I'm not going to hurt you."

Lara sat barely perched on the toilet edge. The room seemed to darken, and become smaller. Her head spun as she tried desperately to think her way out of this nightmare.

"Jackie, give me the gin. Give me the gun. Please get up."

"No, no, and no. You may not say anything. Just listen."

"What's wrong?' Lara asked, staring at the gun.

"Shut up I said! Everything's wrong. I loved Todd," Jackie said in a voice like steel. "You took him away from me."

"Jackie, no, please," Lara said while working her mind for words that wouldn't get her shot. "I want to help you."

Jackie leveled the gun at Lara, "Once again, I told you not to talk." She then began waving the gun around in no particular direction.

"You want to help me? Ha! You could never understand how hurtful it is to be ignored, and rejected time after time. How do you think it feels to be considered a nonentity, worthless and invisible? I can't remember a time in my life when I didn't feel pain. Every damn agent in that office ignored me. You all treated me like your maid. But I showed all of you. I pilfered more money than any of you ever made."

Jackie's voice was at a low growl as she continued. "I had to pay someone to have sex with me. How many women do you know who pay for sex, and love? Only a loser. My pain is real. It hurts so bad right here," Jackie pointed the gun to her heart. "Todd caused the worst pain. I loved him, Lara. I truly loved him."

Jackie's eyes glazed over as she took another swig from the bottle. Pointing the gun at Lara, she re-focused, gave Lara a steady glare, and said, "He was cruel I know, but he was also kind, and good. He'd joke around in the office with me, and sometimes bring me lunch. I felt safe, oddly even loved. Then you came along, and changed everything. He couldn't see anyone but you. That's about the time he started watching, and checking my accounting. I knew he'd someday find out about the missing money."

Jackie's eyes drooped, and her grip on the gun loosened briefly. Then her head snapped up. "I believe he wanted me to know he was watching my work. He enjoyed making me live on the edge. I loved him, and I feared him."

Lara's mind raced as she groped for the correct words. Reaching her hand out toward Jackie she said, "I had nothing to do with his behavior. He was cruel long before I showed up. Come on, honey. Get up, and put the gun down."

Jackie gulped the gin. Her words slurred. Her eyes lost focus. "You may not know this, but I followed you around after Todd's death. I wanted to confront you, to make you say, 'Sorry I slept with the man you loved'."

So, it was her following me!

Every fiber in Lara's body concentrated on Jackie's descent into drunken rambling. She watched Jackie's grip on the gun loosen, then tighten, then loosen as she placed it on her chest.

Maybe she'll pass out.

"I'm not finished with you, Lara," Jackie slurred, looking down into the light blue bottle. "The day Todd died I was the one you heard in the empty house. Remember? I let myself in, and hid until everyone left."

"Oh no," Lara gasped. "It was you. You killed Todd."

Jackie raised the bottle over her head, and smashed it on the rim of the tub. Shattered glass exploded leaving blue shards in and around the tub. A strong odor of alcohol combined with pine needles filled the room.

"Shut up! Shut the fuck up!"

Nausea, and terror swept over Lara. Deep breaths kept the bile down, and controlled her urge to run.

"I promise, I just wanted to scare you two," Jackie sobbed. "I didn't know you were going to leave. I found Todd in the bedroom. It all went so fast."

Jackie jerked the gun up pointing it at the ceiling then back at Lara who put her hands over her head, and ducked. "Shit, Jackie! Watch where you point that thing!"

"All I remember, Lara, is him yelling at me. 'You bitch! I know you're taking money from the firm. You can't make money on your own. You're a thief, and parasite!' Jackie mimicked. "Then he grabbed my throat. His hands were so big. All the time he was calling me a worthless piece of shit. I couldn't breathe. I don't know how I did it, but I broke loose. I pointed my gun, and…" Jackie let out a primal wail, "I'm through, I'm ruined."

Lara sat mesmerized by this pitiful woman who could easily kill her too. Her only chance of surviving was to keep talking until Jackie passed out.

"Please honey, give me the gun," Lara said, extending her hand toward Jackie's arm. "Trust me. Put the gun down. I'll help you get out of the tub so you won't fall, and cut yourself on all this glass."

Jackie sagged further down into the tub, closed her eyes, and waved her hand dismissively.

"I just want this hell to end. Go on." Tears streamed from Jackie's swollen eyes. "Don't worry. I'm okay."

Run!

Knowing Jackie could still use the gun, Lara hesitated, and put her hand out.

"Please, let me have the gun."

Jackie sighed deeply, "I won't do anything. I'll put the gun where it belongs."

Without looking back, Lara ran out the bathroom. The phone vibrated. It's Sonya! Stopping, she glanced at the message:

We're at J's door.

She dashed through the bedroom. A deafening shot reverberated through the suite.

Oh no! I'm shot!

Lara fell to the floor. She heard a man call her name. Where was he? Looking around the room she saw two lamps casting an eerily warm glow. Nothing moved. Silence, complete silence. Feeling no pain, she eased her body to the side checking for blood. Nothing.

I'm not shot! Run!

She lunged toward the couch and the man's voice. "I'm here," she yelled. She ran into Ron, and saw Edie behind him pushing through the doorway into the suite. Edie drew her gun, and followed Ron, leaving Lara curled up on the couch.

Sonya crept in behind the detectives. "Lara, where are you?"

"I'm here, Sonya."

Sonya sat beside Lara, wrapped her arms around her friend, and whispered, "You're safe now."

It was then she heard Edie shout, "Oh shit!"

Lara jumped off the couch, and ran into the bathroom where she saw Jackie's perfectly tailored suit covered in blood. Horror, and nausea swept over her.

"She shot herself!" Lara wailed, turning to Ron whose gloved hand was slowly lifting the gun from Jackie's fingers.

Her hands flew up to the sides of her head. "I thought she was going to kill me! Why did she do this? I wanted to get her out of the tub. I wanted to help her!"

Edie nodded at Ron who put his arm around Lara's shoulders, then guided her back to the living room. "Thank you," she sobbed, sinking into the couch next to Sonya.

Lara felt her chest tighten. How did this happen?

Poor Jackie, poor pitiful Jackie.

"Sonya, I tried so hard to get that gun from her. She told me she shot Todd!"

Lara felt the room spin, and the nausea return. She put her head on Sonya's shoulder, and quietly wept.

"You did all you could," Sonya said, as tears ran down her cheeks. "Jackie has been on this path for a long time."

CHAPTER 36

Edie cleared her desk before plopping down the thick Drake file. Her eyes blurred from lack of sleep. Several times last night she had woken from nightmares of Jackie, lying in a tub, dressed in a blue business suit, splattered with blood.

She rubbed her eyes, and yawned before going through the file. She was impressed with Lara's presence of mind to tape Jackie's gut-wrenching confession. She had heard the heartbreaking tape once, never to hear it again. It was hard enough to read a suicide note, let alone hearing Jackie's voice crying for help. The tape had been transcribed, then put in the file. Case closed.

A knock on her door jolted Edie out of her gloomy thoughts. She quickly rose from her seat, tripped on a pile of files she'd taken off her desk, then jerked the door open. Narcotics Detective, Buzz Cline stood outside smiling like a Cheshire cat.

"You don't need to bang the door down, Buzz. Have some respect this early in the morning," Edie said.

Buzz sauntered in followed by Ron, who leaned against the wall.

"Wait 'til you hear this," Ron said.

"I've got your shooter in the Drake case," Buzz said, taking the empty chair.

Edie tilted her head quizzically toward Buzz. "Really? Who do you have?"

"You remember, the day after Drake's murder, I told you Alex Ricci dealt with some vicious drug lords? Last night the thugs caught up with him."

"Ain't that a shame," Edie said. "Was he badly beaten?"

"No, he was badly shot. Enough to put him in the hospital."

"Is Ricci dead?"

Buzz shrugged. "Not yet. He survived surgery, but who knows how long he will last. Wait 'til you hear this, Edie."

Edie sat back, laid her hands on top of the desk, and smiled. "I'm all ears."

"You know the fight Ron broke up at *Ceres* between Ricci and Billy Parsons? Well, he called me with the details. I put a twenty-four-hour watch on Ricci in case he fled the country," he said. "But instead of getting out of Dodge, that dumb fuck made a delivery of cocaine in the parking lot behind *Ceres*. Something went bad, and he was shot."

Buzz grinned slyly. "We were close enough to grab, and arrest the shooters. Bam, in the slammer, off the street!" Buzz said pumping both arms over his head. "So, get this. While we're waiting for the ambulance, Ricci, who can barely talk, wants to see Ron. I told him Ron was not there, and pretty soon he wouldn't be."

"You've always been such a sensitive guy," Edie said.

Buzz bowed at the waist, then continued. "Ricci said he had to talk to Ron, tell him about Todd Drake's murder. Long story short, I convinced him Ron wasn't coming, and to tell me. That's when he confessed to killing Drake."

Edie shrugged, shook her head, and looked over at Ron, then at Buzz who rubbed his hands together, and then spread them wide.

"Case closed."

"Congratulations, Buzz." Edie said leaning back with her hands behind her head. "Now you can congratulate us."

"What for?"

"Ron and I wrapped up the Drake case last night. Jackie Long confessed to Todd's murder before she shot herself. We have her confession on tape."

Buzz bolted up from his chair. "That's not possible. She was covering for him."

"I think Ricci was blowing smoke up your ass," Ron said.

"What the hell! Why do you believe Ricci's girlfriend?" Buzz asked.

"Everything fits making her the killer," Ron replied. "Forensics just confirmed that the gun used to kill Todd, is the same gun Jackie used to commit suicide."

"That just doesn't make sense," Buzz said. "I've been around for a long time, and I can peg a liar a mile away. I'm telling you, Ricci's confession was real."

Edie sat shaking her head. "Two people confessing to murdering the same man? Something's wrong here. With your permission, and of course the doctor's, we'd like to talk to Ricci before he dies," Edie said.

Buzz ran his fingers through his hair. "Be my guest, but I'm going with you."

•　　•　　•

The elevator stopped at the fourth-floor of Ben Taub Hospital. Edie rushed out, with Buzz and Ron in tow. The nurse asked the detectives to wait while she paged the head of the Intensive Care Unit. After what seemed like an interminable time to Edie, a tall dark-haired man in scrubs approached the nurses' station. She saw the nurse point to the detectives.

"I'm Dr. Welch. Did you have me paged?"

"Yes doctor," Edie said before introducing herself, Ron and Buzz. "It is of vital importance we talk with your patient, Alex Ricci, while he can still communicate. He may have committed a murder. We'll only be a few minutes."

"Mr. Ricci is in bad shape. He may not make it, " Dr. Welch replied.

"We understand," Edie said.

"Alright. Go on in. A nurse will stay to monitor his vitals. Make it brief."

The three detectives entered the Critical Wound Unit where Alex lay barely visible under white blankets. Tubes were clustered on each side of the bed backed by blinking, beeping machines.

Edie quietly moved close to Alex's ashen face. A clear tube holding brown liquid came out his nose. Blood caked on his dry, slightly parted lips.

"Alex. It's Detective Ross. Can you answer a few questions?"

Alex opened his swollen eyes to a slit. He nodded slightly, and croaked, "Yes."

"I'll say this slowly so you'll understand," Edie said. "I'm here with detectives Cline and Yates. We want your statement concerning Todd Drake's murder. You have the right to an attorney. If, during the interview you decide to stop, we will leave. Do you understand?"

The nurse gave Alex a teaspoonful of ice before he whispered, "Yes. I killed Todd."

Edie placed a small tape recorder on the side of Alex's head. "Why did you kill Todd?"

"He owed me fifty grand. For party drugs," he began.

"Alex, last night Jackie Long confessed to murdering Drake," Edie said. "I'm sorry to tell you she committed suicide."

Alex drew in a sharp breath, coughed, and turned his head from Edie. When he turned back tears rolled down his cheeks.

"She didn't kill him."

Edie looked at the nurse, who continued to monitor his heart rate. The nurse gave Alex another spoon of ice, then whispered to Edie, "Just a few more questions."

"Tell me how it happened," Edie continued.

"Jackie made a key to the house. We got there before Lara. We hid. Then when Lara left..." Alex said before closing his eyes.

"Stay with me, Alex," Edie whispered. "What happened after Lara left?"

"Confronted Todd. Bastard wouldn't pay. Insulted Jackie. Lunged for her throat. I shot him in the head."

"Todd was shot in the head, and chest. Did you shoot him in the chest too?"

Alex coughed before adding, "Jackie shot him in the heart."

"That's enough," Doctor Welch said as he entered the room. "If you don't have what you need by now, it'll have to wait."

"We have what we came for," Edie said. "Thank you, doc."

Edie removed the tape recorder from the pillow. She looked once at Alex, whose eyes were closed, and leaned in close so he could hear her.

"Thank you, Alex. Thank you for the truth," she said, and left the room.

Edie followed Ron and Buzz to the elevator. No one said a word until the elevator doors opened on the main floor.

"I'll get my final report over to the D.A. today," Buzz said giving the two detectives a half grin. "I think we all did a damned good job on this case."

He turned to walk away then stopped. "Isn't it amazing what people will do?"

Buzz shook his head, waved a fist with his thumb up, and left.

As soon as they returned to the squad room Ron got Edie a cup of coffee before pouring a cup for him. They silently walked to Edie's office, and sat down. Edie looked over at her partner, took a sip, and sighed.

"That was a shitty way to get a confession. Do you think Alex is going to die?"

Ron stretched out his legs. "I'd say it doesn't look good."

"I think we can close this case," Edie said raising her cup to Ron. "Another one under our belts."

"True, but I'm afraid I'll be harassed for months about Alex's bag of sweetener. I really thought it was blow. Damn! How embarrassing. At least I know I'd never make a good narc," Ron chuckled.

"You can handle the teasing. You're a good cop. None of us are perfect."

"Thanks, Edie. Are you going to let Lara, Sonya, and Megan know about this latest turn of events?"

"I'll tell Lara if you'll call Megan, and Sonya," Edie said.

"Terrific. Now there's two opposites. Sonya the sunshine kid, and Megan the ice queen. Lucky me," Ron said with a wry grin.

"You'll survive," Edie chuckled. "I still can't stop thinking about those two broken people, Alex and Jackie. Their greed disrupted so many lives. What a waste."

Edie's cell phone rang. "Detective Ross. Yes, how's he doing? Thanks for calling." She put the phone down on the table, and looked over at Ron. "That was the hospital. Ricci died five minutes ago."

"Damn! I was looking forward to testifying against that heartless bastard."

"I don't think he was totally heartless. I got the impression he had real human feelings for Jackie," Edie said rubbing her eyes. "That's if you believe a snake has feelings."

Ron took another gulp of caffeine. "On the brighter side, the Drake case brought Lara into my life."

Edie studied her partner. She tried to picture the two of them together.

"I've been blind, Ron. It makes perfect sense. Two single people thrown together in an intense investigation. I'd be surprised if something didn't happen between y'all."

"Don't go off the deep end, and start planning a wedding. We're just good friends for now," he said with a laugh. "I'll let you get your work done."

After Ron left, Edie couldn't stop smiling. She liked Lara. Over the weeks, she had come to respect her. That woman had been through a lot. God knows she's had a terrible time with men. Thinking of Ron and Lara together brought Edie out of the depressing world of violence, jealousy, and suicide that enveloped the Drake case. Smiling, she picked up the phone, scrolled through her contacts, and pressed Lara's name.

"Hi Lara. It's Edie. Got a minute?"

"I'm showing a property now. What's going on?"

"I have to talk with you about some additional information in Todd's case. Can you meet me at *Ana's* at five?"

"I thought it was over!" Lara said with surprise. "Are we okay to meet in a public place?"

"It is over, and yes, we can meet publicly. I'll fill you in on what else I've learned," Edie replied.

"Now you've sparked my interest. I'll be there."

Edie sat back, sighed deeply, and called her husband. "Ted, how would you like to take off this weekend?" Edie smiled as she listened to Ted's warm, inviting voice emanating from deep within his chest. "We won't go far. How does the *Hotel Zoie* sound? Great. Maybe your folks can watch the kids. I'll make reservations."

•   •   •

Lara wondered what Edie could tell her after last night. Try as she might to forget it, the sound of Jackie's voice, the gun shot, the smell of gunpowder combined with the metallic smell of blood, immediately took her back to the Bard's bedroom. Todd on the floor. Now Jackie. Fear and sadness consumed her.

"Lara, how many square feet did you say this house has?"

She looked at the fact sheet in her hand, smiled at her client, and continued her job.

CHAPTER 37

Lara

The cushioned booth at Ana's bar was a welcome place for Lara to ease into while waiting for Edie. She sat back, and breathed deeply trying to relax. Her day started off on a high note when she called her brother, Randy. They talked for an hour. She promised Randy that she would come to Austin in a week for much needed family time.

She had gone back to work only because buyers can't wait, and her buyers needed to find a home soon. After dragging herself to the office she realized working was the best way to get rid of the bloody image that played constantly in her head.

The office had been awash with emotion. Megan came in, gathered the agents together, told them about Jackie, then strode with head held high into her office, and locked the door. Sonya didn't show up at all. She called Lara saying she was taking the rest of the week off. They agreed to meet for dinner.

Lara found Billy in an empty office, where he was quietly crying. When he saw her he got out of his chair, and moved toward her with arms wide open. Her anger melted away. She never could stay angry with Billy, and he looked so pitiful. He said he was checking into a drug rehab facility near Austin. Lara hugged him tightly, shed a few tears, and wished him well.

Meanwhile, the rest of the agents worked in stunned silence except Chaya, who wept whenever someone spoke to her. Lara was relieved when her buyers showed up, and she could get out of the office.

Her eyes wandered toward the arched entry of *Ana's* bar. She saw Edie purposefully walk to the booth.

Edie sat, then waved at a waitress. "Let's order a drink."

Lara looked over at Edie, smiled, and said, "Hello to you too."

Edie sighed deeply. "Sorry, I'm beat. It's been a tough day."

"It certainly has. My office is in total meltdown mode."

The waitress interrupted, taking their drink orders.

"I imagine, as the owner of Drake Properties, Megan is having a tough time. I wonder if her business will survive this," Edie said. "My husband always tells me life isn't fair, it's eventful."

"Megan is tough. I'm not worried about her," Lara said. "As for your husband's wise adage, I'm ready for a life of non-events. I'm thinking about going back to therapy for a mental health checkup."

"Not a bad idea," Edie said nodding to the waitress, who placed their drinks before them. The detective took her jacket off, pulled her shirt out of the top of her skirt, then sat back, and sipped her scotch.

"Now that you're comfortable," Lara said with a slight smile, "Can you tell me your new information?"

"It seems Jackie is not our only shooter."

Lara gasped. "What? There's another one?" Her eyes darted around the bar. "Does that mean the murderer is still out there?"

"No, he died early today, in the hospital with gunshot wounds."

Lara took a sip of her drink. Leaning forward she whispered, "Who is it?"

"Alex Ricci. He was shot in a drug deal that went bad. For some reason, probably because he wanted to clear his name before he met his maker, he confessed to murdering Todd."

Lara drew her hands against her cheeks. "Jackie's boyfriend? The bartender?"

"One and the same. He was in the Bard's house with Jackie."

"Do you believe him?" Lara asked. "He could have gone to his grave covering for Jackie. Have you thought of that?"

"I did, but he confessed after I told him Jackie was dead. I'm convinced he was only thinking of himself, and saving his soul. He did shed a tear when I told him about Jackie. I think somewhere deep inside he actually cared for her."

"Well, that beats all." Lara shook her head. "Last night Jackie told me she let herself into the Bard's house, and hid until I left. She never mentioned Alex being with her." She sipped her drink and shuddered.

Oh my God. They were both there!

"After you left, they confronted Todd, who refused to pay Alex for a recent drug deal," Edie said. "Names were called, tempers raged. Todd turned on Jackie, grabbing her by the throat. According to Alex, he shot Todd in the head."

"Jackie covered for Alex until the end. How tragic. How sad," Lara said.

"It gets more bizarre," Edie continued. "After Alex shoots Todd in the head, Jackie takes the gun, then puts one shot into Todd's heart."

"I'll be damned. I didn't know this happened in real life. It's so, so Agatha Christie."

"First time I've seen a case like this," Edie said. "Normally it's just one enraged asshole. I'm still not sure Jackie planned to shoot Todd, but she kept the gun they used."

"The same gun she pointed at me? The one she used in the tub? Like a souvenir? What a macabre pair," Lara said. "I don't think I could do your job, Edie. How do you sleep at night?"

Edie shook her head. "I once heard a detective describe the people we deal with as the baddest, saddest, and maddest in our society. After all I've heard from you and Sonya, I don't think I could be a realtor. Your whack-o's are free to create havoc in the world. Mine are mostly jailed."

Lara raised her glass to Edie. "Touché."

Lara looked around the bar as it filled with young professionals looking for new friends, new lovers, and some happiness.

"I want you to know that Ron and I are having dinner together tomorrow night."

"Ron told me already," Edie said. "He's a great guy. I've had a few partners before him, and I can say he's the most diligent and focused. He's also fun to be around."

"So, this isn't goodbye. We may see each other at cop parties. Do cops have parties?"

"Of course, we do," Edie laughed. "Perhaps I'll get to know you in a less stressful atmosphere," she said, then caught the waitress' eye, raising two fingers in the air. She looked at Lara who was fidgeting with her cocktail stirrer.

"There's something that bothers me," Lara said. "Am I still in danger? I mean, David is still out there."

"Remember, David is under a restraining order," Edie said. "Not only that, but I'm convinced Ron put the fear of God in him. I guarantee you won't be bothered by him."

"That's encouraging news. Am I completely out of danger now?"

"You can relax. Todd was killed because of greed on Alex's part, and unrequited love on Jackie's end. You just happened to be in their way."

Lara sat still as tears welled in her eyes. Her stomach unknotted, and her breathing slowed. "It all boils down to sex and money, money and sex. The human drama played throughout the world. A play in which I no longer want a major part."

"That may be a motive for murder, but you can't just give up on the entire life drama," Edie said.

Lara wiped her eyes and shrugged her shoulders. "I can forget about having money. I've never been able to hang on to it. What you don't have, you don't miss. But you're right. No reason to throw all life's drama in the trash bin," she said with a wicked grin. "I've decided I'll keep sex."

The sound of the women's laughter made the waiters, and customers smile as if they were in on the joke.

END

ACKNOWLEDGEMENTS

I want to thank my beta readers, Teresa Coleman, Ric Coleman, Rita Doherty and Erik Doherty, who were diligent and unwavering in their critiques. I owe you all my deep gratitude.

My son, Regan, and his wife Peggy, who read and critiqued vital chapters. Your responses were spot on, and invaluable.

My editor at Yellowbird Editors in Austin, Sara Kocek. You helped me pull the story together in an encouraging, professional way.

My writing critique group, Rhonda Wiley-Jones and E. Marie Baker. Two highly skilled writers whose help, and support spurred me on to finish the manuscript, then rewrite and rewrite. What would I have done without you both?

Many thanks to former Assistant District Attorney in Harris County, Norma Davenport. She graciously, and patiently allowed me to pick her brain about the legal end of police work.

My heartfelt appreciation goes out to my Houston real estate co-workers, Marilyn Savage Martinez, and Ann Blankenship, whose professionalism, humor, and love of life are the essence of the characters in this book. Thanks to all the Houston realtors I had the pleasure of working with, and all my past, and present clients.

Many thanks to my current broker, Laura Fore, at Fore Premier Properties in Kerrville, Texas, whose undying support and patience, propelled me to finally finish the book.

Words are not sufficient to express the gratitude I feel toward my supportive, caring husband, Gary, who gave me the gift of time, and space to write for hours on end without complaint.

ABOUT THE AUTHOR

Diane Dickinson grew up in Oceanside, California. She has a degree in journalism from the University of Houston. She worked for two Houston area newspapers as a news reporter, and news editor. She was a freelance writer until a friend encouraged her to become a realtor, a career that led her to write her debut novel. She is a member of The Writer's League of Texas, The Author's Guild and Mystery Writers of America.

Diane has two children, and two frisky dogs. She lives with her husband in the Texas Hill Country, where she continues to write, and work as a realtor.

NOTE FROM DIANE DICKINSON

Word-of-mouth is crucial for any author to succeed. If you enjoyed *Final Transaction*, please leave a review online—anywhere you are able. Even if it's just a sentence or two. It would make all the difference and would be very much appreciated.

Thanks!
Diane Dickinson

We hope you enjoyed reading this title from:

www.blackrosewriting.com

Subscribe to our mailing list – *The Rosevine* – and receive **FREE** books, daily deals, and stay current with news about upcoming releases and our hottest authors.
Scan the QR code below to sign up.

Already a subscriber? Please accept a sincere thank you for being a fan of Black Rose Writing authors.

View other Black Rose Writing titles at
www.blackrosewriting.com/books and use promo code
PRINT to receive a **20% discount** when purchasing.